SCHOOL FOR HOPE

SCHOOL FOR HOPE

Michael McLaverty

POOLBEG

First published 1954 by Jonathan Cape, London
This paperback edition published 1992 by
Poolbeg Press Ltd
Knocksedan House,
Swords, Co Dublin, Ireland

© Michael McLaverty 1954

Poolbeg Press gratefully acknowledges the financial assistance of the Arts Council of
Northern Ireland
Poolbeg Press also receives financial assistance from The Arts Council/An Chomhairle
Ealaíon, (Dublin) Ireland

ISBN 1 85371 172 1

Cover illustration courtesy of The Ulster Museum, Belfast
Cover design by Pomphrey Associates
Printed by The Guernsey Press Company Ltd,
Vale, Guernsey, Channel Islands

Also by Michael McLaverty

Call My Brother Back
Lost Fields
In This Thy Day
The Three Brothers
Truth in the Night
School for Hope
The Choice
The Brightening Day

Collected Short Stories

To the memory of my father and mother

✿ 1 ✿

In the midsummer evenings when they had tidied away the tea-things in the kitchen the two old sisters retired to the sitting-room, and there, with the two windows open to the long-legged sun, they sat in front of the pansy-leaf firescreen that hid the empty grate. Some years ago Elizabeth, the elder of the two, had wrought the firescreen with beads no bigger than a pinhead, but failing eyesight had enforced her to desist from work of such intricacy and, as she was not one who could sit idly in a chair, she was now crocheting a surplice for the Foreign Missions. Mary, the younger by two years, was sitting with her hands folded on her lap, resting from the day's housework and thinking of tomorrow's, and wondering what she could do now that she wouldn't have to do then. She had no need to worry about the outhouses: their yardman, Johnny, saw to that: the cows milked, the eggs collected from the fowl-house, and the yard swept clean as they always had insisted. If she closed her eyes for a moment she could picture it clearly: the white walls with their hems of tar to ward off rats, the galvanized bolts on the black doors, and among the cobble-stones a few white feathers that had escaped the bristles of the yard-brush. Since their brother's death six years ago, Johnny had no need to look after the land; the fifty acres that they owned were let each year to neighbouring farmers, and save for the keeping in order of the orchard and the lawn and the paths, Johnny concentrated on the rearing and breeding of white leghorns. As she sat she heard him trudge into the kitchen with two buckets of coal for the morning's fire, wash his hands at the sink, and presently go humming past the window on his way to the town for a couple of bottles of cool stout.

The sisters sighed simultaneously: they had the house to themselves and they could open the door into the hall without fear of catching the strong smell of Johnny's tobacco or, if they

9

felt inclined, they could sit in the kitchen and not find him stretched out in front of the range with his cap over his face and a fly or two walking undisturbed across his bald head. Mary sighed again, and then raised her head when a thrush sang from the shade of the chestnut trees outside the window; she could not see the thrush, but when the light wind raised the leaves she could see the clusters of green chestnuts sway up and down in stiff rhythm. 'They're no bigger than gooseberries,' she mumbled to herself, 'but in a couple of months or so they'll be as big as apples — they will indeed.'

'What's that you say, Mary?'

'Oh, nothing, nothing. I'm just listening to that thrush loosening his throat.'

She smoothed a wrinkle out of her skirt, and then as if imitating the thrush's song she said to herself: 'Yes, yes, I'll do that! I'll do that! I'll do that now!' and rising languidly she went off to the scullery. In a few minutes she was back with a deep enamel basin, and sitting down in an armchair she spread a newspaper at her feet and began to top-and-tail gooseberries with her scissors.

Elizabeth halted a moment at her crocheting and frowned at her over her spectacles: 'I wish, Mary dear, you'd take that class of work into the kitchen. The drawing-room is no place for topping-and-tailing gooseberries.'

'There's nobody here to see me.'

'That doesn't make it right. If you wouldn't like anyone to see you doing it in the drawing-room then there's something wrong with it.'

'I'm doing no harm. It's bright here in the last of the sun, but it's lonely and dull in the kitchen' — and as she spoke a gooseberry fell from her fingers and rolled over the floor.

'There! I told you it was wrong.'

'If you'd stop your scolding that wouldn't have happened. I'll soon find it, never fear.'

'You'll find it squashed under your heel some fine day — that's

where you'll find it! The carpet, dear knows, is shabby enough
without adding gooseberry stains to it.'

'I'll find it all right, Elizabeth, I'll find it.'

Elizabeth continued her crocheting, her lips audibly counting
as if to quell the annoying snip of her sister's scissors. Now and
again there was the marble-roll of gooseberries as Mary's plump
hand plunged into the basin, and Elizabeth would halt, in spite
of her determination not to do so, and peer contemptuously over
her spectacles. 'Perhaps, Mary, you'll allow me to say that you
should have two basins for work of that nature: one to hold the
docked ones and one to hold the undocked.'

'I suppose I should,' and Mary smiled at the strangeness of
Elizabeth's words, and began to think of the little coal-boat that
docked at the river-quay not far from the house, and of the
poor women and children sauntering out from the town with
baskets to pick up the stray bits of coal that fell from the crane-
bucket at unloading time. 'It's strange one could think of
coal-boats and gooseberries at the same time,' she said to herself;
and chuckling inwardly she bent her head to conceal her way-
ward pleasure. But Elizabeth hadn't noticed the smile; she had
stopped her work, had rested the needle on the surplice and was
now rubbing her eyes with her forefinger. Save for a long rod of
light leaning in a corner of the room the sun had almost left it,
and in a few minutes it would be sheering past the windows and
fingering the tree-trunks with gloves of shadow.

'I hope, Mary, you'll not put all those gooseberries to the
making of jam. You'll keep some for a few tarts, I presume?'

'Tarts! What would we want with tarts? You know that
gooseberry tarts don't agree with you.'

'I wasn't thinking of myself. I was thinking we could have
Helen Lynch and Peter for tea some evening soon.'

'Helen Lynch! No, there'll be no gooseberry tarts for Helen
Lynch — not after her last visit. I don't mind Peter coming, but
her! Last time she was here she did nothing but find fault with
everything I put on the table. She sampled everything but, if

she did, she talked of nothing else but the fine pastry her new cooker makes — delicious and soft, melts in your mouth like thick cream.'

'That wasn't a slight on your cookery, Mary dear. She was only explaining the excellences of her new oven. Helen Lynch wouldn't slight or affront you in any way, I can assure you.'

'Would she not indeed! She's the very girl that would — and it wouldn't cause her conscience a single flutter. Peter is a like-able soul, but that Helen one puts on too many airs and is far too house-proud for my way of going. I declare to goodness since she went into that new bungalow I can't stand her hoity-toity manner. Tarts, indeed! I'd like to see myself baking tarts for Helen Lynch.' She put a gooseberry in her mouth, crunched it, and made a wry face. 'They're sharp and sour this year and they'll run away with too much of my sugar without thinking of tarts for people who don't appreciate them.'

Elizabeth hadn't expected this outburst on poor Helen, and as she lifted her needle again she pretended to concentrate on her work, her mind all the time fumbling for the exact words that would coax Mary towards her plan.

'I should have this surplice ready by the end of October. What do you think?' and she spread out the lace invitingly on her lap and traced part of the pattern with her finger.

'You'll have it ready if you cease visiting and being visited. Helen has little else to do with her time except gallivant about the countryside. Sure everyone knows she has her brother Peter under her thumb as if he were a boy out of the High School. He's like a trained dog the way he gives in to her whims and fancies.'

Elizabeth shrugged her shoulders, adjusted her spectacles low on her nose, and lifted her needle. She sighed, held out the surplice at arm's length, and placed it on her lap.

'Yes, yes, you're right, Mary,' she said with slow flattering emphasis. She paused and stared over her spectacles at the floor. She gave an unnecessary cough: 'There's always wisdom in what you say ... Indeed, now that I come to think of it, Father Lacy said that to me the other evening: "Mary doesn't say much but, when she does, she speaks with the wisdom that comes from the untroubled mind." '

'And did Father Lacy say all that about me? Many a tart of mine he tasted and appreciated in this very house. I'm sure it was the gooseberries put him in your mind.'

'I suppose, in a way, it was.'

'Poor Father Lacy — a more patienter or kinder man never set foot in the parish.'

Elizabeth coughed again and stroked the surplice: 'It's strange you should say that. In fact that's his own estimation of your very self ... "Mary is patient, and when you're patient you're kind. Kindness comes from patience — your sister has it in every finger." '

'And did he say all that, the poor innocent man? He doesn't know the hardened old sinner I am. It takes you to live with a person for years before you can say you know them — and even then one never gets to know them completely. Isn't that so, Elizabeth?'

'That'll do you, Mary. I have lived with you long enough and, dear knows, I could say "yes" to everything Father Lacy has said of you. But that'll do you, you old play-actress,' and she shrugged her shoulders pleasurably and patted the surplice.

Mary, stooped over the basin, raised her head to catch her sister's eye, but Elizabeth seemed to be absorbed in the adroit progress of her needle and pretended not to notice the attentive look that was cast at her. Mary stretched out her hand and gently raised the hem of the surplice. 'It's a lovely piece of work, Elizabeth. Any young priest on the missions would be glad to wear it.'

Elizabeth held it up and displayed the unfolding design. 'It's a new design — a design of my own that I improved on from Carrickmacross lace. I don't think it could be bettered. The

13

chalices come out well, but I'm afraid one or two of the little fish have short tails.'

'You'd have to measure them with a ruler to note the differs — and no young priest would do the like of that.'

'That's true, Mary. There's many of them would wear it back to front and not notice the difference.'

'It's a pity you wouldn't colour the little fish with red and blue thread.'

'I never saw it done and it may not be liturgically correct.'

'I suppose not,' Mary agreed timidly, not knowing the meaning of the word 'liturgically'. 'But it's beautiful all the same. Has Helen seen it since the design appeared?'

'She hasn't. But what does it matter what she says? You admire it, and that's enough for me.'

'Maybe, after all, we should ask her over. It's a month since she was here. She'd have something to talk about when she'd see that surplice and maybe she'd stop telling us how to improve this house of ours.' She put her head to the side and began to mimic Helen's voice: ' "Really, Mary and Elizabeth, you should make a window in that hall above the stairs — it would transform your hall and give it more light. And really you should scrap that old range and buy a cream-coloured cooker like mine. It would make a pleasanter kitchen and a lighter coal bill into the bargain." ' She began to chuckle, but Elizabeth did not join in.

There was a long pause and then Mary said penitently: 'I shouldn't be mocking people behind their backs,' and she stretched her hand under the surplice and readmired the lace-work against the pink flesh of her palm: 'It's lovely, Elizabeth, and I insist that Helen sees it soon.'

'I'm not particular whether she ever sees it or not,' Elizabeth said with controlled coolness. 'Sure what does it matter whether Miss Lynch sees it or not? Hm, as if I'm in bother about her opinion about anything!'

'But she really must see it and have it talked about,' Mary went on. 'Sure when we have a fine crop of gooseberries we may as well make a few tarts. I made too much jam last year, and I have a pot or two of it on the shelf and it's so stiff you could slice it with a knife. Too much jam can go to waste — that's what I think.'

'Well, Mary dear, whatever you wish. If you insist on having her I'll drop her a note and give it to a boy in the morning on his way to school. He can leave it in the house or give it to Master Lynch himself in the school.'

The needle moved now with relaxed dexterity, and when a few gooseberries rolled over the floor Mary shuffled her feet to hide the noise and Elizabeth coughed and pretended not to hear. Mary disliked the idea of giving the note to a schoolboy, for last year the schoolboys had robbed the orchard and tormented poor Johnny, and since then she was reluctant to do anything that would encourage them to make free with the place.

'Yes, Elizabeth, that will do fine,' she said after a long pause.

'What will do fine?'

'That idea of yours about the letter. Give it to a boy passing on the road in the morning.'

'Yes, yes,' Elizabeth answered, not wishing now to be disturbed.

'That sun's left the room. Should we not close the windows before the dew falls?'

'Not at all. The fresh evening air is wholesome, and forby the noise of the window would frighten our thrush from his perch. Let the creature sing out his fill and then we'll close it.'

She bent low over her crocheting and then paused, listening to a motor purring on the road below the house; in a few seconds she heard it crunch on the pebbles on the path and halt abruptly outside the window.

'Quick, Mary, quick with that basin!' she cried, and gathering up the newspaper from the floor she stuffed it under a cushion, and as she waited for the door to be knocked she fixed the corner of the hearth-rug that Mary had kicked over in her hurry from the room.

The visitor was Peter Lynch, and as he strode into the room with Mary fussing behind him she heard his foot crunch on a gooseberry. Elizabeth gave her a furtive look of scorn, and then speaking sweetly to Peter she asked him to snib the window for her against the evening air.

'And why didn't you bring Helen with you? Both of you are always welcome, you know.'

'Helen doesn't know I'm here. My visit is as big a surprise to me as it must be to you,' and he sat down, explaining how he had been having a game of golf on the links and had met Father Lacy on the road home, and that it was on his account that he had made this call so late in the evening: 'And here it is in a nutshell. You know that Mrs. Toner is retiring from the school in September and that we are appointing a new assistant in her place?'

'I never thought Mrs. Toner had reached the age limit. She doesn't look a day older than fifty,' Elizabeth exclaimed.

'She's exactly fifteen times three hundred and sixty-five days older than fifty,' Master Lynch said with easy good humour, and not wishing to be deflected from the words he had rehearsed on his way up to their house he went on: 'Father Lacy has appointed a young girl to take Mrs. Toner's place. And this is where you come in: I was wondering — at least Father Lacy was wondering — if you would be good enough and kind enough to put her up.'

'Oh, Master Lynch,' Mary said in a shocked voice, 'we never kept lodgers in our life. Indeed, we wouldn't know how to handle one.'

'No, Peter, we never kept boarders,' Elizabeth supported.

'But this is a very exceptional girl by all accounts,' Peter emphasized. 'She's a university graduate and she's musical. Her father, a doctor, died when she was young, and so did her mother. She was reared by an aunt. Father Lacy seems to have known her people intimately.'

'But . . .' Mary protested.

'She might be some harum-scarum, some fly-by-night that would break the peace of our home,' Elizabeth interrupted.

Peter laughed: 'If Father Lacy heard you he'd be offended. You don't think for one moment he'd bring a girl of that description into the school — he's too shrewd.'

'He's too soft, you mean. I don't think much of his last two appointments,' Elizabeth said. 'That young Murphy fellow is so conceited he wouldn't bid you the time of day if he met you in a twenty-acre field; and he has the children scared out of their wits into the bargain. And as for poor Mister Brennan I often wonder why Father Lacy brought that lazy man back here, and the sloth oozing out of him like a damp wall.'

'Well, well,' Peter said, locking his fingers together to control a capricious enjoyment of these outspoken comments. 'You've a mighty poor opinion of the school.'

'Now, please, don't misunderstand me,' Elizabeth corrected. 'Everybody knows how hard you work, Master Lynch. I never heard an ill word about you from any party or any quarter since you came here ten years ago. Look at the fine scholars you've turned out,' and she went on, with Mary's help, to name a priest, a doctor, two teachers, and five lawyers that had passed through his hands.

'I didn't do it all myself. A school is a school. Before the boys reach me in the top standards they have to pass through the other classes and, if they are not taught well there, I can do little or nothing,' he tried to say with conviction though it wasn't what he really felt, for since he came into the school he got little or no co-operation from those who taught with him. 'Will you think over the message I brought you — will you do that?' he asked, looking diplomatically from one to the other.

'Master Lynch, we're too old to be dancing attendance on lodgers,' Mary said gravely. 'Sure we've no place here for them but the spare room, and it'd need to be repapered from top to bottom and the floor margins varnished. No, we couldn't think of it. And sure you never can call the house your own with lodgers parked in every corner of it and sprawling all over your armchairs. Oh, dear me, what made Father Lacy think of us — of all people?'

'You'd think I was asking you to house a group of down-and-out actors. It's clear that Father Lacy thinks a lot of her people when he asks you to take her. If you don't get on well with her you can dissolve the company at a week's notice. What could be easier than that?'

Mary sighed: 'Sure, Peter, we could never give anybody a week's notice. Look how often poor Johnny has gone on the spree and we hadn't the heart to turn him out.' She stared at her hands and then suddenly clapped them together with the joy of discovery: 'I've got it! Sure Helen could put her up, now that you've plenty of room in your new bungalow.'

'Mary!' Elizabeth declared in a shocked tone. 'It wouldn't be proper!'

'Proper? Couldn't she stay as well over there as here? She'd be beside the school for one thing. And now that Helen has a new cooker, preparing the table would be a pleasure for her.'

'It wouldn't do at all,' Elizabeth explained, shaking her head solemnly. 'People would talk. After all, Master Lynch is still a young bachelor.'

'I'm not saying he isn't, am I? I'm just saying that Helen could keep her and fend for her better than we could. There's no harm in that suggestion, is there?'

Peter smiled, ran his fingers through his auburn hair, and stretched out his legs. Mary saw the squashed gooseberry clinging to the welt of his shoe, and in her confusion to distract his attention she held out her hand towards the surplice at the side of Elizabeth's chair. Elizabeth glared at her, rolled up the surplice primly and put it on the window-ledge. It was unfinished and she wasn't going to display it now. There was a long silence.

Staring at his sun-bronzed hands and then at his finger-nails Peter said quietly: 'Father Lacy thought, and so did I, that your place would be the most suitable about here for a girl of this type. There isn't another house here nor in the town that we could recommend. She's a charming girl, by all accounts. And, as I have said, she's a doctor's daughter.'

'Give us a day or two to consider it,' Elizabeth said.

'We needn't consider it,' Mary intervened, having sensed the restraint that would press down on their year-hardened habits, and realizing also that they were too old to go changing their ways for a young strip of a girl. 'We can say "no" now, and not have Master Lynch sitting back on his heels and smiling at his good fortune. There's plenty of places in the town that would be glad of her — the hotel, for instance.'

'The hotel would be too expensive. And as for the other places you wouldn't wish her to be settled among labouring men, would you? Men that mightn't shave from a Monday till a Saturday. And then their language! — the girl would leave us in a week.'

'Father Lacy wouldn't take offence if we refused?' Mary ventured meekly. 'I wouldn't like to offend Father Lacy — I would not indeed. He was so attentive when Paul was ill; I'll never forget his kindness on that occasion. And yet I don't know how to accept. And then we wouldn't know what to charge per week, or is it per month? Dear, oh dear, it's lamentable. And, Peter, you shouldn't have encouraged Father Lacy in that idea — you, of all people, that knows us so well.'

'You'd think we had asked you to harbour a fugitive. It's a young lady we're bringing you. In a short time you'll be as fond of her as you would be of a niece.'

'A lady! Sure the meals we serve might not be to her liking.'

'Mary, your cooking is the envy of the countryside. Helen prides herself in that line, but — and I'm her brother — she couldn't hold a candle to yours, not if she had all the latest gadgets from here to Paris and back again . . . You'll take her, won't you? There's Elizabeth and she's dying to say yes.'

'It's a big responsibility,' Elizabeth said with a superior air. 'But if we agree to take her it must be understood that we are

19

doing it to oblige Father Lacy and yourself. The neighbours needn't think that we have any crying need to take in a boarder.'

'As if any neighbour would think that of the Miss Devlins! Elizabeth, I'm astonished at you!' and he laughed so heartily that Mary and Elizabeth were forced to laugh with him.

'It's agreed that you'll take this girl for a while. Nora Angela Byrne is her name.'

Neither of the sisters spoke and he added: 'Father Lacy will be a pleased man when I tell him. Of course he knew he was making his request to the right people — to two of his most respected parishioners.'

'She's a nice class of a girl, from what you say,' Elizabeth softened, 'and she may be good company by all accounts.'

'She may be the divil's own company if she doesn't come in till all hours of the morning,' Mary said. 'That'd be a nice how-do-you-do.'

'It would be a nice how-do-you-do for us all, if that were the case. But it won't be the case, and you won't have any trouble on that score.'

Peter looked at his watch and wound it up. Then he saw the squashed gooseberry at the side of his shoe, and tearing a leaf from a note-book he wiped it off and threw the crumpled paper to the back of the firescreen. 'You never know what you'll trample on, even out on the links.'

The two sisters were too startled and too ashamed to admit the truth, and when Peter stood up to take his leave they escorted him to the door in a daze of bewildered stupefaction. He shook hands with them and said that he always knew there were at least two ladies in the parish and that Nora Angela Byrne might be a third.

When his car had driven off they came inside and Elizabeth sat down as if in a state of complete exhaustion.

'That's a nice present he brought us,' Mary said. 'One never knows what's round the turn of the road.'

'Don't talk till I gather my breath. I'm so weak you could knock me down with a wren's feather.'

'Don't collapse on me, whatever you do. I'll have a lot more to face before this is all over . . . To think that the Miss Devlins have stooped to keeping lodgers!'

'You're very coarse, Mary. Please call her "our guest" or "our teacher friend". There's something very low about "lodger"; it sounds as harsh in my ears as "codger" or "dodger" . . . In any case you shouldn't have agreed to take her when you knew I was dead-set against it from the very first.'

'Elizabeth! You didn't support me when I was saying "no". Not a word did you say.'

'Surely you realized that when I didn't speak I was giving you my silent approval?'

'Sitting idly by is poor help in untying a hard knot.'

'Oh, Mary dear, you shouldn't have softened. The same Peter could coax a fox out of its hole. He's away off now with himself, as happy as a successful auctioneer. What possessed you to say yes to him?'

'We needn't squabble over it. It's done now, and before the night's much older he'll have brought the good news to Father Lacy. We must accept it. But always bear in mind that we can get rid of her if she's not to our liking.'

'That's so. We can always comfort ourselves in that way.'

But Mary wasn't listening to her; she was standing up, one hand fidgeting at the edge of the table, the other fingering the lobe of her ear. She took a hairpin from her hair, stared at it, and put it back again. She crossed to the window and looked out at the darkness bundling around the bushes and at the crescent moon like a silver swing boat above the chestnut trees. She gave a loud anxious sigh.

'Rest yourself, Mary dear, I know by the cut of you that you're going to start in as if this Nora what-you-call-her were arriving tomorrow. We have many weeks to get things in order. Sit down, please, or you'll only upset me and bring on one of my headaches.'

As if she hadn't heard her, Mary whisked out of the room,

and in a few minutes Elizabeth heard the pounding of feet in the spare room above her head.

'That woman will be the death of me,' she said, and lifting the surplice from the window-ledge she unrolled it, and in the dim light from the sky admired the soft lacy pattern and strove to seek comfort from it. But the movement of furniture above her head and the murderous thud of the brush on the floor made her roll it up and hurry from the room. She climbed the stairs, and underneath the oil-lamp on the landing saw the place piled with suit-cases and cardboard boxes. She tried to open the door of the spare room but as there was a bed pulled against it she could only stick her head in and saw to her dismay that Mary with a cloth over her head was brushing the floor by candlelight and hadn't heard her.

'Mary!' Elizabeth shouted. 'Stop this madness at once or I'll go straight over to Father Lacy and tell him we can't take this girl. We have our good health to consider.'

'We have our good word to consider. We'll not go back on that, even if it costs us our health,' and Mary continued to brush vigorously, the dust whorling round the candle flame.

'You're very prudent, I must say. Tomorrow's a new day, Mary. And what's the use of brushing the floor when you know the walls have to be repapered and Johnny goes thumping over the floor and spitting horrid brown spits here, there, and everywhere — thick spits that you'll have to scrape off with an old knife? You're only doubling your work. Listen to reason, Mary,' and she put a hand to her brow, groaned, and said that her poor head was splitting.

Mary laid the brush against the wall. She eyed her sister with puzzled concern, slowly untied the cloth from her head and blew out the candle.

'Yes, Elizabeth,' she agreed quietly. 'We must be reasonable and take things easily.'

'That's what I maintain. Take things in their stride. We mustn't fuss unnecessarily. Sure, after all, what is she but a school-teacher!'

In the kitchen, under the hanging oil-lamp, they stirred up the range and heated some milk for themselves, and though they tried to speak of other things their minds slipped unnoticed back to Nora Angela Byrne, and they wondered what they had done or hadn't done that God should afflict their house with a stranger — a house where no stranger had ever strayed or stayed before.

When she had seen Elizabeth into bed and had given her a hot water bottle she exhorted her for the love of God to put all thought of this girl out of her mind.

'I'll do that, Mary dear,' she said feebly. 'At our age we must do what will suit us and not what will suit Master Peter Lynch. If I had him here for a minute I'd speak to him in a language that he'd understand. It's wonderful the rush of words that can whorl up in your mind when you're lying flat in your bed.'

'It's better to let them whorl down again if you want any sleep,' Mary advised as she stood at the window looking at the stars sparkling among the chestnut trees. 'I must go now, Elizabeth. It's so dark below you can hardly see the bushes. But it's a lovely night all the same. If you look at the stars winking through the leaves it'll make you sleep. Good night, Elizabeth.'

'Good night, Mary dear. Say a prayer that I'll sleep.'

Mary didn't go to her own room. She tiptoed down the stairs, and seeing a light in the outhouse window where Johnny slept she crossed the yard and tapped at his door.

'Oh, it's you, Miss Mary,' he said, standing on one bare foot, his coat off, and a razor in his hand. 'I was just paring a corn.'

'I want you to run into town tomorrow and bring me out some patterns of wallpaper.'

He pointed his razor at the room where his lamp rested on the table: 'Sure them walls have no need of wallpaper. I'd rather have the distemper that's on them for it's my firm and honest opinion that wallpaper gathers every dirt and dust and encourages moths and mice and every mortal disease.'

'Ah, Johnny, it's Paul's old room I'm thinking of. We're expecting a visitor, a friend of Father Lacy's.'

'Wouldn't that be colossal trouble and expense to go to for a bird of passage? And, to tell you the truth, I'm not a great hand at the wallpapering.'

'She may be here for a long stay.'

'Aye,' he said, rubbing his bare foot on the leg of his trousers and awaiting further explanation. 'She must be mighty important if Paul's room isn't grand enough for her. Is she a sort of quality person that wants everything elaborate?'

'She's the new teacher that's coming to take the place of Mrs. Toner in the school.'

He cut the air with his gleaming razor and she told him to close it in case he'd do damage to himself.

'I never heard anybody to be over particular about a schoolteacher. I never did. Look at the cut of Master Brennan, there's as many stains on his waistcoat as there is on a painter's jacket.'

'This guest of ours, that we are expecting, is a lady,' Mary said.

'A lady!' and he whistled with astonishment. 'You're not wanting the room done up at once, for I've a terrible load of sick pullets on my mind? I've some there in a box in the room with me. They need careful handling day and night.'

'In four weeks I'd need to have it done.'

'Ach, when I'm at myself I could wallop it up in half that time. I'll have a look at it tomorrow. But don't dream of tearing off the old paper, Miss Mary. I've always heard it said that new paper slapped on over the old paper keeps out the damp.'

'There's not a trace of damp in Paul's room!'

'I'm not saying there is, Miss Mary. Damp can crawl in like a thief in the night — it can indeed. Into the best-kept houses it can creep: a slate can crack unbeknownst to us or a hair-crack come in the lead gulleys — and then where are you? You've a damp stain there's no accounting for.'

'Tomorrow, get the patterns,' she said curtly, for he was in one of his moods of explaining and counter-explaining that would aggravate a desert saint. 'And do be careful with that razor, Johnny. And I told you before not to put the lamp on the table but to keep it on the wall. Some night you'll burn the place down over your head.'

'I had to put it there to see this brute of a corn that has the life and soul tortured out of me.'

'Good night now, Johnny. And go into town early for the patterns.'

She crossed the yard, quenched the lamp in the kitchen, and taking her own hand-lamp she slipped upstairs. She halted for a minute outside Elizabeth's door and was pleased to hear her snoring deeply. 'The poor thing must be fagged out,' she said to herself as she went into her own room.

She knelt down and said her prayers, praying for direction and patience, and when she was in bed she prayed herself into sleep. And in her troubled sleep she dreamt she had walked in her bare feet to Father Lacy and had told him rudely that they couldn't take this girl, and the priest had shed green tears as big as chestnuts and as they burst on the ground out hopped a swarm of gooseberries. She awoke then with a start only to hear the rain pelting like hailstones against the window.

2

ON a Saturday in September Nora Angela Byrne arrived by bus in the little town, and as the bus halted in the Square two soldiers, who were seated in front of her, gave a pluck to their tunics and a hitch to their belts, and lifted down her case for her from the rack. She allowed them to pass out in front of her, and as she stood in the sunlit Square, timid of her new surroundings, and not knowing which of the two roads in front of her led to the Miss Devlins she heard an old tramp asking the soldiers for money.

'We'll give you some on pay day,' the soldiers said, swinging their yellow canes and marching on.

'And when in the name of God is that?'

'Monday!' the soldiers laughed.

'Aw, the army's gone to hell! When I was in it we were paid every bloody hour,' and the tramp scratched his cropped head, turned round and stared at Nora's case with alert curiosity. She was already poking in her handbag for a sixpence, and when she handed it to him he lifted the case and asked her where she was heading for.

'It's all right, thank you,' she said, 'I can carry it myself. I'm only going as far as the Miss Devlins.'

'That's a brave piece out of the town — a long way to swing a heavy bag the like of that. Follow me. I'm not the man to take money for nothing,' and to her embarrassment he strode off with the case, and she followed, pleading with him not to trouble.

'Trouble? It's no trouble at all. Sure what the hell have I to do except loiter till the next bus comes in in the evening. Come on, girl. The Devlins know me. Mary's a grand woman, but the Elizabeth one is as stiff as a starched shirt.'

She kept two paces behind him through the main street and

tried to smile off her uneasiness when two youths, who were repairing a jacked-up motor car, whistled after them. The barber, through the open door of his shop saw her and the tramp, and he halted in shaving a customer and stared at them over the frosted glass of his window. A publican, rereading his newspaper spread out on the counter, came to the door and stood with his hands under his apron, wondering who she was and where she was going. But Nora was unaware of their prying eyes, for her whole attention was knotted on the best plan of retrieving her bag. For one thing her escort was very dirty and she did not know what the Devlins would think of her or of him if he insisted in accompanying her up to the very door: his hand that gripped her new case was black, his raincoat was spotted with grease as if it had dripped on him from a colander and his bare heels flopped up and down in two odd shoes.

In a few minutes they had left the little town behind them and were out in the silence of the country fields, and there he slackened his pace, took to the middle of the road, and transferred the bag from one hand to the other. The sun was warm, and on the dusty hedges there gleamed handfuls of blackberries.

'I can find my way now, thank you,' she said. 'You can give me the bag now — it's too heavy for you.'

'Heavy? What are you talking about, girl? I could swing that bag for ten miles and not produce two blobs of sweat on that head of mine. Are you for stopping long with Mary and Elizabeth?' he asked, still holding on to the bag.

'Yes — no. Yes — I don't know exactly,' she said querulously.

'You're not a friend of theirs?'

'No.'

'And what in God's name takes you here? Sure there'll be no fun for a fine girl like you with two old blades the like of the Devlins.'

'I'm here on business.'

'Business?' and he gave a whistle of surprise. 'Business — sure that's a man's job. What class of business?'

'Please give me the bag. I'm taking you out of your way. Leave it down for a minute,' and she unzipped her handbag for another sixpence.

'No, girl, you've paid me and my work's not done. Do you think I'd take another cent from a fine girl like you? I would not indeed. I'll see you right to the Devlins' gate. I'd march up with you to the very door only I might meet Elizabeth. Ah, she's the right oul hairpin! What do you think of her?'

She pretended she hadn't heard him.

'What errand are you on?' he probed.

She sighed with impatience, but thinking that if she satisfied his curiosity she could get rid of him she said boldly: 'I'm the new teacher for the Boys' School.'

'A school-teacher, by the holy! Listen to that – a school-teacher. And do you mean to tell me that a lovely prancing girl like you is a school-teacher? I wouldn't have believed it only it has come from your own lips – I would not indeed. And you'll be teaching with Master Lynch and Master Brennan and Master Luke Murphy . . . Do you know what I'm going to tell you?' and he shouted challengingly across the hedges. 'I could teach the heads off the whole bloody lot of them. I could, man. If you were gasping for a smoke there's not one of them except Master Lynch would give you a stale butt. Teaching! I could teach the whole town every day in the week including Sunday, I could indeed. You wouldn't think to look at me that I've an aunt a teacher in Australia and a sister a nun in New Zealand.' He shook his head proudly and raised his cap in salute. 'I'd be at the teaching myself only they tell me I'm not right in the head. Do you know what I'm going to tell you, girl? When I wasn't the height of two turf I sat in the same desk as Master Brennan and I'd my sums done while he'd be sucking the paint off his pencil and wondering to the good God whether he should add, subtract, or multiply. Ah, my lovely girl, I was the bright scholar in them days. Ask Master Brennan if you don't believe me. Joey O'Brien is my name, but I've no fixed abode.'

'I believe you all right. But give me the bag, please, please.'

'I'll give it to you at the Devlins'. We're in sight of it now. That's it there — away to the right among the trees. You needn't ask Elizabeth if she knows me, for she'd give me a character that no judge in the bench would let cross his sacred lips. Do you smoke, girl?'

She shook her head.

'You don't! Sure every whipster of a girl smokes like a coal-boat. Man alive, if I'd a smoke I could tramp with that bag from Fair Head in Antrim to Mizzen Head in Cork.'

He walked off the road to the hedges, and regardless of the dust that lay on the blackberries he plucked a handful and stuffed them into his mouth. He chewed them as loudly as a horse. 'That will kill the wild hunger in me for a smoke.'

She was suddenly frightened by his purple lips and tongue and looked round helplessly for some protection. The bag was at his feet, the brown sweaty handle gleaming like fresh liver. He crouched over it, fingered the label and spelt out her name loudly: 'Nora Angela Byrne — a sweet name. My sister that's the nun out in New Zealand is called Angela. Would you believe that now? She was born when the Angelus was ringing and brought her name with her. I bet you never heard the like of that before.' He stopped and raised his head, listening.

A flock of sheep was approaching, taking up the whole width of the road, and at the sight of them Nora's courage revived. She lifted her bag and pressed close against the hedge to let them pass. A drover, smoking a cigarette, followed the sheep, a dog with two odd eyes trotting at the side. When the sheep had shooshed past her Nora suddenly realized she was alone, the tramp having gone off with the drover. She was afraid to look back, and she hurried on, tugged by a feeling of relief and yet of annoyance, for she was wondering if she had said anything that had insulted him.

The road descended to a small quay where a collier was un-loading coal, a few children with baskets staring at the swinging crane-bucket. She stood for a moment to calm her agitation, breathing in the salty air from the lough, and rejoicing in the braids of it that combed past her forehead. At a nearby stream, that ran under the road into the sea, she rested for awhile, and then dabbled her perspiring hands in the water and wiped the handle of her case. She opened her flapjack quickly, arranged the strands of hair that had been blown awry by the open windows of the bus, and lifted her case.

From an upstair window of the house Elizabeth had been on the look-out for her, and perceiving her bent over the stream she wondered to the good God what the girl was examining and hoped she wasn't the kind of teacher that would bring tadpoles or insects into the house — if that were the case she'd just empty them down the sink for her!

The door was open to the sunlight, and when Nora tapped the brass-shining knocker the two sisters appeared at once in the hallway and introduced themselves.

'So you found your way all right,' Elizabeth said. 'It's a nice walk out from the town when you can make your own time.'

'It is. I enjoyed the walk very much. I love the country at this time of the year with the leaves on the turn and the air so fresh and clear.'

'It's all right in a way, I suppose,' Elizabeth said dryly. 'But it can be lonely here and quiet at times. . . .'

'I'm sure you're famished with the hunger after your long journey. Come now and I'll show you to your room, and we'll have dinner quite soon,' Mary said, as she lifted her bag, and walked upstairs, telling her over her shoulder that her bicycle and trunk arrived safe and sound, and that the bicycle was in an outhouse in the yard.

'This is your room,' she said with bright pride, ushering Nora in in front of her. 'And there's your trunk in the corner. You may close that window if you find the air too strong.'

'I love it the way it is. What a lovely view from the window!'

'It's grand except for those telephone wires outside; they make my eyes dance a jig in my head. You won't have far to go to the school, for that's it there fornenst you on the hill. That grey place with the round window in the gable. It's a bit dirty-looking just now, but when the sun shines on it in the mornings it looks as white as a bee-hive. And just beyond to the left, if you look hard, you'll see a red bungalow with trees around it. That's Master Lynch's, and he lives there with his sister Helen. They're a nice pair and are great friends of ours. Oh, I forgot to mention that the Girls' School is at the other side of the town . . . But I'll not detain you with my chatter, for I'm sure you're dying for a wash-up. There's water in that jug, but if you prefer using the bathroom it's straight across the landing. If they'd only bring the electric light out to us from the town we'd be fairly comfortable and with no complaints. But we're promised the electric soon.'

Left alone Nora unpacked a few frocks, put them on hangers, and hung them in the wardrobe. She spread her brushes on the table, washed her face and hands in the basin of water, and, on combing her hair, wondered what they'd think of the grey patch that was so noticeable in the dividing blackness of her hair. Her aunt had told her it was attractive with a face so young as hers, and advised her to keep the dye away from it. 'As if I'd ever think of dyeing it,' she smiled into the mirror. 'I wouldn't touch it — not if it turned all grey before I was thirty. I would not! I'm not as vain as all that.' She looked at her cheeks: the journey had magnified their pallor, and she supposed too that the encounter with the tramp had added to it. She patted them with her fingers, touched her lips slightly with lipstick, and descending the stairs shyly she stood at the hall door and gazed at the brown-leafed trees and the swallows gathering on the telephone wires.

In the kitchen the two sisters were discussing her appearance, especially her paleness, and Elizabeth was hoping they hadn't brought a delicate girl into the house: a parentless girl, too, that they might have to nurse back to health and wear themselves out in the thankless struggle.

'I agreed to take her and I'll take the responsibility,' Mary declared as she stooped over the range.

'I'm relieved to hear that. You know I was against the project from the very first.'

'We'll not have that all over again — and the girl here in the house with us. You never breathed a syllable against it. You can't deny that — and that's enough!'

'Oh, I could deny it, but this isn't the time nor the place to defend myself. If she's not strong, it wasn't right nor proper for Master Lynch or Father Lacy to foist her on to two old people like us.'

'I'm sure they didn't ask her to furnish a doctor's certificate. For goodness' sake leave things alone for awhile and stop this useless worrying. We did it out of kindness — and that's its own reward. We'll not turn our backs to the plough, after us pledging our own good word. And anyway she might be stronger than we imagine.'

'It'd be a terrible blow, after all our expense in getting the house painted and her room done up in the latest style.'

'Will you go out, please, to the sitting-room and entertain our friend till I get this blessed dinner on the table?'

Elizabeth went into the hall and found Nora in the doorway, her shadow stretched out behind her.

'Oh, there you are, Miss Byrne. I didn't hear you come down. I was helping Mary in the kitchen. You see we have only ourselves here, and have no servant girl since our poor brother's demise six years ago. Up to then, of course, we always had a servant or two, but latterly we found we didn't require one. Two old ladies can fend better on their own. It gives us more independence.'

'I can well understand that,' Nora said as Elizabeth motioned her into an armchair where the sunlight from the window fell directly upon her. 'I'll be able to give a hand when I'm settled in,' she added politely.

Elizabeth pooh-poohed that suggestion, and as she adjusted

32

four pegs on a wooden frame placed on the table she looped a skein of wool around them and began to unwind it, at the same time studying Nora's appearance with a disconcerting intensity. Yes, she was decidedly pale, Elizabeth said to herself: that black hair should be glossier for a girl of her age, and that grey streak in the middle might be another indication of delicate health; her brown eyes were too bright, and though she was tall one couldn't exactly call her thin. But her clothes: the navy-blue tailored skirt, the hand-made shoes, the white silk blouse and the gold cross round her neck, were certainly not bought out of a teacher's salary. No, this girl, Elizabeth concluded, had money behind her.

As she began to question her skilfully about her father she noted that the girl's voice was both musical and unaffected, and she reasoned that, whatever else she was, she was surely a well-reared young lady.

'And he died when you were ten, poor child. He must have been a young man then.'

'I think he was about forty.'

'Forty — dear me, that was very young to die. Our poor brother, God be good to him, was fifty-six when he died. Of course he had angina, and he was lying for almost a year. If a young man dies it's usually from the heart or, God preserve us, from something malignant or, perhaps, consumption. It's usually some ailment of that nature that takes them away from us when they're young.'

Nora clasped her long hands on her lap, and averting her eyes from the thinning skein of wool on the frame she said quietly: 'My father met with an accident. He was flung out of a trap when his pony shied at a barrel of tar on the roadside.'

'How very sad!' Elizabeth said, and sighed audibly — a sigh of relief rather than sympathy. She wound her wool rapidly.

'Those roadmenders are very careless,' she added after a pause. 'I remember once when I was coming from devotions on a moon-lit night in October and I saw something rise up suddenly on the road in front of me. I thought at first it was a horse that had broken loose from a field, but when I shooshed at it and stamped my feet there wasn't a budge out of it. Then the moon slipped out from behind a cloud, and what do you think I was shooshing at? A tar-boiler, if you please, one of those fellows with the long necks on them.'

Nora smiled.

'It was very funny, indeed,' Elizabeth pursued, 'and I laughed to myself the whole way home. And ever since, if Mary sees one on the road, she says: "There's your black horse, Elizabeth." But it'd have been a different laughing matter if I'd run up against it in the dark and destroyed my good clothes on the tar. But I wouldn't have let them off with their carelessness — that's not the kind of me. I'd have made them pay compensation.' And she recounted proudly how, on another occasion, she had made her grocer pay for a new coat she had ruined against the freshly painted door of his shop. 'It was his own fault, of course. He had no Wet Paint sign pinned to the door to warn you. I suppose, Miss Byrne, you never had any experiences like that.'

'None that I can remember,' Nora said. And then she smiled, a smile of conscious irrelevance. 'The only thing strange that has happened to me recently was the removal of my tonsils. I say "strange" because it is such a childish complaint to come to me at my age.'

'Dear, oh dear, that was serious enough for a girl of your years. You must have lost a good deal of blood.'

'I suppose I did. But I seemed to get over it quickly enough, thank God.'

'You must excuse me for a minute, Miss Byrne, till I get another skein of wool and see what's happened to the dinner,' and she hurried off to impart to Mary the uplifting news she had just heard.

'I hope, Elizabeth, you're not being inquisitively rude with your questions. You could have waited a day or two, at least, before being so personal.'

34

'Rude, indeed! The girl told me all about her tonsils and her father's death, without being asked a single question. Rude — I like that!'

'I'm sorry, Elizabeth. It's not in your nature to be rude.'

'It is not indeed. It would have been unmannerly to interrupt the girl when she was speaking of these personal matters.'

'Allow me to say it's very unmannerly to leave your guest alone,' and Mary rapidly stirred parsley sauce that was heating on the range.

Elizabeth swept back to the sitting-room. Nora was standing at the window looking at the trees and admiring a chestnut that had burst open on the ground and its brown leathery skin gleaming like a horse's eye.

'You've a great crop of chestnuts out there, Miss Devlin. I suppose the boys gather them on their way from school?'

'H'm, they don't wait till they fall. They fire sticks and stones into the branches, and last year they broke a window on us with all their clodding; but Master Lynch made them pay up their pennies and put in a new pane. They've left us in peace ever since. He knows how to handle youngsters. But they all like him in spite of everything. I'm sure you'll be very happy with him in his school.' And taking Nora's arm she led her back to the armchair while she herself looped another skein over the pegs and sat down in her former position.

'Dinner will be ready directly.'

'There's no hurry. Don't let me upset your time in any way,' Nora said, sensing a feeling of dry irritability in the old lady's voice. She moved her head into a leaf-shadow that screened her eyes from the tantalizing sun and wished she could escape so easily from the critical gaze of this inquisitive woman. Standing up she asked to be allowed to unwind the wool, but Elizabeth wouldn't hear of such an offer and told her it was very monotonous work and she'd prefer to do it herself. And then, suddenly, when Nora was again seated she said to her: 'Forgive me, Miss

Byrne, for my carelessness, but I forgot to ask about your dear mother.'

A nerve quivered at Nora's mouth, she fidgeted uncomfortably, and Elizabeth regretted having spoken.

'She died shortly after my father. What she died of I do not know.'

'I am sorry for bringing these sad memories back to you. What am I thinking about at all, at all?' she excused, misinterpreting Nora's feeling of discomfort.

Nora felt the colour prickling her cheeks, and aware that the warm nakedness of that flush exposed her embarrassment she bent her head to hide it. She clasped her hands on her lap and wished she had the courage to say boldly, and without any trace of defiance or arrogance, that her mother had died seven years ago in a sanatorium and that she had had an elder sister who had died there too. There's the truth for you, and let it be known to everyone! Have the mothers in despair that a girl like me should be teaching their youngest boys, bending over them and breathing into their very faces. Yes, tell everyone. If I go to a dance be charitable and let them know about me, so that my partners may hold their heads sideways and not let my breath mingle with theirs! But tell them — if you'll believe me — that there is nothing of that nature wrong with me. No matter what they may think, they need not be afraid. Since my little operation for my tonsils my chest has been X-rayed, and there was nothing abnormal in the photo: no spot, thank God, no indication that there would ever be one. All that my doctor has ordered me to do is to avoid unnecessary tension and worry. You can tell them that, if you wish, and tell them also that I have a broken engagement behind me. I was engaged to a cashier in a bank, but he broke it off. He feared the worst when he heard the family history.

Oh, if I could say all that it would be difficult, but it would be the truth and there'd be relief in it, she said directly to her own mind, and gazed at her hands clasped firmly on her lap. Nothing,

36

O God, can excuse a lie — nothing, not even the tortures of the naked truth.

She took a handkerchief from her sleeve and blew her nose, stiffening herself against an inclination to cry. Inquisitive questioning woman! What right has she to know about my mother's death or my sister's? She deserved the lie she got — and any way there was nothing malicious in my telling it. But maybe I misjudge her. Maybe she asked these questions out of sympathy and not curiosity. I mustn't judge people too quickly!

'I'm sorry,' Elizabeth said again, and looked at the open door, fearful that Mary might come in and notice the feeling of disquiet in the room. 'I know how you must feel for the loss of your dear parents. We'll talk no more about these sad matters,' she added, and in order to detain Mary for awhile longer and also to escape from that pitiable strain on the girl's face she excused herself and went off to the kitchen. Her absence would give the girl time to regain her composure.

'Mary, she's a charming girl,' Elizabeth announced in the kitchen, and rested a hand on her sister's shoulder. 'She's charming. But she's a sensitive girl — and you must be careful what you say to her. She's had a good deal of trouble in her day, I think.'

'I suppose that has helped to form her charm.'

'It has, I suppose. But we've had our share of trouble too, when you come to think of it.'

'We have, but I don't think it has given us much charm or whatever you care to call it, Elizabeth.'

'We may possess charm, in the eyes of an outsider, for all we know.'

'Well, if I possess any of it, I'm not going to bother about it, for up to now it has done me neither harm nor good that I'm aware of. However, will you please get Miss Byrne seated at the table before this dinner is spoiled on me. I'll not have much of me charm left if that happens.'

37

'I will do so at once, Mary. Remember to be careful what you say to her. Take my advice and ask few questions.'

Elizabeth went back to the sitting-room. 'Come, dear,' she said, leading Nora by the arm across the hallway. 'We have the dinner ready at long last.' And as Nora felt her arm being pressed she realized she was being sympathized with for the wrong reasons — even from that she could take no consolation.

✿ 3 ✿

THE mahogany table draped with a yellow linen cloth was laid for three people, and with a rapid glance at the shining cutlery and the pleated serviettes standing like fans in the tumblers Nora sensed uncomfortably that these people were making unaccustomed efforts to please her — people who would ordinarily, perhaps, be dining in the kitchen near the heat and close comfort of the range.

Mary seated her opposite Elizabeth, but in the cool leafy light from the window, and with an unobtrusive movement of her hand she made the sign of the cross, and with a contented, 'Now, now, but *I* was long in preparing this,' she offered Nora bread with her chicken soup and said: 'And at what time, Nora — yes, we must call you Nora without any more to-do's about it — at what time did you leave home?'

'At nine this morning. But I had time for a nice cup of coffee on my way through Belfast.'

'You must be starving. Elizabeth and me will do the talking and give you time to eat after such a long journey from home.'

Home! The word sounded strange, for never at any time could Nora refer to her aunt's house as her home. She never thought of it in that way, and, for that matter, she didn't care if she were never to return to it. Her aunt and uncle and their children, she believed, were glad to get rid of her presence about the house, but to be just to everyone, she must admit, that she was also pleased to be shot of them. Ever since her slight operation for her tonsils — three days in hospital — her nerves were not strong, and furthermore the last school she had taught in was not to her liking: for one thing she disliked the strain in it, the selfishness, and the continual snapping and vexing that prevailed among the staff — an environment that her doctor had warned her to avoid if possible. And it was that warning that impelled her to look out for a change; and when this new school was advertised — the Infant Department in a Boys' School — it was her aunt who pressed her to apply for it. The manager, Father Lacy, had married Nora's father and mother and he would probably appoint her because of that strong acquaintance. Her aunt, too, would send a personal letter to him. How sweet of her aunt to do that! Nora recalled that decision with a dry smile, for on that very day her aunt had been in ill-humour because of her eldest son's failure to matriculate — a failure which she accused Nora of fostering because of her indifferent interest in the poor boy's French. Indifference! — that certainly wasn't true. Tom had shown no willingness to learn it all the time she had been coaching him. 'I can do nothing with him,' she had declared to her aunt, 'because where the will to learn is absent I'd rather break stones than try to teach.' 'But you should make him,' her aunt had said. 'Boss him and threaten him! After all, you are his first cousin, and a teacher, and a university graduate no less! Surely you should know the right method and the proper means of dealing with a difficult boy.' Nora had smiled, then, to prevent herself from uttering the blunt truth, that Tom was not graced with brains. Her aunt had noticed the smile, and accused her, there and then, of cold ingratitude. They quarrelled. Ingratitude! It was untrue. Hadn't she done her level best for the lazy fellow? Her uncle knew that, her aunt knew it too, but still they blamed her and not their son.

'Nora, dear, allow me to help you to some more chicken and ham,' Mary interjected, 'or more mashed potatoes or parsley sauce. You're eating nothing.'

'Oh, I've never eaten so much in all my life. Everything is so lovely, and your table is the last word.'

'Drink plenty of that fresh milk. We have lashings and leavings of it.'

'There's nothing so good for the complexion, nothing so nourishing as cream while the cows are still on the grass,' said Elizabeth.

40

'I've never tasted so rich a milk before,' and Nora held out her tumbler to be refilled.

Such relief to be free from her aunt for a while — free to forge out for herself her own life, a new life, unhindered by the cool asperity of her uncle and the monotonous talk of the matriculation examination. But — and she cast a glance across the table — would she be able to get on agreeably with this woman opposite? Father Lacy had written: 'We have managed to get you a nice comfortable place not far from the school. A place, where, I can assure you, you will be well looked after.' Yes, she would be well looked after — there was no mistake about that. Another few meals like this and she'd be in despair about her waist-line. But there's one thing she must do. She must pull herself out of this sensitiveness about her health. These references to food and milk were, she must strive to believe, ordinary friendly gestures and did not imply any polite anxiety about her pallor or appearance. Yes, please God, in time she'd be able to grow into their ways and let these snips and snippets of conversation glide impersonally past her. They knew nothing about her mother and her sister and what they died of, and she'd take good care that they'd never know — she'd not cause them any undue fear if she could help it.

'I can safely recommend Mary's apple tart. Allow me to give you another helping.'

'Really, Miss Devlin, I couldn't touch another crumb.'

'I hope you're not slimming — that would never do in this house,' and Mary wagged a forefinger at her. 'And now we'll have a little cup of coffee to follow.'

'Oh, mercy on us!' Nora sighed; and though she seldom indulged in overeating she forced herself to sample everything she was offered. Mary was delighted, for there was nothing she hated more than cooking a meal that wouldn't be eaten, and she was convinced now that a girl like this with such a healthy appetite was sure to be a healthy girl in spite of Elizabeth's anxiety.

'There are few cooks like Mary left in this part of the country,' Elizabeth said proudly.

'I can well believe that. They all got married, I suppose?' Nora said. But the words had scarcely left her lips when she realized she had blundered.

Elizabeth coughed and tapped her lips with her serviette: 'Mary, of course, had many suitors, and so had I for that matter. But we were too attached to the home and to mother to bother ourselves with young men. And so, we allowed our chances of marriage, one after another, to go past unheeded. Still, we never have the slightest regrets over the course we followed and adopted. Isn't that so, Mary?'

'I don't know,' Mary said uncomfortably.

'I am sure you broke many hearts, both of you,' Nora said, endeavouring to soften the unintentional inference of her first remark.

'Countrymen's hearts are not so easily broken,' Mary smiled. 'They don't wear them on their sleeves — you'll find that out before very long.'

'I'm not so sure about that, Mary.' And then Elizabeth turned to Nora: 'I could name two or three well-to-do young men who left here after Mary refused them in marriage.'

'Don't heed her, Miss Byrne — Nora, I mean. I'm too old now to blush,' and she hurriedly said grace after meals and pushed in her chair. 'Come, Elizabeth, and don't be talking like Jane Austen.'

'You'll allow me to wash these dishes with you?' Nora suggested.

'Not at all, Nora girl.'

'Not at all!' Elizabeth echoed. 'Mary and myself won't be long in tidying up thsee few things.'

'But I always helped my aunt with the washing-up. You'll really spoil me.'

'We'll sit and rest for awhile in the drawing-room,' Elizabeth said.

Nora held back in the hallway. 'You wouldn't mind if I strolled over as far as the school? I feel a bit dizzy after the bus journey, and a walk, I think, would help.'

'Mind!' Mary said, raising her hand in surprise. 'Mind, not at all. Mercy on us, child, you are free to go and come as you please, and make yourself at home here. We'll have supper about eight. Wear something warm going out, for it gets cold now in the evenings with the leaves on the turn, and there's always a chilly mist rising up from the river at this time of year.'

✿ 4 ✿

GOING out into the sunshine she tied on a yellow scarf and walked quickly down the path to the open gate, aware that Elizabeth was eyeing her from the sitting-room. But when she reached the road, where the hedges and trees concealed her from the house, she took her time, breathing in the autumn air and rejoicing in its cold freshness, a freshness like overshadowed water. Around her were the harvest fields, the stooks standing on their shadows, and children's voices carrying far as in the stillness of an evening. But at a turn on the road she halted, gazing at a stream that tumbled into a pool as brown as a chestnut; a bramble branch arched into it and she noticed one thorn wrinkling the water with lines as fine as on a snail's back. The cold mossy smell of the water and the restless specks of froth whirling like ants with their eggs filled her with a quiet and languorous satisfaction that smothered the displeasure of Elizabeth's probing questions. She had lied to her about her family, but she must take care not to let it happen again. She must take a firmer control of herself. After all, she was no longer a child; she was twenty-five, and why should a girl of her age lie to anyone about her mother and sister? They had died in a sanatorium — that wasn't a disgrace but a misfortune; it would be different if it were something they had brought upon themselves through vice and ill-living. Anyway it was nobody's business, only her own. In time she might grow to love this place and the school, and then there'd be nothing more she could ask for or live for. Marriage? No. To fall in love again? No. Like her last affair it would end as soon as she'd confess the truth about her mother and sister.

She braced her shoulders and breathed in the air deeply, rejoicing afresh in its clean loveliness. She lifted a stick from the roadside and tapped the hedges as she went along. A road branched to the right, and climbing it she presently saw the school a few hundred yards in front of her. She leaned on a wooden gateway and gazed down at the grey house through the trees: the ribbed fan light above the door, the two silver birches at the gate, and further to the left the blue estuary with a yacht nodding to its buckled reflection. She turned away and opened her coat to cleanse the fusty smell of travelling from its folds.

The walls of the school were not as clean-looking as seen from the house: there were ball marks on them, cracks in the plaster, and in the yard a trampled crust of bread and a piece of newspaper stained with jam. She went round to the back, raised herself on the window-sills and gazed into the four rooms in turn; her own room she knew by the smallness of the dual desks, the pictures of Red Riding Hood and The Three Bears, and on a window-ledge a statue of the Blessed Virgin with a few bedraggled chrysanthemums at her feet.

On her way out the school gate cringed on two octaves as she pulled it after her — a sound that'd remain with her, she reflected, when many another memory would have faded or, should she say, would be lost if that little sound didn't hold it together. She walked past the school intending to glance at Mr. Lynch's house and walk on into the town and round again to the Miss Devlins' by the road she had taken with the tramp. But the sound of hedge-clippers coming from the garden made her hurry, and when her foot gritted on the road Peter Lynch, his face red from stooping, appeared above the hedge.

'Pardon me,' he said, touching his cap. 'I saw you taking an unusual interest in the school and I was wondering if you'd happen to be Miss Byrne.'

She nodded, and he hurriedly placed the clippers on top of the hedge and came out on to the road.

'I hope I don't look the part, but I happen to be the high and mighty boss of the whole shooting gallery,' and he excused the green stain on his hands and held out to her his little finger. 'To shake hands like that is the sign of a long stay.' He tapped his pockets. 'I've the school keys here, and if you're not in any particular hurry I could show you round the palatial premises.'

He pushed the school gate open with his toe and motioned her in in front of him. Near the main door engraven on a slab in the wall was an inscription from Daniel the Prophet: THEY THAT INSTRUCTETH MANY ON TO RIGHTEOUSNESS SHALL SHINE LIKE STARS FOR ALL ETERNITY.

'A passport to eternity,' he said as he saw her reading it. 'I hope Daniel is near at hand on the day of Judgment — that's all I've got to say,' and he put the key into a keyhole as big as a man's fist. 'It's not a new keyhole we need, but a new door,' and he pushed it open with difficulty because a pebble was wedged in the threshold. In the porch hung a few caps, and a coat with a sleeve inside out was hanging up by its pocket. He arranged the sleeve and hung up the coat by its tag. He's conscientious, she thought, or maybe — and it would be worse— over-officious about frittery odds and ends.

'This is my room — beside the door and the draughts and the married daughters that come up to abuse me for hammering their little sons. Maybe I shouldn't say that. When all is said and done they're as decent a set of children as you'll find in any part of Ireland. That's not to say they're all angels. They're just children and they need a clout or two now and again.'

'You sound as if you like them.'

'I came here ten years ago and I've seldom regretted it. I might like them better than I think I do. We don't know what we really like till we've lost it.'

She was aware of the loud tick of the clock in the empty room and noticed on the blackboard chalked in careful script:

Canst thou not minister to a mind diseased,
Pluck from the memory a rooted sorrow,
Raze out the written troubles of the brain,
And with some sweet oblivious antidote
Cleanse the stuffed bosom of that perilous stuff
Which weighs upon the heart.

'That's for the bigger boys to learn and chew over,' he said shyly.

'Do you think they'll understand it?'

'Bits of it may strike some of them now. But years later, if the lines come to their mind, the full meaning will come with it. That's what I think: for many a time I've understood the meaning of lines years after learning them. But I find that they do like Shakespeare.' And sitting on top of a desk he counted the names of the plays he had tried out on the top standards: *Macbeth*, *Julius Caesar*, *Twelfth Night*, *Coriolanus*, and *Hamlet*. '*Coriolanus*, I think, was the most successful. For some reason or other they love that man who would rather "see a sword and hear a drum than look upon his schoolmaster". Perhaps it's the animal in him that appeals to them, or maybe his rashness and honesty of speech.'

Nora smiled. ' "Before him he carries noise and behind him he leaves tears." '

'Just like me on a Monday morning.'

'Though I had to stew over that play for an exam that's the only line I can quote from it. But I do remember that Coriolanus always spoke what was in his mind no matter what the cost.'

'He was certainly no place-hunter, and he wouldn't get far in any job these days. I suppose it's his truthfulness that attracts the young — they're not good at it themselves, especially if it means a crack across the knuckles.'

'And his treachery?'

'No, they don't like that — only for it he'd be, I think, their ideal hero. But sure we all have our weaknesses, little and big,' and he jumped off the desk and led her into another room.

'This is Mr. Brennan's,' was all he said; and as she recalled the tramp's description of him Mr. Lynch was saying over in his mind: *Vacant heart and hand and eye, easy live and quiet die.* Yes, that about summed him up — an answer without ambiguities. But, perhaps, I shouldn't think that about him, for I may be a bit like that myself if I only knew.

They passed into Mr. Murphy's room. 'Mr. Murphy is the youngest of us — he's been teaching now about four years all told. You'll find him and the rest of us, I hope, an easy crew to get on with.'

'I feel I will, Mr. Lynch,' she said as he led her across to a door in the partition.

'And this is your room,' he said pleasantly. 'It gets the sun throughout the entire day, so if you haven't bright children you'll at least have brightness falling from the air.'

As she stood erect looking at the children's paintings that gave a colourful lift to the walls he noticed that she was as tall as he was; and when she spoke, praising this painting and that, he discovered himself listening more to the sound of her voice than to what she was saying.

'And at what time do you begin on Monday?' she asked, when he had pulled the cringing school gate behind them.

'You're not going off like that. You'll have to meet my sister Helen. She'll be annoyed if I don't introduce you while you're here.'

He lifted the shears from the top of the hedge, ran his finger over the blade, and sauntering up the garden path he spoke loudly so that Helen might not be taken unawares.

The door was open and they stepped into an oak-panelled hall with a parquet floor polished like a convent corridor. He brought her into the sitting-room where there was a fire in the gate, some book-shelves, and a large bay window looking out on the garden.

'Take a seat, Miss Byrne, till I get Helen. I won't be a minute.'

Strange there is no dog, she said to herself when she was alone. A house like this needs a black cocker spaniel to complete it. Before Mother died their own home was in many ways like this one; they had an oak-panelled hall with a brass gong on a table and a few copper ornaments on a high shelf. And they had black mats and, of course, Sponge, the black cocker. But you couldn't have seen him on the rug till he opened his mouth and displayed his pink tongue. And there was a peculiar smell from him — a smell like mossy water, or was it a smell like damp clothes drying too near a fire? And then the way he used to lie so still when Mother was looking for him after discovering his wet paw-marks on her clean hall. 'I hope that Tory isn't in the sitting-room,' Mother used to say with a wink. 'Wait till I get my hands on him.' And how cute he used to be at a time like that: not a stir out of him or a movement from his tail till Mother had gone off; and then he'd sneak out from under his chair, rub himself against my leg and stretch himself luxuriously in front of the fire; and then the way his damp curly coat used to steam and his paws dry in a grey dust. And Mother used to scold me when I scratched his tummy with the toe of my sandal and made the dust rise. And the way Eileen, my sister, used to set me wild by saying that my eyes were the same as Sponge's. Yes, this house needs a black cocker to complete the furnishings.

The door was knocked and Peter came in with his sister. She was active-looking, thin and grey, but much older than her brother, Nora thought.

'You've a lovely place here, Miss Lynch,' she said, after they were introduced.

'I suppose there are worse places.'

'Worse!' Peter exclaimed. 'Don't heed her, Miss Byrne. Helen thinks there isn't a nicer spot in the whole county of Down, or in all Ireland for that matter.'

'Well, let me tell you if I were a young girl like Miss Byrne it isn't to this place I'd come looking for a school.'

'It's not the place that matters so much as the people in it,' Peter said lightly, telling Miss Byrne to sit down until Helen made a cup of tea. Nora protested, saying she had just risen from the table before coming out. Helen held back until Peter insisted playfully that he would make it himself and drink it himself if none of them would join him. He had his way and Helen hurried off to the kitchen to prepare the tray.

Later as she watched him go down the path with this stranger, take out his knife and cut chrysanthemums and tie them with string while the stranger held them in her hands she was suddenly angry with him. 'He's a silly man!' she said to herself, and lifting a dead leaf off the mat she crumpled it in her hand and put it in her apron pocket.

When he came in from the gate she stared at him coldly. 'Well. what do I think of her? . . . Isn't that what you're going to ask? Well, I don't like her. I never cared much for brown-eyed people.'

'Oh, is that so? I thought her a very fine girl. She has a nice speaking voice.'

'Has she! I wasn't aware of it. She didn't speak much to me. Anyway it might be one of those put-on voices which another month or so will show up in its true colours.'

'I don't know how to say it, but I felt all the time you weren't a bit friendly towards her.'

'You felt exactly right. I was ashamed of you making a proper fool of yourself. I wanted to show her there was somebody in the house with reserve.'

'What exactly do you mean?'

'Peter!' and she closed her eyes and shook her head deprecatingly. 'Although you're forty years of age you are still a youth in many ways. You shouldn't have gone out on to the road and welcomed her the way you did. Then you brought her into the school, and, as if that weren't enough, you land her up here into your very home. Not half a day in the place till you're tripping over her with attention.'

'Surely you didn't expect me to let her pass by without a word when I was cutting the hedge.'

'You could have slipped into the garage till she had passed.'

'That's what many a countryman would have done. But I never act on such impulses. And anyway that impulse didn't occur to me, and if it had I'd have turned against it. I never allow myself to avoid meeting people I may happen to see: the impulse to avoid them often comes to me, but I take myself in hand and override it.'

'You've made that young girl feel absolutely at home.'

'That's what I intended to do.'

'You'll not get the work out of her in school that you should get. Familiarity produces indifference. It's your old fault; you're too kind and too familiar with everyone. Ever since you became a principal you've complained to me, time and again, about the lack of co-operation from the others on the staff: their selfishness, their not caring a straw what happens outside their own classroom. "I'll teach my own standard — that only, nothing more" — they seem to say. And now this Miss newcomer will slide into the same selfish groove as the others, because of this silly performance of yours on her first day here.'

'I never knew that hospitality was considered a fault.'

'It's not that. What I mean is that you should be more aloof, a man in authority.'

'A man in authority! Well, well, is that the next of it! I could never be that, except by being untrue to my own nature.'

'Then go on killing yourself as you're doing, and small thanks you'll get for it, either from the children, their parents, or your own teachers.'

'But surely I'm not here just to serve myself or have myself served. I'm here to do my work and to do it as honestly as I can — at least that's what I'm paid for. There's something more important to think about than one's sense of authority.'

'You're lacking in one thing — moral courage. Just the other day you allowed that Mr. Murphy to disobey you when you asked him to take your class for singing.'

'I didn't want to impose my will on him.'

'You should have *made* him do what you asked.'

'To make anyone is wrong; to lead them is better.'

'You're far too servile for my taste. And servility dressed up as humility is loathsome.'

'Humility never crossed my mind.'

'To be well thought of — is that the reason?'

'No, you're wrong there. To avoid tension was one of the reasons. No one can do good work where there's tension. And I don't intend to send anyone away from the school — boy or man — hating it. And surely you don't think I'd expect Murphy to think well of me just because I allowed him to have his own way. In all probability he has laughed and retold it with a twist in it — how he drove me off with my tail between my legs when I asked him to take the singing class.'

He shrugged his shoulders, took out a cigarette and lit it, and as he was throwing the match into the fire he noticed a coat-belt under one of the chairs.

'Your imagination is certainly a humorous one, Peter. To think that that scamp Murphy will stare at me with his usual insolence and have this insult to you feeding his swagger. He has no respect for me, and he'll have less now.'

'As long as you act rightly, what people do to you doesn't really matter in the end. It's themselves they hurt. You take things far too seriously,' he said, lifting the belt and coiling it round his wrist. 'If Murphy were too familiar you wouldn't relish that either.'

'The least he could do would be to be polite to me when he meets me.'

'The least I could do at the moment would be to drive after Miss Byrne with this belt of hers.'

'There's more of the foolishness. Couldn't you keep it for her until Monday?'

'The poor girl might be searching everywhere for it.'

'Let me tell you that that girl has more than one coat to her back.'

He smiled, not heeding her protests, and put the belt in his pocket. She pleaded with him not to go out with it, but he told her not to upset herself over nothing, and taking out the car from the garage he drove off and overtook Nora near the Devlins' gate.

'Your belt?' he said.

'Oh, thank you! I never missed it,' and she felt the back of her coat with her hand. 'But you shouldn't have troubled, Mr. Lynch. It would have done on Monday.'

'I was just running into town and I thought I might overtake you,' he hedged, and gave a toot to the horn. The car sped off and she saw the grass on the banks being flattened by the draught of air from the car and dead leaves hopping on the road.

That evening after Mary had allowed her to tidy away the tea dishes they went into the sitting-room where, under the tall brass reading-lamp, Elizabeth was crocheting her surplice, a surplice that Nora praised time and again because it gave Elizabeth evident pleasure. The blinds on the window were undrawn and as she watched in the dark panes the pink reflections of their hands and the leap of the fire she became so drowsy that she was glad when Mary suggested that she should go to bed.

'There's no call to wait for us, Nora. There's Elizabeth, and she could sit for another two hours if she had anyone to keep her in chat.'

'We'll all retire early tonight,' Elizabeth said. 'Tomorrow's Sunday and we'll all need to be up for Mass. Mary always goes to first Mass, but you should lie in and go to second.'

'I think I'll go to the early one.'

'Of course, no one wishes you to go to second Mass if you prefer the earlier one,' Elizabeth said, an obscure jealousy thinning her voice. 'My only reason for suggesting the second was on account of your extreme tiredness after your long journey. I thought you'd enjoy the extra hour in bed.'

'I'll go to first, if I waken in time.'

'That's right, Nora, just please yourself and that will please us,' Mary said.

Nora didn't light the little lamp in her bedroom because the moon was shining full in the window, at one moment filling the room with light and then shutting it off again like a door closing.

And with the moonlight came the lonely flurry of the wind in the trees, the bump of a chestnut falling, and a man's step passing on the road. She heard the collier blow its whistle, and when she was in bed heard the throb of the ship's engine as it slid out on the outgoing tide. She lay relaxed, allowing her mind to sway out with the ship, and then sway in with the startled waves that would be chattering on the shore, and to sway out again to where the moonlight made a crazy pavement on the troubled water.

✿ 5 ✿

IN a short time her first impressions of the school underwent a change, a certain wavering perplexity descending on her as her acquaintance with the teachers and the children deepened. None of the teachers, except Mr. Lynch, went home at lunch-hour, and it was left to her, as to her predecessor, to boil a kettle of water on a primus at midday and make tea for herself and Mr. Brennan and Mr. Murphy. For the first few days Mr. Murphy displayed a polite deference towards her, but as the succeeding days brought easy familiarity his voice harshened in a manner that disquieted her. At times he mocked Mr. Brennan brazenly, and though he would wink furtively at her she felt that the mockery had a tinge of spite in it. The two men, with their socks in coils above their shoes, usually sat on top of the infant desks while she carried their cups of tea to them, and Mr. Brennan, a stout man in his fifties, never took his eyes off his newspaper while his fingers fistled in his lunch-packet beside him on the desk.

'There's Tim burrowing into that newspaper and not giving us the fruits of his contemplation,' Murphy said one day with an abruptness that startled her. For a moment there was a tight knot of silence in the room and she paused with the cup at her lips.

'The fruits of my contemplation are the obituary notices,' Brennan mumbled from behind the paper. 'That's a column that's never vacant, I assure you.'

'A bright column for all supernumeraries to peruse,' Murphy added.

'The population of the graveyard never decreases no matter what happens. People are always going in and none coming out,' Brennan answered in a solemn tone that made Nora smile.

'I hope you're not thinking of joining the entrants,' Murphy went on.

'One never knows,' Brennan answered without looking at him. 'One never knows. Look at Archie Baxter, hale and hearty, gets a jag of a little fish-hook — and inside a week he's in his grave. That's enough to frighten any mortal man.'

'Sure you don't fish,' Murphy said with comic seriousness.

'I'm only using that as an instance of what could happen to any of us.'

'Oh, I see!'

'I'm glad you do, for there are times when you seem to want everything explained down to the last detail.'

Murphy lit a cigarette and blew the smoke towards him, the smoke breasting the newspaper and billowing over it. 'I can't coax you to have one,' he said to Nora, crossing his legs and at the same time manœuvring Brennan's lunch-packet to the edge of the desk.

'No thanks, Mr. Murphy,' she said. 'I don't think I'll ever indulge in that habit.'

'You're a wise girl,' Brennan said from behind his newspaper, his fingers groping for his lunch. 'About twenty years ago I gave up smoking for Lent and I have never gone back to it since. And what's more I've never regretted it. It'd be a nice calculation in arithmetic to see how much money I have saved by that sacrifice.'

'It may have improved your bank account but it surely hasn't improved your health, has it?'

'I might be in my grave if I had continued at it.'

'You'll die when you're time comes, that's my belief.'

'It's not mine. We have to take every precaution known to mortal man. Wouldn't you be a fool if you did something — take a swim on a day like this for instance — that might put you on the broad of your back for three or four weeks, and at the heel of the hunt maybe plant you in the graveyard?'

'If my pocket could afford the luxury of lying in bed I'd

gladly take that swim. Illness is an expensive item that only you could afford. And maybe Miss Bryne could afford it, too, if we only but knew.'

She glanced towards Brennan to see if he were annoyed, but saw nothing, only the trembling of the newspaper that shielded him.

'Mr. Brennan's health is his own and he has every right to look after it in his own way,' she defended.

'I'm not saying he hasn't, am I?' Murphy answered, rising from the desk and picking off the bread crumbs that clung to his pullover. He yawned and stretched himself. 'I'm going to take care of my health at the moment. I'm going out for a breath of ozone before Mr. Lynch blows his little whistle. I'm tired waiting here for a peep at the newspaper.'

'Here it is! Why didn't you ask me for it?' Brennan said, but Murphy strode out of the room pretending he hadn't heard.

'He's an insolent fellow,' Brennan muttered to himself and opened out the paper again.

Nora collected the cups and saucers, and as she poured water over them the sight of cigarette-ash floating in the water repulsed her; she was ready to say something critical of Murphy but withheld it on catching sight of lipstick on her own cup. 'We never see our own faults,' she said to herself, pouring hot water into the basin. She could hear the children's voices leaping up in a gleeful glitter at the open window, and she cleaned the cups hurriedly to get out to them.

Mr. Brennan folded up his paper. 'Do you know what I'm going to tell you, Miss Byrne? Before you came here, Mr. Murphy was as dry as that duster on the easel. He did nothing at lunch-time except manicure his nails with a pared matchstick. Now he's showing off before you, the mockery is usually at my expense but I don't mind. He's young, and it's better to let him have his fling.'

'You're very tolerant, Mr. Brennan.'

'I'm just indifferent. It's no way to be, but as I haven't a good heart the doctor told me to be careful and not be flying off the handle at the least provocation. Ah, there's nothing like being careful. Look at that poor fellow dying from the jag of a fishhook. But, of course, if you thought of all the diseases that the flesh is heir to — tumours in the brain, cancers of the stomach, and T.B. and the God knows what — you'd have no peace day or night. Of course, Miss Bryne, you don't mind my reading the newspaper.'

'Not at all — as long as it pleases you.'

'But it doesn't please me. I have already read it. I use it to protect myself from having discussions with that argumentative Murphy. He gets on my nerves, and too much arguefying with the likes of him is bad for my heart. When I get into a rage I can feel the blood bolting in my forehead. If you want to live long, Miss Byrne, go slowly and take no risks — that's my advice.'

'But that wouldn't be living at all, Mr. Brennan. You wouldn't be growing. It would just be a dumb decay. I, for one, wouldn't relish that.'

Mr. Brennan stared at her and said nothing, while his hand involuntarily opened out the paper again.

'It's my belief,' she went on, 'that those of us who are to die early live a lifetime within their short span. Nature seems to compensate them in some way. Look at St. Theresa of Lisieux or Keats or Katharine Mansfield or J. M. Synge.'

'I never thought of that,' he said. 'Maybe after all there's a long life before me yet, for I'm no Keats, no St. Theresa, and I'm sure I'm different from the other two you mention . . . Would you like to live long, Miss Byrne?'

'Oh, I don't know,' she said, pulling on her coat. 'For one thing I've never taken out an insurance policy in the hope that I would.'

'If you ever think of taking out one let me know. I've a cousin in that line of business and he'll see you right.'

'Are you coming out for a breath of Mr. Murphy's ozone?'

'I'd rather sit and rest myself. I'll get as much ozone as will do me in my walk home at three-thirty.'

Out in the playground a fresh wind was swirling the brown leaves and lunch-papers into one corner, some children were sheltering from it while a few were playing handball, and others had pieces of paper on a string and were running with them over their shoulder and shouting: 'Look at my kite!'

At the foot of the playground she saw Mr. Murphy striding back and forth with his hands in his pockets, and now and again with a toss of his head fling back a lock of hair that blew over his forehead. She did not join him but moved to a circle of boys who were gathered round Mr. Lynch. He was playing chestnuts with them and they shouted 'Oh' when he scored a hit and 'Aw' when he missed, but when his chestnut split in smithereens they all cheered and scrambled for the bits that fell on the play-ground. With pretended disappointment he threw the bare string to Miss Byrne, and clapping his hands together he asked a few boys to gather up the lunch-papers from the yard. He put his whistle to his mouth and at the first two blasts the whole mass of children had arranged themselves in rows, and with their feet marking time they marched through the door ahead of their teachers. In a few minutes the playground was deserted, and gulls and crows were alighting on it to pick up the uneaten scraps of bread.

That afternoon Father Lacy paid his first visit to the school since her arrival. He had been on retreat in Roscrea Abbey and later had gone for a holiday to Donegal. She had never met him though she knew from her aunt that he had been a close friend of her father's. And she wasn't surprised when it was her father he mentioned as soon as he had shaken hands with her and wished her every happiness in the school.

'You take after his side of the family I'd say. You wouldn't remember him much, I suppose?'

'A little, Father Lacy. He died when I was ten.'

'I knew him well, very well,' and he spoke of their long

friendship extending from their college days. 'And your poor mother, I knew her too. It was I who married them.'

'Yes, my aunt told me of that.'

'I lost a good friend in your father. His death was a tragedy,' he said, fingering his watch-chain. He paused. 'You had an elder sister — what is she doing now?'

She felt her face redden as she said: 'She died, Father — in a sanatorium.'

'Oh, yes, I remember now. She was Eileen, wasn't she?'

'Yes, Father, Eileen she was called.'

'I see,' he said in a low voice. 'God knows, you're left lonely enough,' and noticing that she was twisting the strap on her wristlet watch and was silently embarrassed he stretched out his hand to a boy in the front desk and ruffled his hair: 'Give me a few of those curls, Jackie; this grey thatch of mine could do with a few of them . . . Miss Byrne, could you lend me a pair of sharp scissors for a minute?'

Father Lacy made a pretence of cutting the boy's hair with the handles of the scissors and the class stood on their feet shouting out directions.

'Ach, these scissors are too blunt, they wouldn't cut a cat's whisker! I'll come in tomorrow with Mr. Lynch's hedge-shears — they'll do the job for me.'

He asked them about their dogs and their horses, and then he turned to the blackboard and told them to watch him closely and he'd give sixpence to the boy who'd give the best answer. He put his thumb on the board and said 'Monday', then his index finger and said 'Tuesday', then another finger 'Wednesday', another 'Thursday' — and then he paused and said: 'What comes next?'

'Friday!' they chorused.

'You're all wrong: it's my little finger that comes next.' He shook hands once more with Nora, waved his hat to the class, and left the room.

She was pleased with herself and with him, for without

hesitation she had told him the truth about her sister, and had not bungled at it as she had done when asked the same question by Elizabeth. And as she handed out the pastel books, humming to herself, her exultant mood affected the children and they chatted freely with one another.

'Oh, quiet, quiet, please,' she said smilingly. 'Quiet! Father Lacy doesn't know how bold you are . . .' They sat still and listened. 'Today I want you to draw a harvest scene: the stooks in the field and the sun shining. Close your eyes first, think hard of a harvest field, and then try to put down what you see. I'll give a nice orange to the best.'

'Yes, Miss,' they said, and as they bent over their books she sat at her own table, paying no attention to them, but thinking of Father Lacy and wondering how much he really knew of her and her family. She could never conceal anything from him and had no inclination to do so. She was sure he knew all about her mother's death. But what would happen if, in casual conversation, he let it fall to Elizabeth and Mary or to Mr. Lynch? No, no, he wouldn't do the like of that! Maybe she should warn him not to? What would he think of her, or say to her, if she made a request like that? 'My dear girl, an affliction of that kind is a misfortune, not a disgrace. It is not like the leprosy of sin, something of your own choosing' — something like that he would be sure to say to her. No, she could never bring herself to request a silence from him on that point. And even if Mary and Elizabeth did get to hear of it they would hardly challenge her about it: Mary wouldn't, but Elizabeth — she could never be sure what that lady would do!

She resolved not to think any more about it. She got up from the table, and was moving down the aisles between the dual desks when the door was knocked and Mr. Lynch entered. He lifted up a few of the pastel books, and smiled with approval at the splashes of colour: they all had yellow stooks, some waisted and some shaped like bell-tents; some had white shadows while others were blue and a few red; some had attempted to draw a cart, others a dog or two, and all had the same kind of sun — a daisy's head with a few petals.

'They're all splendid, Miss Byrne,' he said when she joined him at the head of the room.

Suddenly there was a roar from Mr. Murphy in the next room, then the sound of a boy crying, a thumping of a fist on the blackboard and a shout: 'Look up here, you parcel of donkeys, till I explain it over again.'

Mr. Lynch smiled: 'He shouldn't let it get on his nerves like that. What will he be like when he's Mr. Brennan's age?' He stood beside her with a sheet of paper shaking in his hand: 'This is what I came in for, Miss Byrne: I'm doing a bit of reorganizing and I was wondering if you'd be willing to take my class for singing. It would be for two half hours a week and I could take something with your class while you'd be taking mine. Maybe you'd like to think over it for a while?'

'I'd love to take them, Mr. Lynch,' she said at once.

He wasn't accustomed to getting immediate answers to any of his suggestions and he was unable to constrain his pleasure: 'Oh, that's fine!' he said. 'I have a voice like a crow, and it would only do their young voices harm listening to the likes of me . . . Thank you very much, Miss Byrne. You can let me know in a day or two what you would like me to teach your class in exchange.'

He wrote something down on his sheet of paper and went into Mr. Murphy's room. He had chosen, he knew, an awkward moment to approach Mr. Murphy but then, on reflection, he seldom saw Murphy in a relaxed or pleasant attitude before his class. It had to be done and he'd get through with it as quietly as possible. He tried to appear calm, but in spite of himself the paper in his hand was shaking.

'I'm reorganizing for the school year, Mr. Murphy, and I was thinking of taking the four best boys in your class to come into mine right away. They'd only be marking time in this class for a whole year.'

'And you want them to bolster up your own class and weaken mine,' Mr. Murphy said bluntly. 'I couldn't do the like of that.'

'I was thinking of what is best for the boys themselves. After all, the school exists for them; they don't exist for you or for me.'

'I'm not going to let you have them.'

'Surely you don't think they would strengthen my class. It would take them at least two months to catch up with the tail-end of the bigger boys.'

'Would you admit that they'd weaken mine if I handed them over?'

'They would — a little. But that shouldn't signify: we are doing what is best for the children themselves — that's the main consideration.'

'And the inspector — when he comes on his rounds what will he think?'

'He'll side with me when it is explained to him.'

'I wish I could believe that you'd explain it to him for my advantage.'

'Ah, well, in that case if you won't take my word for it, it's not worth while discussing it further. But, of course, you don't mean what you say.'

'To speak frankly, Mr. Lynch, I always speak what I mean. I have a bad class and I am sick and tired to death with them as it is.'

'I thought you were content here.'

'I am when I'm left alone and when you mind your own business and your own class.'

'So it's not my business to organize the school and to do what I think is best for the children in it?'

'It is, but not at the expense of my class. I might agree if I could trust the inspectors to see things humanly.'

'The young men they appoint nowadays are not educational policemen like the old brigade. However, it takes an old tradition long to die, and it's a pity to see a young man like you being affected by it.'

'You have a higher opinion of them than I have.'

'I have more experience of them, and it is on that that I have formed my opinion and wish to form yours.'

'You're trying to re-educate me — is that the next of it?'

'You needn't drag in cheap abuse of that kind, Mr. Murphy. Have some trust in what I suggest.'

'I have trust in myself — that's the main thing in this job,' and he lifted a piece of chalk as a signal that he was finished with the discussion.

Mr. Lynch shook his head hopelessly: it was useless to press the point further. It would only lead to tension, to ill-feeling. He must have patience. 'All right, Mr. Murphy, we'll leave it at that. Maybe you'll reconsider it and let me know?' and before he had time to get out of the room Mr. Murphy was shouting at his class ᵗo pay attention.

✿ 6 ✿

THAT afternoon on her way from school Nora was pleasantly drawing up in her mind a group of songs that she would teach Mr. Lynch's class. She'd not attempt anything grandiose at first: the old favourites would do to begin with: *The Minstrel Boy, The Skye Boat Song, The Last Rose of Summer, Linden Lea* and, perhaps, a section from *Samson and Delilah*. She would have three-part singing. It would be a joyous half-hour for her, for she could ask for nothing more delightful than listening to boy sopranos. She would send, too, for her portable gramophone and introduce them to some orchestral and instrumental music, and to some of Elizabeth Schumann's Lieder. There was nothing like putting them in contact with the best.

She began to hum to herself and to take delight in the windskip of the leaves on the dry road. Three young boys overtook her, giggled to themselves, and ran past her with their schoolbags bouncing on their backs. Shy because of me!

> The noisy geese that gabbled o'er the pool,
> The playful children just let loose from school . . .

Strange I can't remember the next lines! She stooped to prise a pebble from inside her shoe and turning round saw Murphy striding after her, his face red, and a handkerchief in his hand.

'I'm taking the long road home,' he breathed, 'for I didn't want to be slouching home with Brennan.'

'I suppose I'm the lesser of the two evils?'

'No, a change from fusty boredom. At least you'll talk but he won't. I've never met such a solidified bag of cement in all my life as Brennan! Some day I'll slip a mouse-trap into his lunchpaper when he has his nose stuck in *The Irish Recorder* — that

65

would make him do the hop, skip and jump in fine Olympic fashion.' He wiped his brow and tucked his handkerchief in his sleeve. 'I'd a grand slam with Lynch this afternoon — it was great gas while it lasted,' and he began to retell it, mimicking Mr. Lynch's voice and calm manner. 'But I soon scattered him. I told him he could reorganize as much as he liked, but not at the expense of my class. I'd have let him down easy if he hadn't come off with that platitude about the school existing for the children. It was that that set me on my high horse.'

She told him she had agreed to take the upper class for singing.

'You did not! Och, that lets us all down. Some weeks ago he asked me to take it but I refused point-blank. It's not your duty to teach his big lumps.'

'And who's to say what is my duty except Mr. Lynch himself? He can't sing and he asked me to take them, and I gladly agreed.'

'He can sing well enough for the type of children he has to deal with. And furthermore he takes a keen interest in music and thinks nothing of motoring up to Belfast for an orchestral concert. Oh, you'll have a nice handful putting his croakers through their doh-me-soh-dohs. He'd have a healthier respect for you if you had rebelled.'

'But then I wouldn't have had the same respect for myself. Respect from others for bringing disrespect on yourself is not a relishable quality.'

'He'll play on you, once he finds you side with him in all his whims and fancies. Of course it's for your own good I'm warning you. Always look to Number One! You're too soft.'

'It's not softness. I want to do what is right by myself and by the school. If I don't do that I feel miserable. You don't realize, Mr. Murphy, what it is to teach in a school where there's nothing but wrangling from day to day. I taught in one and I was glad to get out of it.'

'Surely, Miss Byrne, you don't think I'm wrangling. You have to claim your rights.'

'We have our obligations. We can't wriggle ourselves out of that.'

'Lynch has no backbone as it is, and you're on the way to spoiling his character completely. Man alive, if you only heard him speaking to the parents when they come up complaining. He gets red from the neck up, and he adopts a cringing attitude that I wouldn't accuse poor Brennan of in his dullest moments. When they come up to me with their complaints I soon send them to their kennels in quick time. Softness is killing teaching in that school. What we need is a man with energy, strength, domination — someone that will steam-roll the cheek out of the children and snap the door on the heels of their whining parents. They're spoiled at home and Lynch continues the spoiling in school.'

'I must admit that I like what I know of him.'

'When you see more of him you'll change your opinion.'

'I hope I won't have to do that. You're too hard on him.'

'I'm too hard on myself, you mean. It's easy to take the easy way in teaching and be easy on yourself. Guard the old blood pressure — as Brennan would say. But it is my belief that if you take it easy the class will take it easy — and where are you? Nothing done; no progress; nothing to show at the end of the year except slovenly work, slovenly answers, and brazen cheek. Lynch always complains of the boys I send him forward: they'll do nothing for him, he tells me, without being beaten into doing it. That, for me, is a confession of an easy-going nature.'

'But you can't expect Mr. Lynch to change what's natural in him.'

'I'm not asking him to. But he shouldn't complain about the boys I send on to him. Children here don't want to learn and you have to use the rod. You'll find that out before you're much longer in the school.'

'He believes in making things personal. It's personality that counts in teaching, he told me: a teacher's memories, experiences, enthusiasm, his love and belief in what he teaches.'

'You must become as impersonal as a machine, that's my

belief. Try to joke with the class and they'll take nothing serious for you.'

'But that would be a hell.'

'It's not exactly that: it's just a foretaste of hell. The boys are only laughing at Lynch — listen and laugh is their motto; not listen and learn. They treat him as an old cod and he doesn't know it. Brennan is an old cod and is under no delusions about his deficiencies. Talk to Brennan about personality with a capital P and he'll stare at you with his dead eyes and say, "Aye" or maybe, "No", or if he is in an energetic mood he might flick his newspaper and follow it with a silence as deep and as hollow as an extinct volcano. Not that Brennan has any volcanic tendencies!' He laughed at his own joke. 'Do you know what I recommended to Brennan one day as a cure for his nerves? Hard work. "Throw yourself into it," I told him. "Take your chalk and your cane and skip about the room like a ballerina. Let yourself fly like an elastic catapult! Jump into your work like a Grand National steeplechaser, roar and rant, and you'll find no self to brood over." "Yes," said Brennan, in his invalid voice, "there'd be no self to brood over, for I'd be in my grave after such a barbaric performance." '

He recounted all this to her with the ease and dexterity of a conjuror producing rabbits from a hat, and as she listened to him, smiling, she thought that he had missed his vocation — that he should have been a doctor. But on second thoughts, she professed to herself that he wasn't endowed with a 'bedside manner'. Suddenly she burst out laughing at her incongruous thought.

'Are you laughing at what I said about Brennan?' he asked.

'Oh, no, Mr. Murphy, I was only laughing at a thing that came into my mind.'

'Give's a share in the thing, for I don't suppose, when I get into our one-horse town, I'll find anything to amuse me over the week-end.'

'It was nothing of importance — nothing that would really interest you.'

They reached the Devlins' gate; it was closed and a tiny brown leaf was trembling in a spider's web between the green spikes. The leaves were falling in ones and twos from the chestnut trees, and Johnny was brushing them off the lawn with a bunch of twigs tied with string. Nora was still smiling to herself, her fingers stripping the lower leaves of a silver birch that tapered like a spire above them. He coaxed her to tell him what she was laughing at, but she shook her head playfully and remained silent.

'You're as close in your manner as Lynch himself.'

'I'll tell him what you said,' she teased. 'He's visiting here this evening.'

'He is not!'

'He and his sister are coming. They are great friends of the two Miss Devlins.'

'I see a fire in the sitting-room window. By all accounts it's to be a big affair.'

'I would invite you, only it's not my place to do so.'

'Invite me! God above!' and he laughed so loudly that Johnny ceased his brushing for a moment and glanced down at him. 'Invite me — I wouldn't be caught dead in such frowsy company. Mary and Elizabeth Devlin, Helen and Master Peter Lynch — all you need to complete the antiques is Brennan and his old mother.'

A shower of leaves fell from the silver birch, and one alighted on Nora's head. 'The Babes in the Wood,' he said, picking the varnished leaf from her hair and turning it over in his hand. 'It's shaped like a heart.'

'It's more like the ace of spades, if you ask me.'

'If I were romantic I'd be putting this carefully away in my breast-pocket.'

'I wouldn't accuse you of such easy sentiment, Mr. Murphy.'

'Me! I have a truly poetic soul though you mightn't think it,' he said, and catching sight of the apple trees at the back of the house he made a theatrical gesture and declaimed:

'To bend with apples the moss'd cottage-trees,
And fill all fruit with ripeness to the core.'

When she told him that she had just been speaking about Keats
to Mr. Brennan he laughed louder than ever, and Johnny, leaning
on his broom, glared down at the gate and wondered if they were
laughing at him. But just at that moment Elizabeth came to the
hall-door. Murphy ceased laughing and said with mock gravity:
'Elizabeth appears arrayed in black, a golden brooch about her
gorgeous throat . . . Adieu, kind friend, adieu, I can no longer
stay with you,' and he hurried off, shaking the leaf that was still
in his hand.

'That Murphy fellow has put a long journey on himself today,'
Elizabeth greeted her at the hall-door. 'I never knew him to
come this road before. I don't care for him, I needn't tell you.
He hadn't the manners to call a greeting up to me, but runs off
like a stray pup.'

'He may be a little brusque in his manner, but he means well,
I think,' Nora said.

'Means well! I never care for men who guffaw so haughtily . . .
I must call Johnny for a bowl of soup before he stumbles over
that witch's broom of his.'

Nora went up to her room and lay down on top of the bed.
She wondered why she was so pleased and what she was really
smiling at. She reviewed the whole day, pondered on Father
Lacy's visit, and speculated on each of the teachers in turn.
Every one was different from the other: Father Lacy was austere,
but tender and kind — a combination perhaps of real saintliness.
Mr. Brennan had a lone man's faddiness about his health — the
marks of many a country curate. Mr. Murphy could amuse,
attract, and repel her at the same time; he was restless, buffeting
and whirling all before him like an autumn breeze. She didn't
believe she could ever take him seriously. Mr. Lynch she liked —
at least she'd form her own opinions about him and not be
infected by anything Mr. Murphy said of him. She could pair

them off: Mary and Elizabeth, Helen and Peter Lynch, Mr. Murphy and Mr. Brennan — no, that wasn't the right pairings: Mary and Peter would blend better, Elizabeth and Helen, Mr. Brennan and Johnny, and Mr. Murphy and Caius Marcius Coriolanus!

She smiled, stretched herself on the bed, and rested her head on her arms. The window was open and she could see the leaves falling, and one alighting on the sash and tumbling into the room. She heard Johnny's slow step on the path, and then presently heard a flittering of flame, a cough from Johnny, and saw the white smoke rise up and obliterate the trees. She breathed in the burnt smell of the leaves — it was lovely, and it would last the whole evening and into the next morning.

She got up and as she helped Mary with the cooking, she sang gaily and affected Mary with her joyous mood. But prior to the arrival of the visitors she dressed herself in a cream frock with brown collar and cuffs and sat in the sitting-room, where she had to rouse herself to admire and re-admire Elizabeth's surplice, which was now finished, washed and ironed, and was to be the main exhibit of the evening — an exhibit which Nora would be glad to see on its long journey to the Foreign Missions.

Because the evening was still and a red moon rising the Lynches walked over to the Devlins', and when the three elderly women had arranged themselves in armchairs near the fire Peter found himself seated beside Nora on the sofa, and in a few minutes was showing her a bundle of snaps of holidays spent in Brittany, and talking mostly of Vannes and declaring that it was an old town with character and that it was places like that that always came back to his memory and not the famous beaches of Perros-Guirec or Carnac or Quiberon.

Mary was quietly watching their pleasurable absorption and she motioned to Helen with her eyes and smiled knowingly. But Helen had no need for the hint; she had been covertly listening to their conversation and not to Elizabeth's retelling of a trip she had once made to Lourdes — a pilgrimage that Helen had patiently heard out to the end on many previous occasions. She could afford, in all charity, to close her mind on it and concentrate on the pair sitting too closely together on the sofa. What was it she disliked about this Miss Byrne? — she asked herself. For one thing she disliked her ivory complexion, and for another thing she could never care much for dark brown eyes — eyes that could conceal every emotion. And that elongated face belonged more to the horsy people you saw in flashy magazines! And that grey streak in her hair — how anyone could think that attractive was beyond her! It was a pity Peter didn't show a little bit of reserve. She coughed loudly a few times, and with the corner of her eye perceived no indication that Peter was aware of her presence in the room.

Elizabeth produced her surplice and spread it slowly on her lap for Helen's admiration. But Helen's mind was so distracted and her comments so dry and perfunctory that Elizabeth, with stiffening indignation, stowed the surplice in a drawer and sat down, struggling with bitter disappointment. Helen was jealous of her lovely work — she was sure of that!

She sat calmly for a moment, and then noticing that Helen's attention was on Peter and Nora she leant forward, lifted the poker and jabbed the coals in the fire. Mary glided away to make the tea, and shortly afterwards Elizabeth rose, and gently taking Helen's arm she said with affected sweetness: 'Come, Helen dear, I'm sure you'll be delighted to help me to lay the table.'

She closed the sitting-room door on her way out, and when they were in the seclusion of the dining-room she wasn't surprised to hear Helen say: 'Tell me, Elizabeth, what do you really think of this Miss Byrne? I'm sure you're tired of her!'

'Not at all, Helen. What put that in your head?'

'Do you not find her strange?'

'Not a bit. She's like a niece of our own, and fits into the house as neatly as a new hearthrug.'

'Do you know much about her'?

'Me? Of course, Helen — I know everything about her'. And

as Elizabeth had the gift of elaboration, and could believe ever afterwards that she had not departed one syllable from the truth, she related in detail all that she had imagined of Nora's parents and upbringing: her father, she declared, was the finest medical practitioner of his day in the county of Derry; her mother — she dissembled with full-blown confidence — was a highly educated lady and was the daughter of an eminent veterinary surgeon who had swept all before him in Edinburgh university. 'Nora, of course, was well provided for, and her aunt, who took her in charge, wished to send her to Oxford, but the girl refused to go — preferring the local teaching and the local climate. And no one could blame her for that!'

'I just knew she was well off by the cut of her wardrobe!'

'My dear Helen, I don't think we've seen the one-half of it. She has left as much behind with her aunt as she has taken with her. She dresses very attractively, I must say. And, by the way, I saw that Murphy fellow coming home with her today; I earnestly hope that he wouldn't be trying to inveigle his way around her.'

'He's a very good-looking boy and I wouldn't be surprised if they did make a match.'

'If Nora ever married, it wouldn't be for good looks, I'm sure. She'd aspire to something more permanent — taste, mind, refinement. Your Peter, for instance.'

'Peter has no notion of marrying. And anyway he'd be too old for her — fifteen years at least separate them.'

'That's not a big gap!'

'I don't think Peter cares for her.'

'If that's the case he can hide it very well! Did he express his dislike to you, Helen dear?'

'He had no call to. I know every twist of his little finger. He's not good at pretending, and forby he's not the marrying kind.'

'All men are the marrying kind when the right girl comes along. If you like I could drop a hint or two on his behalf.'

'You need not trouble yourself, Elizabeth. Peter is quite capable of doing his own speaking if he wished. But he doesn't wish, and it would disturb him very much if an unpleasant rumour of this kind floated round the countryside.'

'I know when to speak and when not!'

Mary entered with the tea-pot and told Elizabeth to call the others. And when Peter and Nora came into the dining-room Helen noticed their joyous mood, and unable to suppress her displeasure she gave a forced laugh and said: 'Peter, Elizabeth has been telling me that Miss Byrne has found an interesting escort on her way from school — none other than Mr. Murphy.'

'He only came this way today,' Nora said, smiling. 'I don't suppose he'll make a habit of it.'

'You didn't quarrel, I hope?' Mary said.

'Not a bit of us!'

'I can't stand that Murphy fellow,' Elizabeth said. 'To see him striding up the aisle in the chapel of a Sunday puts me in no mood for praying. The swagger of him, and the way he sweeps out his handkerchief and blows his nose with such loud luxury. And then, when he is collecting, he shakes the plate under your very nose to affront you.'

'You take a keen interest in him,' Mary said.

'I do, but it's not for the good of my soul. I'm glad I am not teaching in the same school with him,' Elizabeth went on, pouring out the tea at the same time.

'There's nothing wrong with him. What do you think, Miss Byrne?' Peter said.

'He can be amusing. The other day he told me there was one man above all he'd like to have had a chat with — Lazarus, if you please.'

'Lazarus who?' Mary asked.

'Lazarus — the gospel Lazarus! Mr. Murphy thinks it's tantalizing that there's nothing known of what Lazarus saw at the other side. Was there nobody to ask him what he saw, what he felt, what he remembered? Mr. Murphy feels that if one of the gospels had been written by a woman this mystery would have been solved for us. I only wish I could tell it to you the way he can — he has an amusing way with him.'

'I'm sure he can be amusing at other people's expense besides poor Lazarus's,' Elizabeth commented.

'You're too severe on poor Murphy,' Mary said meekly. 'I'm sure he has his good points. He's a handsome-looking boy, for one thing.'

'I'm sure Miss Byrne would prefer his company to ours. I am sure she finds us a little old-fashioned,' Helen said with a dry smile.

'Oh, no, Miss Lynch; I couldn't enjoy the evening better than I am doing.'

'Murphy is an ill-bred little pup!' Elizabeth said in a vexed tone.

'Tush-tush, Elizabeth. Let us enjoy the meal and leave Murphy out of it,' Mary pleaded. 'And after this Nora will play a few pieces for us on the piano.'

'Hear, hear!' Peter said, tapping a spoon on the table. 'That's what we all want to hear.'

And so after tea they all went into the sitting-room, and while Nora took her seat at the piano Peter stood beside her, turning the pages of her music. She played for them Debussy's *Clair de Lune, La fille aux cheveux de lin*, Two Arabesques, and Beethoven's *Pathétique*. She sang for them *Down by the sally gardens*, and at Mary's request, *Believe me if all those endearing young charms*.

Yes, she was a good obliging girl, Mary reflected: not one of those stuck-up girls that you had to coax, leaving you sorry afterwards for coaxing them! It was a delightful evening, and they must have another one soon and ask Father Lacy to join them. She mustn't forget to mention this to Elizabeth.

'You must be tired, Nora?' she found herself saying out aloud.

'Not much, Mary. Music doesn't tire me,' Nora said, putting her sheets in the piano stool and settling herself on the sofa.

'Indeed, you must, Miss Byrne,' Helen said, getting to her feet. 'We must go now, and not keep you out of your beds any longer.'

'It's early yet, Helen,' Elizabeth protested, 'and sure tomorrow is Saturday and none of us has to rise early. Sit down, dear.'

'Come, Peter, we mustn't be selfish. We have had a good night. And there's Mary dying with sleep.'

'I am not indeed! I'm just getting into my stride.'

Despite all their objections, Helen would not stay, and moved out of the sitting-room to get her coat. It was a lovely night for their walk home; the moon was as bright as a new shilling, the tree-shadows as solid as planks on the lawn, and the smoke from the burning leaves warming the chilly air.

'Good night!' the three of them called from the lighted doorway. 'Good night and thanks,' Peter called back, and when the light from the closing door had swept through the bare hedge he found himself cut off abruptly from the pleasant evening.

They walked in silence for a while. Then behind them the collier's whistle blew loud and sharp in the frosty air, and when its echo had fanned away behind the little hills Helen said: 'They lost no time in unloading her today. The crew will all be at home in Scotland by tomorrow night.'

Peter made no comment. She spoke then of the chilliness of the night, but he knew that these obvious commonplaces were not what she was really thinking, and he felt, too, that she knew he was hurt by her behaviour this evening.

'And the Miss Devlins were so kind!' she said.

'They were — very kind.'

They walked to the turn of the road that led uphill towards the school. The collier blew again and he could hear the pound of the engine and the thrashing of the screw. Helen sighed, her breath white in the light from the moon. He sensed that she was waiting for him to speak of Miss Byrne, but he suppressed that desire and said: 'You had no call to bring Murphy's name forward tonight. It only involves me in discussions that I dislike.'

'I thought, perhaps, that Miss Byrne might be fond of him and I wanted to praise him. Surely there was no harm in that?'

'I don't see that a walk home from school with Murphy means anything.'

'It may lead to something, and I was showing Miss Byrne that I was interested in her.'

'It would be a good thing if you minded your own damned business once in a while. And while I'm on the point, I didn't like the unmannerly way you mentioned it. We had hardly seated ourselves at the table when you let fly.'

'It was rather unmannerly of you — of both of you — to sit so detached the whole evening from the rest of the company. Did that not occur to you?'

'The rest of the company haven't the same interests as Miss Byrne and myself.'

'It's news to me that you have anything in common.'

'We have both an interest in music for one thing. And what's more, she's a highly agreeable girl. Today she took me out of a fix by agreeing to take my class for singing.'

'I thought you were going to make Murphy take it.'

'I don't *make* people do anything. I make suggestions — that's all. I told you that before!'

'I don't envy her her job. Your boys are too big for a young girl like her to handle.'

'She was delighted to be asked.'

'I hope the delight stays with her.'

'You seem to wish it won't!'

'You're in a very sulky mood tonight, Peter.'

'It's you that's in the nasty mood. You have been in it the whole evening.'

'Me! I have never been in better form . . . And what's more you never raised your eyes once to admire Elizabeth's beautiful piece of lacework this evening.'

'I leave that business to the old women. What the blazes do I know about lacework?'

77

'You've no call to be rude over it!'

A cat pressed itself under the school gate and crossed the road; another followed and they went through the hedge into his garden. Peter stooped for a few stones and Helen walked on ahead into the house. He stayed out for a long time hunting the cats, and when he came in she had gone to bed.

For a long time she heard him tapping at the piano, trying to play one of Miss Byrne's pieces.

'Dear me, but he's a foolish man,' she sighed to herself and cowled the bed-clothes round her head. She turned her mind to Mary's supper and to Miss Byrne's apple-tart that Elizabeth had praised so highly. Such stuff to praise! Why, a child in the Girls' School could do better. The pastry was so leathery that when you tried to cut it it curled up at one end. And then, Peter asking for another helping! It's no wonder he's in a sulky mood! That Nora one may be able to play the piano and take a singing class but she's no hand at cookery — that was certain!

✿ 7 ✿

WHEN Mr. Lynch came into her classroom to intro-
duce her to his boys for the singing lesson she was seated at her
table, a tuning-fork lying in front of her, her hands relaxed on
her lap in an effort to curb her unreasonable excitement. And as
he walked ahead of her through the adjoining room she glanced
at Murphy and he winked furtively and gave her a comic grin
of commiseration. And when Mr. Lynch stood in front of
Standards VI and VII and appealed to them to do their level best
for her she lingered shyly near the easel on which hung a
tattered modulator chart. The boys surveyed her with overt
pleasure as her nervous hands smoothed her hair or fingered the
pearl earrings that she was wearing for the occasion.

Mr. Lynch's introductory speech rambled into unnecessary
repetition; no one paid any attention to what he was saying, not
even Miss Byrne herself as she lowered her eyes to escape from
the unflinching gaze of these big boys.

'In a few months I hope I'll have the pleasure of listening to
a group of songs,' he concluded, and smiling to Miss Byrne he
strode off to take her class for painting.

There was a tentative buzz of talk and an unnecessary shuffle
of feet as the boys eased themselves in the dual desks. Nervously
and politely she asked them their names, but when she reached a
boy with bald patches in his red hair he shouted: 'Buster Maguire!'
and immediately there was a spontaneous laugh from the whole
class.

'You weren't christened Buster, surely?'

'No, Miss.'

'Then what precisely is your Christian name?'

'Please, Miss, Michael Malachy Maguire.'

'I hope you'll be as musical as your name.'

There was another laugh from the boys. She felt a telltale

flush on her cheeks and she ceased her questioning, clapped her hands for silence, and signed to them to stand. She asked one boy to open a window and immediately a half-dozen boys scrambled across the floor to oblige her.

'One is enough, please,' she said. They nudged one another but none backed away, and they all bundled round the window, pushing it up, and taking time to survey the playground before resuming their places. She began with breathing exercises, but noticing that some of them held in their breaths till their neck-veins swelled out like ramrods, she desisted at once and lifting a ruler turned to the modulator. There was a sound of a school-bag falling on the floor and Maguire whimpering with feigned concern: 'Please, Miss, somebody's spilt my books on the floor.'

'Wipe them up,' another said.

'Let them lie there, please,' she ordered, 'you can gather them at the end of the lesson.'

Maguire ignored her, and she waited patiently till he picked up the books, blew imaginary dust off each of them, and stowed them in his bag in meticulous order.

'Take this note — softly now! Doh-oh-oh!'

'Doh-oh-oh!' they sang back.

The ruler ascended the chart: Doh-me: ray-fa: me-soh: fa-la: soh-te: la-doh. The ruler paused at high doh before descending: doh-la: te-soh: la-fa: soh-me: fa-ray: me-doh.

The low doh was so down-at-heel that she herself had to smile; they began to laugh, then, and she had difficulty in quietening them.

'Sing the scale by yourselves — slowly and softly, please.' And while they were singing it she passed down among them, checking the boys whose voices had broken or were breaking, and these she placed in a group at the back of the room. One boy, pale with stone-blue eyes, and wearing a ragged jersey, had a lovely voice and when she asked him to sing the scale alone he did so with a quick enthusiasm that surprised and pleased her. Maguire resented being cast among the non-singers, and because he maintained that he could sing she asked him to try the scale by himself. The harshness of his voice caused the whole class to laugh and he stopped and cried with affected indignation: 'Miss, they're all laughing at me and I can't go on.'

'It would be better, Malachy, if you would stand aside for today.'

'But, please, Miss, I'm a champion singer.'

She glanced at her watch — there were still ten minutes left. She began to arrange the singers in three sections: the trebles in front, the 'seconds' in the middle, and the 'thirds' standing on the seats at the back. Up and down the modulator fled her ruler, but try as she could to become completely absorbed in the task she was aware of a discordant humming issuing from the corner where Maguire sat with the other non-singers. He thrust out his lower lip and scowled at her, and wherever she turned, his eyes followed her, staring and defiant. At three o'clock by her watch she was yearning for Mr. Lynch's entry to relieve her. But she was determined to make no complaint about any of them. She would hide her distress. She wouldn't admit failure to any-one, and perhaps in a short while she'd be able to win them over to a delight in singing. She'd have patience. She allowed her eyes to rest on the pale boy in the front seat and he smiled back and lowered his head; and it was this boy she singled out for praise when Mr. Lynch entered the room.

'You needn't tell me anything about Larry Mullan,' he said loudly. 'Larry always does his best.' Then he turned and whispered to her: 'But he'll never live, poor fellow, to scratch a grey head. There's consumption in that family — and what's more they were all clever. But Larry's the best of them — and the best in my class, for that matter.'

'Poor child,' she said in a low voice as Mr. Lynch drew from under his arm a few paintings he had got from her class. ' "Mother out with the Baby", I gave them to paint,' he said. 'The colouring is lovely, but one wonders why they all give their mothers lips and teeth like a mouth-organ while up in this class they'll give you presentable-looking figures but common-place colouring. The loss, I think, is greater than the gain.' He held up one of the paintings for his class to admire but they only laughed at it, and to their disappointment he didn't hold up the rest but handed them to Miss Lynch: 'It's like casting pearls . . .' She smiled and hurried back to her own room.

Her class was shouting and streaking one another with paint brushes and she lifted a short cane and slapped a few of them and threatened to go for Mr. Lynch. Listening to their sobbing she relented and wondered why she had beaten them so hastily. She tried to soothe the ones she had slapped by allowing them to give out the reading books for the last lesson of the day. And while they read aloud for her she did not listen to them or correct their mistakes, for over and over again she heard only one thing: 'There's T.B. in that family.'

On her way home Murphy joined her and as she talked about her singing class she praised Larry Mullan's voice.

'The same fellow didn't sing much for me when he was in my class,' Murphy commented. 'His voice won't be of much use to him; the whole family is rotten with consumption.'

She felt her face redden but kept looking straight ahead of her. 'That's a harsh way of speaking of any illness,' she said without looking at him.

'It's the common phrase around these parts.'

'That's all the more reason why you shouldn't use it,' she said. 'It's a brutal phrase. I am sure you never heard Mr. Lynch use it.'

'I don't give a snap what Lynch would use or what he wouldn't use. I am only repeating what I've heard scores of times. Of course if I had known it would have annoyed you I wouldn't have come out with it.'

'Annoyed me!' and she looked at him squarely: 'I don't wish to be teacherish, but it's you should be annoyed. Thank God neither of us has that illness, but if we were ever unfortunate enough to be infected by it we wouldn't like people to say of us what you have said, would we?'

'I wouldn't give one rap what they'd say,' he said, laughing. 'I would just call for Brennan every week and we'd walk out to the graveyard and I'd show him the nice spot where I was to be buried and I'd express the hope that he'd be lying next door to me.'

'Both of you will have years and years of retirement pension before that happens.'

'Why do you say that?'

'I just feel it,' she said, smiling to him as she turned up the path to the Devlins.

On her next singing day, which was Friday, she stayed on in her own classroom until Mr. Lynch arrived to take over. She could hear the noise of his own class as she was passing through Murphy's room. 'That's a rowdy mob you're going in to,' he said to her. 'It's a pitch-fork you need for them, not a tuning-fork. I wish I had them for a few weeks, I'd flay the life out of them.' She said nothing but hurried into the room and closed the door behind her sharply. They didn't cease their chatter, and she frowned at them and clapped her hands for order. The windows were closed, but she didn't ask to have them opened. She requested the non-singers to stand aside. She saw Maguire at the back hiding behind another boy.

'Malachy Maguire, would you please stand aside with the rest?'

'But, please, Miss, my ma said I was a good singer.'

'Is your mother the teacher or am I?'

'Yes, Miss.'

'Yes — what?'

'You're the teacher, Miss.'

The boys laughed and nudged one another as he trailed his feet across the floor and slumped into an empty desk. She tried to ignore him but was conscious all the time of his sullen stare. She asked them what songs they had learnt in the other classes. They all could remember *The Minstrel Boy*. She got them to try it. But they galloped through it, not heeding her demands for slowness and softness. She decided to teach them something new: something they'd never heard before — freshness, perhaps, would hold their attention.

As she began writing a few bars of Tonic Sol-fa on the blackboard a buzz of talk broke out behind her. Without turning round once to check them she continued writing in her careful script. A pellet of paper struck the board, but she pretended not to see or hear it. When she had finished and was turning round to face the class she suddenly saw Maguire stuffing an elastic catapult in his pocket. She asked him for it.

'It's mine,' he said crossly. 'I bought it. I didn't fire anything out of it.'

'Don't take it out in my class like a good boy.'

He began to pare a pencil with a razor-blade and to scrape up the parings with a screeching sound. She stiffened herself against the loathing that struggled within her.

She got them to sing the bars on the board and then to hum it a few times. She gave them words for the music and asked them to write it in their jotters.

> Spring, the sweet spring, is the year's pleasant king,
> Then blows each thing, then maids dance in a ring,
>
> Cold doth not sting, the pretty birds do sing:
> Cuckoo, jug-jug, pu-we, to-witta-woo!

They acknowledged the words with a smile of curiosity. In time she would win them over to her side, she thought. She got them to sing the words, and their voices for a while drowned the noise of the shuffling feet of the non-singers. Maguire scratched his head, swayed to and fro, and tapped his finger-nails on the desk; a few of his companions imitated him, and her scanty confidence shrank to a knot of anger. But, again, she did not complain to Mr. Lynch when her half-hour had ended.

On the next few singing days Maguire was absent. Most of the class responded then, taking delight in the new song. It was

84

a difficult song, but she felt they would master it. She got Larry Mullan to sing the first three lines of each verse, the class singing out the refrain. They enjoyed it, and even Mr. Murphy paused in his teaching to listen to it, and his whole class smiled as they heard: Cuckoo, jug-jug, pu-we, to-witta-woo.

After two weeks Maguire was back again. The boys were slack and inattentive then, fidgeting and smirking at his antics. She sensed he had turned them against her. When she wrote a passage from *Samson and Delilah* on the blackboard a pebble, shot from a catapult, struck her hand. She blushed, said nothing and didn't look down at her hand though she felt it smarting where the pebble had struck. She hated the anger that flashed through her like a pain. She hated their contempt and their insult. She hated her own weakness, her inability to keep order. She wouldn't complain. She'd endure it, but at Christmas she would look out for a new school. Wearily she turned from the board. The smaller boys smiled at her — a smile of sympathy, of collaboration. She glanced at the non-singers and saw Maguire placing a knife, a blade, and a tin box in front of him. She rushed down and snatched them before he realized what had happened.

'I'll give these to Mr. Lynch,' she said calmly.

There was silence then and she was surprised to see Maguire take a book from his bag and open it before him on the desk. His scowl had gone, and as he bent his head over the book the sight of the ugly bald patches in his hair roused her pity for him. They were all staring at her with fear and then she noticed they were staring at her right hand. On the back of it there was a circle of blood, the size of a shilling. She pretended not to see it and said nothing to Mr. Lynch as she handed him the objects she had taken from Maguire.

'Was Maguire giving you trouble?'

'No,' she said bravely, 'I took them from him in case he'd do damage to himself.'

'He'd be good riddance if he did,' he whispered back.

Going home that day she was alone and was glad of it. Anger

left her weak, disharmonized her, and if Murphy had been with her she felt she'd have hurt him by her words; she would have accused him of viciousness towards Mr. Brennan, of brutality towards his pupils, and of an unreasoning hatred of Mr. Lynch. Thank God he wasn't with her. She would have said things to him that she would have regretted later.

She braced herself to walk quickly, but her body would not obey her. She rested at a wooden gate and drooped her arms over the top bar. She breathed in the air deeply and gazed around to still the throbbing in her mind. A stubble field stretched before her, and the low sun shining on the strings of gossamer that covered it made it gleam like a wet fish-net spread out to dry. In one corner starlings bathed in a puddle of water, and the fine spray set up by their quivering wings looked as if they were standing in the white smoke from a fire. She shooshed at them and they flew up to a bare ash tree, and as they spread their wings to dry in the sun they gleamed like jet, and she could hear their incessant chatterings as she trudged away from the field.

Without taking off her coat she sat in an armchair in the sitting-room and gazed with half-shut eyes at the fire burning brightly in the grate.

'You're tired, Nora,' Mary said, coming silently into the room.

'Tired!' Nora started and shook her head wearily. 'Indeed, I am. I am glad, Mary, you don't know what this after-school tiredness is like. Not only do the children drag and dredge you the day long, but the stale air in the room also adds to the fag and the fatigue. I only wish I could sit here for a whole day without stirring — that's the way I feel. But, thanks be to God, it won't be long now till the Christmas holidays.'

'But you shouldn't allow it to get you down like this. You're not a horse. You must go easy on yourself, child. You're too conscientious.'

'It's hard to go easy, Mary. Even to keep a class attentive is a strain. But when you have to deal with the unwilling hand it's a torture. And the singing class — not a word of this to Mr. Lynch for I wouldn't for the world let him know I'm disappointed in them — the truth is that they're hard to control. And there's one boy in particular who's a heartbreak — a Malachy Maguire. It's he that can set the class in such an uproar that they'll do nothing for me.'

'A Maguire — a piebald-headed fellow: you may as well try to get a goose to sing. I never knew any of them Maguires to have a note of any kind! — music or money.'

'It's not that, Mary. It's his manner. He's very troublesome.'

'Oh, the blackguard! And what does Peter say about that rascal?'

'I haven't complained, yet. I don't like to do it.'

'Well, I'll do it for you.'

Nora entreated her not to, and made her promise solemnly that she wouldn't. Mary agreed but on condition that Nora herself would complain on the villain at the first opportunity. 'You must complain,' she insisted. 'Your health is at stake. It's your duty. And Peter will understand. Some of those big boys have no sense of what is just and decent. And anyway they're far too big and grown-up for a young girl like you to handle.'

'Teaching, Mary, is a wearying and wasting job. Let no one say it's easy. We teachers are old before we're thirty-five. We do our best and our best haggards us. We work hard — and as Mr. Murphy says some inspector may come along some fine day and reduce our work to shreds. There are days, Mary, the singing days, when I'd gladly walk past the school instead of going in. Freedom, on those days, lies outside the gate. Oh, the one who said that teaching was a vocation spoke truly. All vocations need sacrifice. I have tried, these past few weeks, to live up to that, and although I didn't intend to complain to anyone, I'm complaining to you in spite of myself. And is there anything more sickening on this earth than one who is always complaining?'

'And why wouldn't you complain! There's nothing so

relieving as a good long talk. And you'll really have to complain to Peter — make no mistake about that!'

At the dinner-table Elizabeth noticed Nora's listlessness, her sighs, and how the corners of her mouth turned down, and she hoped in her mind that the girl was not struggling with some attraction for that Murphy fellow. She suggested this to Mary when they were alone in the kitchen, but Mary shook her head knowingly and said that it had nothing whatsoever to do with Murphy.

'What is it then?' Elizabeth said, determined to have her mind set at rest. 'If you know anything don't stand there, silent as a fool. Out with it, please.'

Mary stared at her, stammered and began: 'It's a little secret. And you'll not breathe a word to any soul?'

Elizabeth sat up. 'As if I'd do the like of that!' — and she settled herself patiently for a long story, expecting to hear that it was a love affair between Peter and Nora. But on hearing that it was nothing except a silly bit of annoyance about a noodle like Maguire she tut-tutted with deep disgust: 'To think that Miss Nora would allow herself to become upset and ill over such a playboy! I never heard such foolishness in all my life. It's a pity she didn't come to me with all her troubles. However, I'll see Peter and Helen and give them both a dressing down!'

She gathered up her work-basket and was sailing off to the sitting-room when Mary caught her arm: 'Please, Elizabeth, say nothing to Nora this evening. She'll be vexed because I told you.'

'Vexed — because you told me! Is that the way to treat your sister — to keep silly secrets from her like a convent schoolgirl? I wouldn't tolerate such stupid privacy in this house!'

She sailed into the room where Nora was seated in front of the fire, a book face-downward on her lap. Elizabeth didn't take time to sit down but leaped into an attack on Master Peter Lynch, on his school, on the singing class, on every Maguire she had ever known, on Murphy and on Mr. Brennan, and on the slothfulness of old teachers and the insolence of the young; and she ended her discourse with a withering denunciation of Peter Lynch for bringing such open-handed destruction into the heart and soul of an innocent young girl — a parentless girl too, when you come to think of it.

'Please, Elizabeth,' Nora said with an aggrieved expression, 'I would rather you wouldn't say anything this time.'

'Wouldn't I! I wish I'd known before this — and you losing your appetite and your good looks. I'd walk over to him this minute only the roads are frosty. While you are in this house you are our guest, our charge, and we'll see that justice is done to you and for you. Singing, indeed! I'd sing a few of them if I had them for a few minutes. And when I see Mister Peter I'll let him know what state it has you in. Your health, child, is more important than teaching singing to the likes of the Maguires!'

Mary was standing in the doorway, wringing her hands, sorry now that she had confided in Elizabeth.

'It would be better that I tell him myself,' Nora said penitently. 'I wouldn't want him to think that I told outside all that happens in school.'

'And why wouldn't you tell us?' Elizabeth bristled. 'We're not the type that would gossip it round the town. You must be more open with us, Nora dear. We are different from the townsfolk. We're established in these parts for years. We have a name that has influence and respect — that's the reason Father Lacy asked us to take you.'

'I'm sorry I have annoyed you with it all,' Nora said, 'indeed I am.'

'Nothing vexes me so much as to see a young girl vexed,' Elizabeth added.

'And that's how I feel about it too,' Mary said mournfully as she came forward from the door. 'Elizabeth has always such good sense in these matters, not like poor blundering me. And of course, Nora, you'll be quite able to speak up for yourself to Peter; he'll understand and he'll give his good-natured smile when he hears it. Let us talk no more about it tonight — it's no use making monsters out of molehills.'

'Yes, there's sense in what Mary says: no use making mountains out of molehills,' Elizabeth said, and sat down with her work-basket on her lap.

When Nora had gone to bed Mary slipped up to her with a hot lemon drink.

'Nora, child, you're not vexed with me?' she whispered to her in the moonlit room.

'I'm not, Mary, I'm not,' she said as Mary sat on the edge of the bed. Mary sought for her hand and held it tightly in her own.

'I don't know what's come over me,' Nora went on, and her voice trembled. 'I don't know why I should have upset you and Elizabeth over my own little bit of trouble. I should have kept it to myself.'

'You're too hard on yourself — and God knows that's the truth,' Mary said, squeezing the hand to her breast. Suddenly Nora burst out crying and Mary put her arms around her and smoothed her forehead as she would a child's.

'And you'll tell Peter, and you'll tell him soon. Poor Elizabeth means well. She's sharp, but she means well. She didn't mean to hurt you — you know that, Nora, don't you? And sure all this will pass in God's good time, and you'll be happy in your school again. And some fine evening soon, we'll look back at all this and we'll have a good laugh to ourselves, the two of us . . . Come now, Nora, take this lemon drink while it's hot. It's the boy that'll make you sleep.'

'You're very kind, Mary. As kind to me as any mother could be.'

'I'm only a blundering old woman,' she said, and was glad that a cloud darkened the moon and hid her few old tears. She continued to sit on the edge of the bed, saying nothing, just stroking the hand that lay in her own and only wishing that she was lying beside her throughout the night with her arm around her. Reluctantly she arose and pressed Nora's forehead and made the sign of the cross on it with her thumb: 'You'll sleep now and put all this trouble out of your mind.'

'I will, Mary. I'm only keeping you from your bed. Good night now — and thanks.'

Mary stole out of the room and Nora fell asleep. But during the night she wakened and wondered what time it was. She sat up with a start, and heard the wind in the trees and saw the blue quivering stars shine their eel-cold light on the bare branches. Below in the sitting-room the clock chimed and she counted the three strokes. Her heart thumped loudly and she wondered what on earth had frightened her. She lay back slowly on the pillow, turned her head from the window and stared at the liquid reflection of the curtains on the wall. She tried to sleep, but the singing class came before her, and she opened her eyes to dispel the loathing for it that was reasserting itself. She couldn't go on like this. She couldn't! She couldn't! Friday would resolve it for her, one way or another.

Friday came. Her resolution had not faltered. All morning she had found herself ill-humoured and upset with her own class, unable to endure their natural restlessness. And when a burst of rage came from Murphy in the adjoining room she shuddered and clenched her hands and wished she could flee from the school. But, she counselled herself, all this dejection of spirit and this desire for flight would pass as soon as she had settled, once and for all, with Maguire.

At lunch-time she spoke little either to Mr. Murphy or Mr. Brennan, and Mr. Brennan, noticing her unusual abstraction asked, when he was alone with her, if he or Murphy had said anything that had offended her. She laughed, then, and said she wasn't aware that she was being dull and that he mustn't mind her silence.

On going out to the playground she joined Murphy and tried to force herself out of her mood of selfish absorption. She watched the bigger boys carrying sheets of white ice and breaking them on the playground to make a slide. Everything around her was white, she told herself: the air was white, the breaths of the running children, the slates on the school, the branches of the trees, and it seemed, somehow, that the voices of everyone were white, too. Murphy strode beside her, blowing into his hands, and occasionally taking a slide on the slippery ground. She smiled at him, and for a moment she stood quite still, no longer feeling isolated or detached from the breathless shouting of the children and the drumming sound of their feet on the frosty ground.

At the end of the lunch hour she felt better, and at a few minutes before two-thirty she went forward to Mr. Lynch's room just as he was preparing to leave for hers.

'I see you don't want to waste a minute of your half-hour,' he said with unconscious irony. 'I could give you an extra ten or fifteen minutes with them if you like.'

'No, thanks, Mr. Lynch. I can manage all I have to do in the half-hour.'

'Whatever you wish,' he said. 'You have just to make the suggestion and I'll alter the timetable to suit you.'

When he had closed the door behind him the detestable hubbub broke out as usual, and to strengthen her confidence she drew herself erect, her face stiff and colourless. She swept round quickly to the board and in less than a minute had pinned a chart to it with the words and music of *Linden Lea*. She had made up her mind not to lose control of the class by writing on the blackboard, and so she had prepared the chart the night before.

'Now,' she said, gripping her ruler firmly. A fierce rigour of control possessed her and she felt that even the boys had sensed it. 'Don't heed the words until we grow accustomed to the music printed above them.' She halted and signalled with her ruler to Maguire. 'Go to your usual place . . . Hurry, please, and don't let me have to tell you this, day after day.' She waited coldly for his usual ritual: the slow disentangling of his school-bag from the form and his pretence to be looking for something below the desk. 'I'll give you some assistance across the room if you don't hurry.' He shrugged his shoulders and lurched across to the other non-singers.

She tapped her tuning-fork and gave the note. They all repeated it, held it as she indicated, and then as it trailed softly away a 'Boo-oo-m' from Maguire swept across the thinning fan of sound.

She suddenly rushed across to him, and a comb wrapped in tissue paper fell from his hands and he pounced on it before she could get it.

'Did you make that noise?'

'No,' he growled, and lay back against the desk and shrugged his shoulders. The ruler in her hand quivered and she wrestled against the impulse to crack it across his knuckles.

'Take out a book and read it! I'm going to stand no more of your nonsense!' She looked down with disgust at the bare patches on his head: like ringworm on unhealthy cattle, she said to herself, and then winced with repulsion from the cruelty of her thought. She turned from him, sick with an evil loathing not to touch him with her hands; she shut her eyes for a moment and prayed that the loathsomeness would leave her.

As she stood in front of the class again she saw him slide the ink-well cover back and forth. He was pitiless with her. She had forgiven him time and again, had shielded him, but today she would crush his confident impudence.

'We'll begin again,' she said, her voice trembling. She tapped the ruler along the notes on her chart, but she paid no attention to what they were singing or how thay sang it. One thing only she heard and that was the sliding of the ink-well cover and then the rolling of a pencil along the desk. She still held back. She would wait until she would get something definite, something that would convict him without doubt or equivocation. She watched him lay his head on his hands in an attitude of sleep and give a loud snore that set the class laughing. Go now! Don't wait any longer! She gazed down at him. Maguire didn't look up though he knew everyone was staring at him and that the class had fallen silent on his account. He seemed to enjoy it, and still resting his head on his arms which were stretched out on the desk he gazed with one surreptitious eye across the room, raised his knee furtively and tumbled his books on the floor.

She fled from the room and returned at once with Mr. Lynch.

'Come here, Maguire!' and he gripped him and spun him round the floor like a top.

'My books fell, Sir,' he said timidly.

'I'll take care they'll not fall again.'

She told him how he had hummed through a comb and upset the class.

'Turn out your pockets, Malachy,' he ordered in a hard voice.

Maguire turned out one pocket in which there was a brass wheel of a clock and a piece of elastic. Mr. Lynch tapped the other pockets with his cane, and made him turn them all out till the comb wrapped in tissue paper was disclosed.

'Why is it wrapped up like that?'

'To keep it clean for my head, Sir.'

'You can go, Miss Byrne. I'll deal with him. You'll have no more trouble with him or any of the others. Do you hear that — all of you? I never suspected for one moment that you'd let me down like this. You'll not insult a young lady who is doing more than her best for you,' and he raised his voice till it could be heard in the four rooms of the school.

She slipped out of the room quietly, sorry now that she had brought this to pass. Murphy stopped her on her way through his room and asked what was the row about. He smiled when she told him and he advised her not to take it so seriously.

'There's nothing like a good thumping row on a cold day like this,' he said to her. 'It generates heat and warms the old blood stream.'

'Maguire forced me to do it. It's been going on . . .' but before she had finished she heard the smack of Mr. Lynch's cane and she hurried into her own room.

Her class was silent, stiffened into an alertness of fear as they heard Mr. Lynch's voice and then a stumbling like a horse in a stable and a boy squealing. She sat at her table feeling faint. Then she got up and stood leaning against the wall at the back of the room.

In a few minutes Mr. Lynch came in. He was paler than she had ever seen him, his auburn hair in disarray, his hands trembling and a handkerchief squeezed tightly in one of them.

'I suppose you think I've murdered him,' he said, and wiped the blood from a few pin-scratches on the back of his hand. 'I gave him four good ones and accompanied it with as much noise and thunder as I could muster. You'd have thought by the way he squealed that I was killing him. But I'm afraid I've got the worst of it. Every place I gripped him I seemed to catch a pin.'

'I'm really sorry, Mr. Lynch. I am indeed.'

'Nonsense. One can't manage a school without a scene like this cropping up now and again. It'll not do him a bit of harm and into the bargain it'll sober the rest of them.'

'But it has upset you greatly.'

'Och, that doesn't matter. We can't shut ourselves up in a box. We have to face things squarely even when they do distress us. You can't go on teaching and expect things to go smoothly all the time. Life would be too easy then, and there'd be something wrong with it and with us, if that were the case.'

Larry Mullan came into the room with his hand raised: 'Please, Sir, Maguire has run home.'

'All right, Larry . . . I'll go now, Miss Byrne, and if you hear that Mrs. Maguire has called, don't come forward unless I send for you. The father won't come — he's working in England.'

But when three-thirty came and the school was dismissed Mrs. Maguire had not called, and as Nora wished to be alone in her walk home she lingered about in her room, tidying up her press and allowing Murphy to get out ten minutes ahead of her.

As she hurried along the road, drops of melted frost hung from the bushes and her feet splintered the white ice in the ruts. From behind a hedge she heard someone shout after her: 'Badger! Badger! Badger!' and she felt her nerves tizz with indignation. She hated the injustice of it and it made her more conscious of the grey streak in her black hair. She didn't look back, and like someone calling a disobedient dog she heard the exasperated voice become hoarse and dry with calling after her: 'Badger! Badger!' It was Maguire's voice — she was sure of that and she was sure also that he was alone.

She slipped quietly up to her room and lay relaxed on top of the bed until Mary would call her for her dinner. There was a tight pressure at the back of her head and she turned on her side to escape from it, and as she lay there she saw the drops of melted frost hang on the telephone wires like notes in a musical score; they slid along the wires, joined with one another and fell weightily on to the ground. She could see the schoolhouse and behind it the trees brushed out against the red hearth of the sky. She shut her eyes and didn't care whether she ever set foot in that school again. She had made her complaint, but the complaint had made her miserable and had distressed Mr. Lynch. But, before God, there was nothing else she could have done. She had had enough patience, God knows, and she couldn't have allowed it to go any further. She had herself to consider in this matter: not only her health but her position in the school. If she had allowed it to continue the singing class would make a poor show for her when the inspector would come round. No, she did the right thing and, please God, she'd have no more trouble with Maguire. Let him shout whatever he likes at her, she'd ignore it. Yes, she'd put that behind her.

'Badger!' she said to herself and laughed. She got up from the bed, looked at herself in the mirror, and pressed her hair flat with her hands. 'Badger,' she said, and looked at the grey streak dividing the blackness of her hair. 'Badger,' she said again and laughed to herself as she crossed to the bathroom to wash before dinner.

Mary and Elizabeth were delighted to hear that she had complained and were glad, too, to hear her go to the piano that evening and play piece after piece and occasionally burst into song. And while she was seated at the piano Peter Lynch drove up in his car to ask if Johnny or any of them had seen Maguire. He explained to them that Maguire's mother had called at the house to tell that her son hadn't come home from school and that she had heard that her poor boy was half-killed by a flogging he didn't deserve and that for all she knew he might have drowned himself by this time. As he recounted this Peter stood on the floor, turning his hat in his hand, and because he wouldn't sit down Mary and Elizabeth and Nora stood with him.

'Don't let it worry you, Peter,' Elizabeth said. 'That Maguire woman is a great oul scaremonger. Indeed the town-ones are all the same. They love notice. A death in the family and they're in their element: they're the centre of everything for a few days. Indeed if the funeral arrangements could last for a week they'd prefer it to a Christmas . . . Sit down, Peter, and don't bother yourself any more about him.'

'I can't, Elizabeth. I'll drive into the town. Maybe Tim Brennan or Murphy will have some news of the playboy.'

'He'll not drown himself,' Mary said mournfully. 'Please God, he wouldn't do the like of that.'

'Mary dear, you're nearly as bad as Mrs. Maguire. The water's too cold for drowning — and every Maguire I knew was apt to take good care of himself. The rascal's hiding in some hay shed and he'll be a hang sight warmer there than in his own home. If I had my hands on him for a minute I'd increase his warmth . . . But do sit down, Peter, and Mary will get you a nice cup of tea.'

'It's all my fault,' Nora put in. 'I seem to exist to cause trouble. I should have ignored him.'

Thereupon Elizabeth broke in and revealed how Nora had worked herself into such a state these past few weeks that it was pitiable to look at her, eating nothing, playing no music, reading no books, and sighing her heart out.

'And to think I never even noticed it,' Peter said. 'Why didn't you tell me, Nora? I would soon have settled it.'

Nora glanced at him and then glanced quickly at the others: none of them was aware, only herself, that he had used her Christian name; he had never done so before and she realized that he was more worried about Maguire than he pretended.

'I'd better be going. The sooner I hear where the playboy is, the more contented I'll be.'

'Go on with him, Nora,' Elizabeth said when she saw Nora holding back.

'May I?' she said to all three.

'You must. Two searchers are better than one. Peter will be glad of your company.'

The snow was falling as they drove into town. The road was already white with it, and as Nora watched the flakes flow rapidly towards the headlights she kept repeating: 'I shouldn't have complained and troubled you like this.'

'You had too much patience with them — that was your only fault. You were too good to them and too good for them. But don't think any more about it. I've had a few cases like this before now.'

The Square was white with snow and their car cut two parallel lines across it as they drove up to Brennan's house. There was a light in the window, and a bowl with two goldfish was shadowed on the yellow blind.

'The only pets he possesses,' Peter said in a hushed voice. He knocked at the door. Black bubbles rose from the mouths of the fish and disappeared on the surface of the water. He rapped again, and either the rapping of the door or someone moving within the room agitated the two fish, for they sped round the bowl with thin files of bubbles rising from their tails. The door was opened cautiously.

'It's only me and Miss Byrne,' Peter said.

'Quiet now, my mother's just gone up to bed and she'll be wondering who's come in.'

He brought them into the parlour, which was as dreary as a railway waiting-room. A gas fire was burning with a saucer of water in front of it. Peter asked if he had seen the Maguire boy.

'No, I haven't seen him. At least he didn't pass that window before I drew the blind. He usually looks at the goldfish, and the other day he put a dirty spit on that window and it nearly made me sick when I saw it sliding down the pane. And the rascal saw me staring at him all the time. He'll come to no good. I hope now he wouldn't do any harm to himself.'

'Not at all,' Peter said, 'that's not the kind of him.'

'You never can tell,' Brennan said slowly, looking from one to the other. 'I remember reading once of a little boy who mitched from school through fear. And do you know what he

99

did? He went out to the stable and hanged himself with a stocking.'

'Maybe Murphy will have heard something,' Peter said, getting to his feet.

'He might, he might,' Brennan answered, standing up too, relieved that they were going. 'I don't go out much in the frost. There's what I do be reading.' He waved his hand to his row of encyclopaedias, and from a round table lifted a bulging portfolio in which he had pasted hundreds of cuttings from newspapers.

'I'll swear you have some mournful items in that lot,' Peter said as he saw him turning the leaves for Miss Byrne.

'Look at that one I have just put my finger on at random,' Brennan said, his eyes brightening. "Three children die from eating fungus." You can't watch children — you don't know what they'll be up to next.'

'We'll have to go, Tim,' Peter said and moved into the dark hallway where he stumbled against the hat-stand. And when the door was closed and the goldfish were once again swirling round the bowl Peter shook his head hopelessly: 'I must be in a bad way, Nora, when I thought of calling on him. He'll be telling me on Monday morning that I wakened his mother . . . I wish to the good God I could waken him.'

They called at Murphy's, but Nora didn't get out of the car, and she saw Murphy come to the hall door with a hand of cards in his hand and saw someone lift the parlour blind and try to peer into the street. Murphy was laughing and he came over and thrust his head into the car: 'It's nice and warm in there, Miss Byrne,' he said, shrugging his shoulders playfully. 'I'd love to jaunt round with you, only I'm in the middle of a card-school . . . Old dame Maguire called with me and I told her to go and chase herself. But she didn't do that, she went over to Brennan's and though she knocked for about five minutes she got no answer. I suppose Tim was having a siesta at the time — anyway he didn't open the door and I saw her going away muttering her prayers.' Murphy laughed at his own joke, and then hearing the parlour window being knocked for his return he said quickly: 'Hope you'll find him before midnight — dead or alive: one thousand pounds reward. Good luck to the hunt. I must go now and not hold up our game any longer.'

'That fellow combines a light heart with a quick tongue,' Peter said, settling into the car again. The snow was still falling, but finer now, like dandruff, and as the headlights lit up the road Peter spotted old Joey O'Brien trudging towards the town with a bag on his back.

'Hello, Joey,' Peter called to him as he halted the car beside him.

'Who's calling me?'

'Do you not know me?'

His bag of empty bottles rattled as he laid it down on the snow. 'It's Master Lynch, begob. And I see you've company . . .' He stuck his head into the lighted car and a cold air came in with it. 'Ah, ah, I've met this lassie before. Wait now, wait now: Angela, Angela, that's her name — the same name as my sister that's the nun in New Zealand.' There was a large drop at his nose and just as it was about to fall he withdrew his head and let the drop fall on the road.

Peter asked him if he had seen Maguire in his travels — the one with the bald patches on his head.

Joey scratched himself against his clothes and rubbed his rough hands loudly. He had seen him a wheen of hours ago picking up coal at the coal-quay.

'And did the blackguard bunk out of school?' and he raised his eyes to the dark sky. 'He'll come to no good for doing the like of that. Look at the style of me,' and he pointed to his old rain-coat fastened with a safety pin. 'If I'd stayed at school I'd be the champion of champions, the scholar of scholars, the teacher of teachers, and not the tramp of tramps — a man with nothing in my pocket but holes, and my poor head as empty as the bottles in my bag.'

Peter gave him a shilling and Nora handed him one too.

'May God Almighty bless the pair of you and wither your sins,' he shouted, 'and may you get married and have many a bouncing child. . . .'

'Thanks, Joey, thanks,' Peter laughed, putting his hand to the wheel.

'You're welcome! Give Maguire a good beltin' when you catch him. Obey! Obey! Obedience is a child's greatest prayer and he hasn't to go on his knees to say it. I know what I'm talkin' about . . . My sister that's the nun wrote that in a letter.'

Peter sounded the horn, and Joey withdrew his head from the window and stood watching the smoke from the exhaust glow red in the tail-lights as the car sped away from him.

They drew up at the coal-quay but there was nothing there only the untrodden snow, the quiet slap of the water they could not see, and above them a pewit crying in the darkness of the sky. Peter shook the heavy gates of the coal-yard and called out: 'Are you in there, Malachy?' His voice echoed in a strange and foolish way; it seemed to enlarge the silence, and in it he could hear Nora's breathing as she stood beside him. Suddenly he noticed her giving a shudder of fear and he realized, then, how deeply she felt it all. He said nothing to her but went to the iron gates again and shook them violently, sending a shower of snow down on himself. He brushed the snow from his sleeves and began to laugh: 'I'm a damned fool, Nora, to be parading about here like a drunken sea-cook. And I'm a worse fool to be taking you out on such a mission. We might as well be on the moon for all the life there is here.' He put two fingers to his mouth and whistled, and heard it echoing into the dark spaces of the estuary. He whistled again, and the whistling left a tizzing sound lingering in her ears.

'We'll call off the hunt,' he said in a fierce gaiety of spirit, and she wondered if the mood were assumed in order to ease her mind. 'If some of the boyos in the town knew I was hunting for Maguire around here they'd have a fine laugh to themselves. Indeed they'd make up a song about it.' They got into the car and he sounded the horn at nothing at all; he sounded it again and laughed. 'It's something like this they'd sing about me,' and his fingers tapped the steering-wheel:

> And out of the car the master leapt,
> While the snow it fell, so cold, so cold;
> But Maguire, the blackguard, was snug in the hay
> While the poor old idiot searched the bay
> For a floating body upon the say —
> Ta-ra-ta-ra-ta-bum-te-aye.

She laughed with him and he released the brake and whizzed away from the quay.

'That's the way, Nora. Don't think any more about it.' He left her at the Devlins' door, but he wouldn't come in and when he had driven off she was puzzled by his behaviour, and later when she was in bed she tried to comfort herself by re-calling his humorous lines but found now that her rush of joy had vanished. He had tried his best to quieten her mind, she felt; and it had made her wonder all the more how deeply he, as head of the school, was taking it. But, one thing was certain, she wouldn't stand aside and let him bear it all. Tomorrow, Saturday, she would have the whole day to herself and she'd make it her business to seek out this Mrs. Maguire and tell her truthfully what had happened in the school. She would tell how she had endured Malachy's behaviour day in and day out, until at last he forced her to complain to Mr. Lynch. If she hadn't done it she couldn't continue teaching in the school. He may be a good boy in his own home, she would add, but in school — and all the boys could support her — he certainly was not. Yes, tomorrow morn-ing she'd get up early and cycle to the Maguires'.

But she slept badly, and in the morning Mary brought break-fast up to her and told her to lie in.

'It's a lovely fresh morning, Nora,' she said, pushing back the curtains and pulling down the window. 'The cold has gone and so has the snow, thanks be to God.' And from her bed Nora could see the sunlit wintry fields, a few patches of snow under the black hedges, and the school on the hill as white as a beehive.

'Is the tea strong enough?'

'It's lovely, Mary,' and she stirred it with the spoon, but stopped on hearing a loud knock at the front door. Mary tiptoed across to the window and looked out. She put a finger to her lip and turned to Nora: 'S-sh! It's Mrs. Maguire.'

'Hand me my dressing-gown, Mary. I'll go down and see her.'

'No, no, let Elizabeth deal with her. She can be a nasty customer when she's roused.'

The knocking came again, and in a few minutes, through the open window, they heard Elizabeth's voice stretch out uninvitingly: 'Good morning, Madam!'

Mrs. Maguire mumbled something and Elizabeth answered sharply: 'Nonsense! Johnny tells me your son sleeps out at night very frequently. This morning I learnt from him that he even found him on our premises on one occasion.'

'No, it wasn't my Malachy he found. This is the first time he done the like . . . My heart's broke with the worry of it . . . I'd like to speak to the new teacher. . . .'

'She's not in. Better call at the school on Monday. No one comes visiting teachers at their private residences.'

'Do they not? Well, I've come and I'm not moving one foot till I see her.'

'I'm afraid that on this occasion you'll have to move your two feet — you can't see her in my house! Don't detain me from my work any longer. And when you find your son I hope you'll deal with him as a mother should and beat some respectable manners into him.'

'How do you know what way a mother should treat her son?'

'Be off at once before I send Johnny for the sergeant.' The door closed sharply and the window shook.

'Ah, you thin oul bitch! You cranky, crabbed, crusted oul

cat . . . Up to your neck all of you against my wee Malachy . . . can't stand the look of his poor head — that's what's wrong . . . I know it . . .' She shouted it all at the closed door, and only when she had banged the gate of the path did Mary sneak towards the window and glance out.

'Oh, dear,' she sighed, 'it's well you were in your bed, Nora, and hadn't to face that dragon.'

About an hour afterwards when Nora did get up they wouldn't allow her to go into the town on her bicycle in case she'd meet some of the Maguires. They sent Johnny in instead, and when he came back Mary was waiting for him at the gate. There was no talk about the Maguire fellow from any quarter he told her; the whole talk of the town was the low price offered for turkeys this year, and the people that had turkeys to sell were going to withhold them till they got a just price.

'They'll hold them up too long and be left with the whole lot on their hands,' Mary said, walking with him up the path.

'That's what will happen, Miss Mary. That's what will happen. That's what I'm after telling them. It's as well, Miss Mary, we didn't rear any more but the two for our own use. And you weren't going to listen to me at the time.'

'You're right, Johnny,' Mary was saying to him, impatient to get inside with her news. But just then Peter's car swung up the path, stopped at the front door, and Peter jumped out.

'The blackguard's found,' he said, and he linked Mary's arm and went into the sitting-room where Nora and Elizabeth were awaiting Johnny's return.

'Yes,' Peter said, smiling, 'he's found,' and he linked Mary the whole length of the room to an armchair. 'He has turned up like a bad halfpenny,' he went on, plunging his hands into the pockets of his overcoat and striding about the room.

'Where?' they all asked together.

'Where! There's not one of you could guess. Come on — I will give you three guesses each. No, I'll be fair and give you twenty-three each,' and he rubbed his hands vigorously and hunched his shoulders. 'It's the best I've ever heard. You'll laugh when you hear it.'

'Och, tell us. Don't keep us in swithers any longer. I wouldn't bother my head guessing,' Elizabeth said.

'I'll not tell until you all make a guess or two,' and he strode to the window and spun round on his heel. 'Come on, Nora, set the ball rolling.'

'He was at home all the time.'

'No — you're miles out,' and he opened his coat and loosened his scarf. 'Try again.'

'If you don't tell me this instant I'm going off to the kitchen,' Elizabeth said. 'Was he in the school?'

'The school! — not at all,' and he raised his hand like an auctioneer expecting another bid. His eyes were darting with roguishness. 'He was ... He was in ... He was ...'

'Och, to the divil with the "he was",' Mary said. 'Tell us where he was in plain English and have done with it.'

'In Scotland — that's where he was!'

'Scotland!'

'Yes, Scotland. You'll take the high road and Maguire will take the low road. That's where he was. The sergeant had a telegram this morning. The boyo had stowed away on the collier on Friday.'

'Mercy on us. Did you ever hear the like of that since God made you? And poor Nora worrying herself sick over an article like that!'

'Well, well, well — Scotland!' Elizabeth said. 'It's a wonder he wasn't famished and foundered going that distance. They'll have something to talk about in the town this day.'

'They will, but I'll not hear any of it,' Peter said. 'I'm for Belfast. Any of you like a spin up to the city?'

Nobody answered for a minute, and then Mary looked across at Nora and told her she should go for the run.

'Yes, of course,' Elizabeth said. 'You'll not get a better chance this side of Christmas. Yes, Nora, you should go, and while you're getting ready I'll make out a list of a few things that you could get for me.'

In about twenty minutes Nora was ready, and when the car was backing away from the door Mary and Elizabeth both shook a warning finger at her and told her to come back at a respectable hour and not to be running off to Scotland. Peter sounded the horn at them in farewell but Elizabeth held up her hand and came out on to the path and asked Nora for about the sixth time was she sure she had the list.

'I have, Elizabeth,' Nora said with smiling patience. 'There it is tucked safely in my glove.'

'I think it'd be safer in your bag.'

'All right, I'll put it in my bag. But don't worry. I'll do your messages the minute I arrive.'

The two sisters came inside. It was past midday and they decided, now that Nora had gone to Belfast for the day, not to bother with preparing much dinner.

They sat, then, at their ease before the fire and talked for a long time about the Maguire affair, realizing that out of it a deeper intimacy between Nora and Peter was growing. Mary, for her part, declared she was happy that things were shaping that way, but Elizabeth counselled her never to speak of it except with caution. That growing friendship, she was sure, would displease Helen, for didn't Helen announce on many an occasion that Peter was not the marrying kind? Elizabeth, whatever else she'd do or say, was not going to allow an idle word on that score to cross her lips. She liked Helen and she liked her friendship, and she wasn't going to do anything that would damp or chill that friendship. It was wiser not to meddle in anything that bore the slightest tint of a love affair. She'd let Nora and Peter drift about in their own way without help or hindrance, word or gesture, encouragement or discouragement from her. That was the policy to pursue — it was always better to go warily, for if things turned out ill no one could shake their heads with scorn at the Miss Devlins.

'All the same I'd like very much that Nora and Peter would make a match of it,' Mary said.

'And who, pray, is talking of marriage? That word never crossed my lips,' Elizabeth turned on her. 'If they go together to Belfast to do a day's shopping before Christmas, surely you don't think they're off to buy a ring. Mary dear, you've no experience of these matters.'

'I wish I had,' Mary said. 'I only read of the like in books and it's not the same thing.'

'The books you read are that silly dreamy sort that go to your head. But they're not meant to stay there. They were written to fill up an evening for you.'

'Am I not allowed to think of Nora and Peter in that way — as two sweethearts?'

'Certainly not! And if you do, please keep your thoughts under lock and key. Don't let me — and above all don't let Helen — hear you dream out loud.'

'It's a poor life if we can't express ourselves on the good we wish for other people. A good that was denied ourselves.'

'I don't want to hear any more nonsense from you, Mary. But if you'd tend to that fire and kindle a little one in the dining-room before they come back it'd be the most sensible thing you'll have done this whole day. And while you're on your feet you could bring me my sewing-basket for it's time I was knitting Father Lacy his Christmas socks.'

Later when Mary had lighted the dining-room fire and had laid the table, and was again seated in the sitting-room under the light from the big brass reading-lamp there was a knock at the door and she hurried to open it thinking it was Nora and Peter. But to her disappointment it was Helen.

'I just walked across for I was wondering if Peter were here. He was never as late as this before, and if the roads turned slippery or a fog came down he'd be in a nice pickle.'

'They haven't come back yet, Helen. But they shouldn't be long now.'

And in the hall Helen glanced at the bright fire in the dining-room and at the table laid for four.

She entered the sitting-room, bearing in her looks and the fox fur round her shoulders the coldness of the air outside. She couldn't possibly stay for supper, she told them, for she had a Christmas cake in the oven and she couldn't leave it for any length of time. She'd just sit for a while till Peter would come; she would take off her fur but not her hat. Elizabeth coaxed her to stay and pleaded with her to take off her coat so that she'd feel the benefit of it when she'd go outside again. Mary let them wrangle it out between them, and just when Elizabeth had succeeded in getting Helen to open her coat the lights from Peter's car fled across the walls of the room.

'That's them now,' Mary said, and saw Helen lift her fur from the table and drape it round her neck. It'd be too bad if she'd take Peter away from the nice supper she had prepared for them.

'Hands up!' Peter said to Mary as she opened the door, and he pointed a toy gun at her with a cork stuck in its muzzle. He pulled the trigger and the cork popped out, and as Mary looked around for the cork Peter held up the gun with the cork dangling from a piece of red string attached to the trigger.

'You were near yourself that time, Mary,' Peter said, and the three of them went into the sitting-room laughing and carrying parcels. He was going to fire the gun at Elizabeth, but on seeing Helen his buoyant mood was suddenly choked. They piled the parcels on the table.

'Miss Byrne has bought up half the toys in Belfast,' he said. 'She has a toy for each of the little boys in her class — what do you think of that?'

'They're only cheap little things and are hardly worth the trouble of carrying all that distance,' Nora said.

'You're very late,' Helen said. 'I thought you had met with an accident. I have had your tea waiting for you this past hour and more, and I haven't taken my own yet.'

'Well, then, you will both join us,' Elizabeth said. 'It'll be very unfriendly if you don't.'

'But I can't, Elizabeth. I have a Christmas cake cooking in the oven and it'll be ruined on me if I don't hurry. Mary understands the tragedy that would be — and the ingredients so expensive this year.' She stood up, buttoning her coat and fastening the clip of her fur.

'It's too bad rushing away like this,' Elizabeth said. 'And Mary had such a lovely supper ready. Could you not stay?' and she looked first at Peter and then at Helen. She hoped Helen would suggest walking home alone, but Helen said nothing and walked towards the door. 'We'll be glad to come some other evening. Good night all,' she said, looking back into the room as Peter followed behind her.

His evening was spoiled and he got into the car and sat beside her without speaking.

'You needn't drive so fast,' she said when they were speeding along the road. 'You've given me enough worry this evening without adding to it now.'

'I have been often later than this and you weren't out scouring the countryside for me.'

'I suppose you had too much pleasurable distraction to think of me and how worried I do be when you're out late and heavy frosts on the road.'

He turned swiftly in at the open gate and the mudguard grazed the gatepost. He switched on the light in the garage, and she held back lifting up tools from the garage shelf and putting them down again.

'I thought you were in a hurry about your cake,' he said, and he plunged his hands into his pockets, feeling the toy gun in one pocket and a small parcel in the other. The parcel puzzled him for a minute till he suddenly remembered it was Elizabeth's crochet cotton that Nora had given him to keep in a safe place.

'Well,' he said, 'why aren't you rushing into the house to look after that precious cake of yours?'

'I have no cake in the oven, if you want to know. I just said that to keep you from sponging on the Devlins. They'll soon get tired of you running in and out.'

'So you have no cake!' he said, without raising his voice. He clenched his fists in his pockets to control his anger. 'I hate a lie — and especially one like this.'

'You can call it what you like. Surely you didn't want me to blurt out: "Mary and Elizabeth are tired of you; they've enough to fend for without you joining in as an extra boarder." '

'It wasn't Mary and Elizabeth you were considering.'

'And who was it, pray?'

'It was pique made you do it. You were wild when you discovered that Miss Byrne was with me in Belfast.'

'Wild! H'm, as if anything Miss Byrne would do would madden me. I wouldn't give her that much notice. I wouldn't think you'd have the effrontery to elope with a young girl — if that's what you mean.'

He looked at his watch. 'I'm going back. I've just discovered a small parcel in my pocket that I forgot to give to Elizabeth.'

'I could give it to her coming from Mass in the morning.'

'Elizabeth couldn't wait till then. You know how fussy she is.'

'Peter, don't go back. They'll think we've quarrelled.'

'Appearances shouldn't upset you. I'll tell them you were just in time to save your cake!'

'You've no loyalty towards your own sister.'

'I have, but not when she tries to mould me to her own hard will. And anyway Miss Byrne and myself have a lot of toys to sort out for the Christmas tree in school.'

'That can all wait.'

'And so can the cake! Did you not see how down-in-the-mouth Mary was when we turned our backs on her supper? Are you going to come back with me and add to her joy? You've a good excuse at hand.'

'I'm not! I know when to accept a kindness and when not to. I know also that they'll soon tire of you.'

He got into the car and backed it out of the garage and in the blaze from the headlights saw her put the key in the front door.

✿ 9 ✿

Now that Christmas was approaching, the whole school relaxed, and when the teachers arrived in the morning they gathered in Mr. Lynch's room, and with their backs against a radiator they smoked and chatted or had a quick glance at the newspaper. The children who came early played about in the playground, and those who came late found themselves early because the ringing of the bell was delayed.

There were no monotonous choral sounds from any of the classes, and in each room, at all periods of the day, the pupils were engaged in painting Christmas scenes or indulging in silent reading. In Nora's room there was a more noticeable and noisier appreciation of the coming feast: from roll-call in the morning until the clang of the last bell in the afternoon her boys, each with a scissors and coloured paper, clipped and cut and pasted as they made clowns' hats, pirates' hats, crowns, helmets, lanterns, and false faces; and as day followed day the windows were looped with coloured streamers, and from the ceiling dangled paper lanterns and coloured balloons which nodded as restlessly as the children themselves. From the top of the press Nora took down the Christmas crib where it had lain in its box since the previous year: the tiny plaster statues were unwrapped from their tissue paper and dusted, and the ox, minus one horn, and the ass, its chipped sides redaubed with grey paint, were placed at the back of the cradle of straw which held the Infant Jesus; cotton wool sprinkled with imitation frost was spread at the entrance of the cave, and above it was a six-pointed star lit by an electric battery which Mr. Lynch had rigged up for the occasion. Staring at it daily the children would get lumps of plasticine and knead and model figures of the same size as those they saw in the crib: and even when they made an ox with its four legs in a straight line Nora didn't reprove them, or when she saw them

113

modelling the shepherds and the heads falling off and being stuck on again with a fierce pressure that bandied the legs of the models she smiled furtively, enjoying these grotesqueries and the pervasive joy that followed.

A few days before the holidays some of the bigger boys from Standard VII helped her to erect her Christmas tree. They put the base of the tree in a butter box and pressed mould around it, and to keep it from falling they tied four strings to the trunk and nailed them taut to the four corners of the box. Each morning Nora arrived early and tied toys to the branches, and when her little boys came in, trailing off their heavy coats, they gathered round the tree, pointing their fingers at the grey aeroplanes or at the red motor cars with rubber tyres, or at the cork guns, or at the tiny brown savages armed with spears; those nearest the tree would touch the tin candle-sockets that held the red candles, and then Nora would have to send them to their desks where they would continue to nudge one another and point their fingers at the blue transparent wax fish with red fins that peeped out from amid the topmost branches.

Time and again when she was seated at her table counting up the attendances of each boy for the previous quarter someone would slip up to her and whisper: 'Please, Miss, won't you give me one of the red motor cars?' or someone else would ask for a gun or one of the fish. She would smile her consent, make a note of their desires on a piece of paper and slip it into the cockpit of an aeroplane or the driving-wheel of a car.

At the end of the day before the break-up for the vacation every toy on the tree had its owner's name affixed to it, and as the boys unwillingly got ready for home she clapped her hands and said to them: 'You'll all be at school tomorrow?'

'Yes, Miss.'

'And you needn't bring your schoolbags ... And there's somebody coming into this room tomorrow and he'll not be visiting any of the other rooms because the boys are too big. Guess who?'

'Baby Jesus,' somebody said.

She shook her head, and then more answers were fired at her, each as ridiculous as the preceding ones.

'It's Santa Claus himself that's coming,' she announced.

'And he's coming to our house, Miss.'

'Oh, he'll come to all your houses if you keep very good. . . . And don't forget to come in time in the morning.'

The next morning the air was frosty, white ice lay in the ruts of the road, and before she came in sight of the school she could hear the shouts of the children in the playground, and when three of her boys saw her they raced towards her to carry her attaché case. The room was gloomy and she had to switch on the lights. The early ones dusted the seats and the window-ledges, and then stood around the Christmas tree and set an aeroplane swinging when they got her back turned.

At eleven o'clock they were given bottles of lemonade and buns. They drank from the bottles in long gulps and only took their mouths away to recover their breaths in a long 'Ah'. And when one bottle fell on the desk and bumped on the floor there were cries of: 'Look what he done, Miss.'

'I didn't, Miss, he knocked it down himself.'

'Be careful now,' she said. 'Take your time or you'll choke.'

There were crumbs on their jackets, crumbs on their chins, and crumbs on the desks and on the floor, and the lemonade streamed out of the sides of their mouths like mandarin whiskers.

In the afternoon the Christmas tree was dragged forward to a cleared space in the middle of the room, and as Nora lighted each candle on the branches a long 'Oh' rose spontaneously from her boys, and presently there was no light in the room except the lights from the candles and their reflections in the polished sides of the new toys. The greyness at the windows had fled, and it seemed as if the mystery of a starry night was held captive in the little room. They stood in a circle round the tree, their eyes big with wonder as they watched their toys or the drops of red wax trickling down the candles and hanging in strings from the lips of the tin holders. And then they sang: *See amid the winter snow* and *Rudolph, the red-nosed Reindeer*, and in the excitement didn't hear the bigger boys being released or the same boys climb up on the window-sills to peer in at the mystery they had remorsefully outgrown.

The outside world grew still, the flames on the tree grew brighter, and their teacher hovered round it in a green dress with black buttons shining like plums that you could eat. But there was one boy who was not looking at her: he was eyeing his wax fish with unusual consternation for he had seen its red tail move and its blue body squirm, and its jaws fatten. He shut his eyes, but when he opened them again his fish was crying — a tear slid out of its bulging eye, slid under the chin and hung there like the barb on a cod fish. He could suppress his fear no longer and he screamed: 'Please, Miss, my fish is crying.'

'Crying, Tommy! Where, child?'

He cried as he pointed at it and they all gathered round him. She touched his little fish and withdrew her hand sharply, for below the fish a candle had been slowly melting the blue wax body. She blew out the candle and fastened the fish to a lower branch, and the boy smiled as he saw her fan out the tail with a gentle pressure of her fingers.

A light was switched on in Mr. Lynch's room — a signal to her that Santa Claus was coming. It was switched off again.

'Link your hands and bow your heads and sing loudly: *Jingle bells*,' she commanded.

Round the blackboard, as if he had descended from the chimney, came Santa Claus dressed in red, a hat on him with a tassel, a white beard, and a bag on his back.

'Santa Claus, this way, please,' she said, and Santa Claus came forward, shook her hand and held it while he nodded to this side and that.

'Be seated, my good children,' he said in a deep voice — a voice so perfectly camouflaged that Nora herself had to smile and look away from him to the butter-box that had its silver paper hanging off one side. He stroked the white beard. He turned his kindly face towards her, and the eyes, shining in the candlelight, looked so steadily at her she had to lower her own to escape from the embarrassing look. At that instant she read in them, she thought, more than friendliness, more than curiosity. And then he suddenly linked her tightly by the arm and led her into the centre of the circle, laid his bag of toys on the floor and bowed to her like a partner in an old waltz.

'And now, my dear little boys — what have we here?' and he unwound the twists from the neck of his bag, plunged in his hand, and drew forth toy after toy with each boy's name attached on a hanging label.

'Don't open your little parcel till you get home. And since your teacher has told me you're all good boys I'll be coming to your houses later on. And don't forget to leave a cup of milk for me on the table and a little bit of fresh moss for my reindeer.'

The children stared at him in silent amazement, saw him clasp his hands like St. Joseph in the crib, saw his eyes shine like stars in the light from the candles, and then saw him place his hand on their teacher's shoulder and they knew that he was pleased with her and with all of them.

'And now give three cheers for Father Christmas,' she said, and they cheered so loudly that their breaths wavered the candle flames and sent drops of grease dribbling on to the floor. Then suddenly he was gone, and their own teacher was standing at the Christmas tree clipping the strings that held their dangling toys.

She allowed them to blow out the candles, and presently there was no light in the room except the star above the crib and the grey light stealing mysteriously back to the windows. They coughed as the greasy smell of burnt wax floated around them, and in the smoky air as they secretly tore the paper from their parcels Mr. Lynch entered the room, switched on the light and brought their day to an end.

When they had all left the room and their last shouts had

dwindled away in the distance he helped her to drag the Christ-mas tree to a corner of the room, and though he told her not to bother with the brushing up of the floor but to leave it for the cleaner she didn't heed him and he told her she was just as pernickety about tidiness as his own sister Helen.

'But what on earth would the cleaner think of me if I left the floor in that state? It won't take a minute.'

He sat on top of a desk, and idly plucked bits of white fluff from his sleeves and shoulders.

'The act went off well?'

'It did indeed,' she said, resting her hands on top of the brush. 'But the time you joined your hands, the wide sleeves of your cloak fell down and I was sure some of them would have seen the colour of your suit.'

'They were too busy watching the beard and the bag of toys. I never saw them so happy-looking in my life ... The tree is a grand custom. But I'm sorry to say it didn't begin with me. It was the tradition here when I came and I'm glad you're keeping it up. But you'll be broke with all the expense you went to — half of it would have been more than enough.'

'It was nothing. There wasn't a single expensive toy on the whole tree.'

And as they arranged the desks again in their usual order she kept telling him about the fish that was supposed to cry; and then when he had finally switched off the light above the crib and they were standing about on the road outside the school he asked her to come into the house for a little cup of tea and he'd run her over in the car after it. She swung her attaché case in front of her and shook her head: 'I'd rather not go today. Some other day but not this one.'

'All right,' he said, stemming his desire to coax her. 'We'd be glad to have you. Helen will be disappointed.'

'You'll make up a nice excuse for me,' and she smiled directly at him, and then quickly looked across the frosty fields where a light from a cottage was beginning to shine forth.

But it wasn't of Helen she was thinking — it was of himself. There was something about him that held her, and was at the same time a cause of an attractive fear. It was foolish to think she could play with him with flippant attachment. Could she say to herself with regard to him: 'Knowing what I am or what I may become I can't get married?' It was all right to hold a self-sacrificing idea like that in the mind — but it was only half of the struggle: she couldn't deny that! There was a not-wanting but it existed in words only — words that could be swept aside by a fascination stronger than her own half-hearted will.

No, there was no use allowing things to drift; no use thinking she could turn back or turn easily away from him if there were love between them. Now was the time to act before she entangled herself in a torturing disappointment that would hurt him as deeply as it would hurt herself. She recalled his remark about Larry Mullan: 'There's T.B. in that family — he'll never scratch a grey head.' Yes, there's the core of it all! Everything that mattered was plain and straight before her — and there was no use equivocating further. But, then, what if she was mistaken? What if there was nothing behind that look of his in the school-room, nothing behind this invitation only kindness, nothing in his calling her 'Nora'?

She shrugged her shoulders, and her attaché case bumped against her knees. The light in the cottage across the fields grew brighter.

'Well, Nora, are you reconsidering it? You're coming in for a few minutes? I give you my word I won't detain you beyond your going.'

'I've already considered it. Some other day I'll be glad to go if you ask me, but not this one. I've a lot of packing to do before I go off tomorrow. Your sister will well understand what that means.'

He turned the ring of keys in his hand. 'You've a good long journey before you tomorrow. Will you travel by train from Belfast or by bus?'

'By train — it's faster and more comfortable.'

'You'll need to be at the station long before she pulls out. The trains are always overcrowded at this time of the year.'

'I'll be leaving here by the first bus in the morning and that should give me ample time to get a seat in the train.'

'Take good care of yourself,' and he shook her hand. 'And I hope you'll have a very happy Christmas.'

'And I wish you and your sister the same . . . And thank you for all your kindness to me.'

'It's you I have to thank for all your help and co-operation — the singing class and the combined operations in searching for the stowaway!'

She swung off down the road. He stood and watched her, hoping she would turn round and wave to him, but she went on, up and over the hill, and when he could no longer see her he could still hear in the frosty air the sound of her quick steps. He put the keys in his pocket, and as he went up the path the light in his sitting-room was switched on and threw a square of light on the level lawn.

Helen came from the sitting-room when he entered the hall.

'So she didn't come with you after all your talk?'

'No, she has too much packing to do.'

'I knew she wouldn't come and I told you not to ask her, but, of course, you wouldn't listen to me. The girl doesn't wish to get her name mixed up with a man years older than her.'

'I'm sure that wasn't the reason she didn't come,' and he brushed past her and hung up his hat on the hat-stand.

'Don't drag your feet on the parquet floor I'm only after polishing — you're scoring it.'

'I'm not dragging my feet. And where is it scored?'

'There — you'll see for yourself if you hold your head sideways against the light.'

'Ach, it's too much like a convent corridor! Some day I'll break my neck on it and then you'll be satisfied. The house has to be lived in!'

'That's my thanks for keeping it in order. If it were dirty you'd have something to complain of.'

'Too much order is a constraint.'

'If you're in a lecturing mood I haven't time for it. And if you're in a disgruntled mood — and that amounts to the same thing — I haven't time for it either.'

The door of their small dining-room was open and he noticed that she had the table laid for two.

'So, I see, you were absolutely sure Miss Byrne wouldn't join us on this last day of the school year.'

'Yes, absolutely.'

'A woman's intuition is never wrong?'

'Never, especially when it concerns one of her own sex.'

'There's a lot about your sex that puzzles me,' and he crossed to the bathroom to wash away the grime and dust of the school from his hands.

When he was seated at the tea-table he told her of the Christmas tree and of the fish that cried.

'It was the happiest day the youngsters ever had since I stepped into the school. Miss Byrne has certainly a nice way with those young ones — you can feel it as soon as you step into her room.'

'I suppose I'll hear no other name mentioned until these holidays are over but Miss Byrne, Miss Byrne.'

'All right, I'll not mention her name at all, if it is going to rile you like this.'

'I wouldn't be so cruel on you as all that. You can't deceive me, Peter. Ever since the first day she came here I felt you were struck on her. And I'll never forget the way you sped after her with her belt. But take my advice and don't do anything rash or you'll be the sorry man and uncomfortable for ever in your school. Luke Murphy is more of an age and a match for her than you.'

'Will you give over talking like this — about nothing? Your imagination is having a holiday. Will you be your age and stop talking like an Elizabethan maiden?'

She tried to justify herself, to talk of her intuition, and of what she knew was taking place in his own mind of which he himself had no knowledge. He smiled, but refused to be inveigled into a discussion that gave her unusual fluency. She went on with her warnings, and when she had finished he rose from the table, pushed in his chair and said calmly: 'I must go now and have a quiet read to myself.'

'It would be better if you'd come to confession with me this evening and not put it off till Christmas Eve when you know the chapel will be crowded. You'll not relish sitting for an hour or two in a chapel that could do with a bit of heat. St. Theresa said you can't pray unless you're comfortable.'

'I don't know what St. Theresa said, and you needn't conspire to look after my soul the way you're conspiring to look after my friendships.'

'I wish it were only a friendship!'

He said nothing, closed the door behind him quietly, and on going into the sitting-room filled his pipe and sat down in an armchair. He could hear the clatter of the dishes as Helen washed them hurriedly, and then in a few minutes he heard her go out and bang the front door behind her.

'She's in a lovely mood for examining her conscience!' he said to himself, and getting up, switched off the light, and sat in the glow from the fire.

Am I, or am I not, in love with Nora? He paused at his question, smiled, but couldn't answer it. It needed another question to support it: Is she, or is she not, in love with me? That's the important question! She certainly has shown no sign of it — never: not even when she was most disturbed as on the night of the Maguire affair did she transgress beyond the formal 'Mr. Lynch'. He had given her a lead in that respect but she didn't take it. Perhaps, after all, he was too old for her. He was forty and she was twenty-five: when he'd be fifty-five she'd be forty, and when he'd be at the age for retiring she'd have turned fifty. The older one got the disparity seemed to narrow: it was like those problems in algebra he often gave to his class: *A father is now six times as old as his son, but sixteen years hence he will be only twice as old: find their present ages.*

He took the pipe from his mouth and smiled. He should set them one like this: *A man is twice as old as his sweetheart, but in twenty years' time he'll only be one-and-a-half times as old: find their present ages.* Love by algebra or the mathematical lover discusses X. No, he mustn't be flippant about it! Whatever else he'd do he'd be sincere. He needn't pretend to himself that Nora didn't really matter to him. She did — and he knew it. He'd miss her during the Christmas holidays and he'd be glad when they'd be at an end. He had never felt like this towards any girl, and he only wished she could feel like this for him.

But he sensed at times there was something elusive about her — that deep within her there was some secret that she wished to hide. Perhaps there was somebody in her home town that loved her; if he were sure of that, he could then leave her alone, and be kind to her in a friendly way and with no other motive in his mind.

He had, up to the present, no grudge against life. His life wasn't the kind a novelist would write a book about. His mind wasn't tormented enough for that: not enough gloom in it — a kind of life French writers would regard as in deplorably bad taste. And yet he tried not to become stale in his ways and in his teaching. Freshness lay in change, he often told himself, and to change often meant struggling with the difficulties of hardening habit.

He tried to use a different set of books each year with his Standards VI and VII: a different Shakespearean play, a different selection of poetry, a different book for reading, and with these went a variation in his methods of teaching. It was true that it made his work more difficult but, then, it added the one thing he desired: change — the desire to break away from the mechanical, the bane of all teachers from the kindergarten teacher to the university professor. The changeless men, they could be called, and all justifying their unchange by asserting that what they had to give was fresh each year for the different set of faces that confronted them. Such an attitude was, for him, a death in life — a winter without a spring.

There was no reason in the wide world, then, why he shouldn't change his life completely by marrying — by marrying Nora Byrne if she'd have him. From Helen he got little or no companionship — she was wedded to the house; but, to be just, he must say she was perfect, too perfect, on that score. And then there was Father Lacy twitting him at every turn: 'Don't leave it too late, Peter, whatever you do. Better to marry sooner than later.' 'I'll do that, Father,' he used to say, 'as soon as the right girl takes me.'

A smouldering coal fell out of the grate and he lifted it quickly with his fingers and threw it back into the fire. Yes, if Nora Byrne could grow to like him there might be no call for Father Lacy to twit him any longer. But then if there were any possibility of her accepting him he'd have to sell his car in order to pay for the wedding. Somehow he seemed to have been born with a strange contempt for money — most of his monthly salary went to the paying off the mortgage on his house and the instalments on his car, and into the bargain he had a mania for buying books. Was it any wonder that he had great difficulty in making his monthly salary hold out from one pay day to the next? If at the end of any month he found he had still a few shillings left in his pocket he regarded it as a fine achievement. At the same time, he must say, he found a certain joy in paying his bills each month. 'Pay our debts first and enjoy ourselves afterwards,' he often said to Helen — and in this matter of spending money he found her a willing partner, for she was never done going to auctions and buying pieces of brassware, and even last year went as far as buying the grandfather clock that he could hear ticking now in the hall. Was it any wonder that after more than twenty years' teaching he had not a penny to his name in the local bank? He had, it is true, a small sum of money after his name in their books but it was in the minus column. The bank manager was always glad to see him at the beginning of a month, but never at the end of a month. There was no doubt about it he must pull himself together on that line: he could stop buying books for a while — that would be something to start with. He had books in every room in the house except the bathroom. Helen had said that he had over twelve hundred volumes and that if he read twelve a year it would take him a hundred years to read what he had, even if he didn't add another copy to his collection. 'They are my intimations of immortality,' he had said to her.

'If you knew the layers of immortal dust they gather, you'd bring less of them into the house,' she had answered as she slapped the dust off a few of them at the open window.

At the New Year he'd start an economy campaign — that'd be his first New Year's resolution. And he must take out an insurance policy with Brennan's friend. But before then he must see to his few Christmas presents — the usual handkerchiefs for Father Lacy, slippers for Helen, a pipe or tobacco for the bank manager, and a little diary for Nora would not be amiss. Helen would see to the Miss Devlins. But really at the New Year he must pull himself together — a man like him who didn't drink, except on festive occasions, should be better off financially and not be pulling the devil by the tail at the end of every month. He gave a sigh of satisfaction, joined his hands on his lap, and in a short while had fallen asleep with a smile on his face.

The light in the room being switched on wakened him. Helen had come back from confession and with her was Elizabeth.

'Yes, I knew you'd nearly let the fire go out, and me bringing Elizabeth in to warm herself after a long sit in that cold chapel.'

'I never heard Elizabeth complaining of the cold in my life,' he said, as he lifted a big piece of coal from the scuttle with his hands and put it on the fire.

'Peter! You'd think there wasn't a tongs at your very elbow.'

'Leave him alone, Helen, the poor man's not fully awake yet. I've often seen Nora Byrne fall into a sound sleep after coming from school. Your job, Peter, is not as easy as some people imagine.'

'They get a long holiday to recuperate,' Helen put in. 'Not like us poor housekeepers whose work is never done and seldom seen or praised. Rest yourself, Elizabeth, and I'll make you a nice cup of coffee and Peter will run you over in the car after it.'

'I wouldn't dream of taking a tired man away from his fireside on a cold night like this.'

'No trouble at all, Elizabeth; I'd drive you ten times as far and think it a privilege.'

When Helen came in with the coffee she overheard them talking of Nora and she let the tray down quietly on the table and said nothing. Peter got up, took a small table from the embrasure of the window, and placed it between himself and Elizabeth. 'This will save us from balancing the cups on our laps.'

Elizabeth opened her coat, took a small scarf from around her throat to display her new lace collar. Helen noticed it at once. 'Such a lovely piece of work,' she said. 'It's exquisite! You put some work into that, Elizabeth.'

Elizabeth smiled pleasurably. 'It really didn't take me long once I got down to it.'

'It's a pity the young girls nowadays have no interest in beautiful work like that. It would be worth Miss Byrne's while to learn it when she'd have an excellent teacher like yourself to show her the way. But I suppose she wouldn't be bothered with it?'

'I suppose she wouldn't,' Elizabeth said, wishing to be agreeable.

'From what I hear she has too much interest in Luke Murphy. He's her match in years and he's nice to look at, but he wouldn't appeal to me,' Helen said.

Over the rim of her raised cup Elizabeth glanced at Peter, but she saw nothing only the top of his head as he stirred his coffee reflectively. Helen was standing between them, and she once more bent towards Elizabeth and fingered the lace collar. 'It's a crime and a sin to see work like that going unnoticed and unlearnt. If I were a young girl how glad I'd be to learn work so rare as that. It's no use talking, the young girls worry about nothing these days. I'm sure the Maguire affair never took a feather out of Miss Byrne?'

Elizabeth paused, and perceiving that Helen was still eyeing the lace collar she said in a low voice: 'I don't suppose it did,' and then she wondered if this contradicted anything she had previously said to Peter.

He looked over at her and then at Helen: 'Let me tell you that Miss Byrne's the type of girl that won't let her distress be seen — that's what I think anyway,' and he tapped his pockets and excused himself till he'd fetched some tobacco. He stayed out of the room for about ten minutes and when he returned, Elizabeth got to her feet and said she really must be going or poor Mary would have Johnny out scouring the roads for her.

In the car she complained to Peter that it was a shame for her to be bringing him out on such a cold night. But Peter brushed her complaints aside and announced it was only a pleasure and that he was sorry it wasn't a longer distance.

Swinging up the Devlins' path he could see the upstair windows lighted but no light in the sitting-room except the sporadic light from the fire on the frosted windows. Despite Elizabeth's continued coaxings he refused to go in for a little chat, and while they were engaged in this friendly tussle Mary appeared at the hall door. Both tried, then, to persuade him but he refused to budge from his seat at the wheel and told them to hurry into the house and not catch cold. He tooted the horn playfully and drove off. They stood at the hall door till he had left the drive and was out on the road where he once again sounded the horn to them.

'Strange he didn't come in,' Elizabeth said, closing the door against the cold night air.

'He knows we're busy and knows that Nora's up to her eyes

in packing. If she had appeared he might have joined us on her account.'

'A few things that Helen let fall this evening makes me think she's not one bit fond of Nora.'

'Well, she'll have to grow fond of her. Some day she might be closer to her than she'd imagine,' and Mary whisked into the kitchen to finish ironing a few of Nora's blouses.

Later when everything was packed and Nora was in bed reading by the light of an oil-lamp on her table Mary made an excuse to come into the room with a few handkerchiefs that she had just discovered, and sitting on the edge of the bed, where she had always liked to sit, she talked of the New Year and the attempts they were making to have the electric light carried out to them from the town.

'That'll be a great comfort for us all, Nora,' she said, looking at the closed case with its hanging label and feeling sorrow at the coming departure. 'You'll get to like this place, Nora. It's lovely here in the spring of the year.'

'But I love it as it is, Mary. I do, indeed. And I think nothing of working with oil-lamps. What makes you talk like this?'

'Och, I don't know,' she sighed and plucked a tiny feather from the pink eiderdown. 'I was just thinking that there might be something here you dislike or that the Maguire rascal upset you too much and that maybe you'd run off during the Christmas holidays and get married.'

'So marriage is a kind of escape,' she laughed and pushed her book under the pillow. She loved her for her transparent love and only wished she could tell her outright that she would rather stay here during Christmas than with her aunt in Strabane.

'Oh, Nora, I'd love to see you married. I would, indeed. But I wouldn't like you to be married and living away in Strabane where we might never see you again.'

'And where would you like me to be married and settled?' she asked, enjoying the talk, and feeling Mary's comfortable weight warming the bed.

'I'd like to see you married and settled here.'

'Now that you've gone so far would you select a husband for me?'

'You'd have to do that for yourself,' and she lifted Nora's hand and held it firmly in her own. 'But mind you, I wouldn't go past Peter Lynch . . . But maybe, for all I know, you have two or three sweethearts at home — am I right?'

'No, Mary, you're wrong. I've none — and that's the truth.'

'None — at any time?'

Nora hesitated and Mary pressed her hand firmly.

'Nora, Nora, I was right. The men in Strabane are not all fools. And he'll be there when you go back. He'll have great welcome for you. What is he like? But, maybe, you don't want to tell me, though if you did I wouldn't breathe it to a living soul.'

'There's nothing to tell, Mary. Two years ago I was engaged but it is now broken off.'

'Broken off — for good?'

'For good or ill — it is broken completely. I'll never take it up again.'

And bit by bit Nora divulged how she became engaged to a cashier in a bank. She described his appearance, his manner, but when she came to the reason for its breaking off she jibbed, grew confused, and strove to smother her evasions in a heap of trivial talk that discomfited herself as much as it bewildered Mary. Some day she would tell her the whole truth, but not now.

'Isn't it strange, Nora, that I felt all along that some great disappointment had befallen you? I didn't voice it to Elizabeth for I knew she'd have given me my answer. But deep in here', and she thumped her breast, 'I felt it, and I often wondered to myself what it was. And now that I know I'll tell no one. I'll put the seal of the confessional on it. But I'll pray that it will be healed up again.'

'You needn't, Mary,' and she raised herself on the pillow and Mary put her arms round her. 'I don't want it healed. It is better the way it all turned out. He didn't really care for me . . .' She paused, was going to say it was the money her father had left her that he cared for, but she checked herself in time and surrendered to Mary's warm motherly pressure against her breasts. She sighed loudly: 'Deep down in his heart he didn't care for me.'

'The cheek of him! He's a right pampered article whoever he is. I wish I were speaking to him for a few minutes I'd let him know who he thought he was. I never did care much for those bank men at any time. You'll find, please God, it was all for the best. And in God's good time you'll find someone after your own heart.'

She smiled and closed her eyes: 'Good night, Mary. You are very kind.'

Mary tucked the clothes around her, and the water gurgled in the hot water bottle as Nora stretched her feet.

'Now don't worry, girl, about catching the early bus, for I'll have you up in time and I'll see that Johnny is up to carry your case into the town for you. But if it's raining you could run in on your bicycle with my old raincoat on you and Johnny will take it from you at the Square. Good night now.' She lowered the wick in the lamp and blew down the funnel, and in the darkness as she put her dry hard hand on Nora's brow Nora remembered the way her own mother used to do the same and how she used to finger her mother's ring, trying, but always failing, to slip it over the fat joint.

'You'll sleep now, Nora. And it won't be long till you're back amongst us again. I'll be counting the days till your return.'

When the door had closed and she was alone in a silence that was warmed by a faint smell of burnt wick she suddenly felt a rush of love for this woman who gave her as much affectionate attention as her own mother would have done. She had only been here a few months and yet she seemed to have known this motherly woman all her life, and could feel more at home with her than with her aunt. Anyway it wouldn't be long till she'd be back again, and the days would be then on the turn.

✿ 10 ✿

ONE evening a few days after Christmas Mary and Elizabeth were awaiting their usual visitors: Peter and Helen and Father Lacy. They were invited for seven o'clock and it was just now past six, Mary and Elizabeth having seated themselves at the fire after saying the Angelus. The brass lamp was lighted on the polished table and their Christmas cards were standing two deep on the mantelshelf. Mary had been cooking all day and she was tired. She sat quite still, smoothing her crinkled fingers that had never worn a ring. She sighed and raised her eyes to Nora's card that stood in a place of honour right in front of the black marble clock.

'I wonder what's Nora doing at this very minute?' she said, her eyes still on the card.

'Getting ready for some dance or other,' Elizabeth answered, without arresting the brisk progress of her needles from which dangled a man's black sock. Mary lifted Nora's card and sat down again. Elizabeth glanced at her over her spectacles, and fancying that Mary was in a moping sort of humour she asked was she quite sure that everything was in readiness for the supper.

'Everything, Elizabeth. The table's laid inside, and the water's plumping on the range.'

'Have you taken Johnny's lamp away from him?'

'Yes, I brought it in an hour ago and I left him a candlestick with a stump of a candle in it, so if he comes home tipsy tonight again you need have no fear that he'll upset a lamp and burn the place down over his head. But drunk or sober he's always sensible, poor man.'

'This thirst of his is lasting too long. I must speak to him myself one of these days for you're far too soft with him, Mary.'

'Wasn't it very kind of Nora to think of him, too, at Christ-

131

mas? He says the new pipe she sent him is the talk of the town.'

'The talk of the pub, he means.'

'He's well pleased with it, and he tells me he never met such a cool-smoking pipe in all his born days.'

'A present that's unexpected is a present over-praised.'

'He told me she's the sweetest girl he ever clapped an eye on.'

'You shouldn't encourage a man of his years in talk like that, Mary dear.'

Mary closed her eyes sleepily, and opened them when a tail of flame buzzed disturbingly out of a piece of coal in the grate. She gave a long sigh: 'If I had married I might now have a daughter the age of Nora.'

'Goodness, Mary, you frighten me. What on earth put a thought like that in your head?'

'It just came in of itself. I was staring at the fire and somehow I felt lonely — and the thought jumped in. Indeed, Elizabeth, it's a pity we didn't both get married and have children around us at Christmas time.'

Elizabeth gave her a hard stare and wondered if Mary were really awake. She coughed and prodded the buzzing coal with the poker.

'And then that story you told to Nora on her first day here.'

'What story are you talking about? I told the girl no story whatsoever.'

'The one about me having two suitors.'

Elizabeth cleared her throat. 'Your imagination is running wild tonight. You shouldn't have taken that glass of sherry at your dinner for it has upset your mind. As if, Mary dear, I'd make up a preposterous story of that nature.'

'But you did, Elizabeth. Surely you remember it: we were having our first dinner with Nora and she was sitting opposite you, and the sun was shining in the window. And there and then you came out with the story. I didn't wish to contradict you or to stop you at the time. I was pleased with the story, but I knew you were only fibbing and trying to make a good impression on our new friend.'

'I don't remember it at all. But if I did make up a story, I'm sure the suitors I chose for you were of good position and of excellent demeanour.'

'The pity of it is that they weren't real. Many a time I regret I didn't go off with somebody when I was younger — even the likes of poor Johnny would have done. You miss a lot of life when you're not married.'

Elizabeth took the finished sock from her needles, took off her spectacles, and put them slowly in their case and snapped it shut. 'Really, Mary, your conversation tonight is not very elevating. For a woman of your years it's bordering on the scandalous. I don't know what to think or make of you this very day.'

'You misunderstand me, and there's no need to get vexed about it. There's no harm in saying I'd like to have been married and have a daughter like Nora. I'm lonesome since she left and I only wish her holidays were up.'

'You're too much attached to Nora. Indeed, speaking my own mind, I don't miss her one bit.'

'How could you say the like of that, Elizabeth? And her company so fresh and bright, and her singing and the piano . . . And the lovely black kid gloves she sent us at Christmas! She's a dear, thoughtful girl, and I hope and pray she'll get married and settle down in the parish. Wouldn't that be lovely! And, maybe, she'd leave her children with us for awhile and teach them to call us "Aunt Mary" and "Aunt Elizabeth".'

Elizabeth raised her eyes to the ceiling and put a hand to her forehead. 'Mary Devlin! I've never, and God's my judge, heard such talk from you in all my life! Have you been reading some trashy book that's stuffed your head with nonsense?'

'I have been reading the thoughts in my own heart and I'm letting you hear them. Since the day Nora stepped across our threshold I grew to learn that we have both missed something in life we were meant to enjoy. My chance may have come and I was too blind to see it.'

'So you're not content with what God has destined for you? There's no such thing as chance!'

'There'd be no such thing as chance, if we prayed for direction and acted always with the right intention. How do we know that we've always done that? It's possible we were too stupid, and too proud, and so turned away from a road that would have led to a deeper happiness. However, I am content with what I have, even it's through my own fault that I have it in so small a measure. But if I had to live my life again I would marry some decent good-living man, even if he had only an acre or two of land.'

'And poor mother — what would she have said? To think that a Miss Devlin should marry into a hovel. She'd turn in her grave if she heard you now.'

'It's the man I'm talking about — not what he has, but what he is. A healthy man with a clean red face; and we'd walk up the aisle of a Sunday, up to the front seat, and he'd go to the men's side and me to the women's side, and then we'd walk home together after Mass and I'd make a fine breakfast for him. And I'd knit him socks in the same way as you're knitting socks for Father Lacy. Do you see now what I mean?'

'I do not, thanks be to God.' And Elizabeth glanced round at the closed door of the room, and then at the windows where she saw nothing only the mist on the cold pane. 'I'm glad no one hears your rambling talk, only your poor old sister. We'd be the laughing-stock of the countryside if anybody else over-heard you . . . I don't want to hear any more of it, and when our visitors arrive don't dare to speak so intimately and so foolishly in front of them.' She got up from her chair and wrapped the black socks in a neat parcel.

A coal fell on to the hearth and Mary lifted it with the tongs and threw it to the back of the fire. She lifted Nora's card and held it sideways to the light: it was a reproduction of a Dutch interior, and in it a girl was standing at an open window reading a letter. Mary peered keenly at the portrait, trying to discover from the girl's face if the letter had brought some disappointment. At one moment she detected a sadness in the girl's expression, but when she studied it again she felt she was mistaken and that the girl was smiling in a lonely sort of way. She glanced, then, at the girl's fair hair and at the dish of green apples that had been left down carelessly, and she marvelled how any man could paint apples and curtains and dresses so truly. It was a lovely quiet picture — just like Nora herself. In the inside of the card was written: 'To Mary and Elizabeth with best wishes for Christmas.' Every time she read that she was filled with deep joy because her own name was placed before Elizabeth's, and she was sure that that was how Nora spoke of them: 'Mary and Elizabeth.' She smiled and placed the card carefully back in its place on the mantelpiece. She took out the black kid gloves from their box, put them on, and held her hands up to the light. 'How well she knew our size, Elizabeth. And to think that we only sent her a pair of fowl.'

'They were lovely fowl — the pick of the flock. I'm sure her aunt's family were right glad to get them. It's strange, now that I come to think of it, I never heard her speak much about her aunt and uncle.'

'Something tells me her heart's in this place. It would be great if we could keep her, and it would be great if we could get the electric light brought out to us soon. Remind me to ask Peter to raise this matter at the county board or whatever board is in charge of these things.'

'I think I hear a car now, Mary,' and as she spoke the car lights swept across the windows, and they both hurried to the door. It was their three visitors: Father Lacy, Peter and Helen, and when they were going into the sitting-room Mary drew Peter aside and asked him if he had done anything for her about the electric light. He assured her he had already raised it in the right quarter and that something would be done about it early in the

New Year. He sat back in his armchair, smoking his pipe and sending the smoke-rings up around the array of Christmas cards. 'She has a right regiment there, Father Lacy,' and he pointed the shank of his pipe at the mantelshelf. 'And all in different coloured uniforms.'

Mary lifted one of the cards and handed it to him. 'That's from Nora, and along with it she sent us each a pair of black kid gloves and a pipe and tobacco for Johnny. Wasn't that thoughtful of her?'

'Gloves to the Miss Devlins!' Helen laughed. 'The Miss Devlins that could hand a dozen pairs to a stall at a Fancy Fair, and never miss them.'

'But these are the finest of kid, Helen,' Elizabeth put in, and asked Mary to show them to her.

'One couldn't expect anything but generosity in excelcis from a daughter of Doctor Tim Byrne,' Father Lacy said, and went on to tell of their friendship when they were boys together at St. Malachy's College and how that friendship had continued undiminished after Tim got married and after he himself was appointed curate miles away from him: 'It's seldom school friendships continue in such divergent circumstances. But ours did and would to this day if he were alive. But poor Tim, God have mercy on him, met a tragic death. He was the heart and soul of generosity. A fine doctor and a great loss.' Father Lacy paused, and perceiving that they were all listening to him except Helen, who was leafing through a Christmas magazine, he went on to describe Doctor Byrne's wedding — one of the first weddings he had ever officiated at and therefore not likely to forget it. And he spoke, too, of his friend's contributions to medical journals and of a theory he had on the prevalence of cancer in areas where people do not use enough vegetables, and how he was still engaged in these researches, here and abroad, when he met his tragic end.

'Was he a wealthy man, Father Lacy?' Elizabeth ventured.

'He was far too generous, Elizabeth. And generosity and

wealth are a most unusual combination. He had a large practice, but what became of it I do not know.'

Peter puffed slowly at his pipe; he was aware that Helen was eyeing him, and he strove to mask from her the joy that Father Lacy's conversation was giving him. But, then, believing that his silence might be coldly interpreted as indifference or lack of interest he found himself saying: 'Miss Byrne must have inherited her father's generosity,' and taking the pipe from his mouth he elaborated in detail how she had prepared the Christmas tree in school and the expense she had gone to in providing every boy in her class with a little toy.

'I'm glad to hear that, Peter.'

'She's a grand girl in every way, and easy and agreeable to work with. But isn't that always the case? The more intelligent the teacher the less likely he is to nourish grudges, having something else to nourish.'

'She takes after her father. He was a most agreeable man. When all is said and done you can't make a silk purse out of something that is not silk.'

They all laughed, and Elizabeth looked at Father Lacy and said: 'Her mother died young, too, I believe?'

'She did, she did. But I didn't know her as well as I knew the father. I only met her for the first time on their wedding day.'

Elizabeth sat back, waiting for him to continue and was disappointed when she saw him turn to Peter and ask how the golf was getting on.

'I'd get along better if you'd take up your clubs again, Father. None of the teachers is interested in it.'

'Why don't you ask Nora?' Mary said. 'She'd be glad to go over the bunkers with you or whatever it is you call them things with the red flags.'

'You should ask why doesn't he invite me to take it up!' Helen exclaimed.

They all laughed, except Mary, who had gone off to the kitchen. Father Lacy rubbed his palms together. 'Upon my word I'd love to see Helen swinging a club — a man's cap on her, and a golfing jacket and skirt. A sight like that would cheer any man's heart.'

'Younger than me take it up,' she defended.

'Indeed they do. You, Mary, Elizabeth, and myself could make a great foursome — but it would be at croquet or bowls.'

Helen expected Elizabeth to defend her age, but when none of them jumped in to support her she saw herself as a figure of fun: a comic, vulgar postcard of a lady with a kilt and a man's cap, and thin legs with bristles on them like a thorned stick. She was surprised at Father Lacy, and annoyed that Peter could be so complacent-looking at this insult to his own sister. Her neck and face reddened, and she was raking her mind to say something hurtful to Peter when Mary came in and called them into the dining-room.

Elizabeth had placed the brown parcel of socks on Father Lacy's plate and a lace-centre for a vase on Helen's, and as she watched them unwrap the paper and display their little presents she smiled her innocent pleasure.

'Thank you, Elizabeth,' Father Lacy said. 'If they wear half as well as your last pair, they'll do,' and he bowed towards her and smiled, anticipating what would follow: a long panegyric on the quality of the wool and how she had skilfully reinforced the heel with a secret stitch of her very own.

'And look at the softness and beauty of this piece of lace,' Helen added. 'And to think that the young nowadays are no longer interested in making these things.

'Yes, be a maker and you've learned the secret of the Miss Devlins' contentment,' Father Lacy said.

'Miss Byrne should take up lace-work, now that she has the right person to teach her,' Helen said primly.

'She has the piano, Helen. And that's enough for anyone with school work to do. Isn't that right, Peter?' and Mary smiled across at him as she poured wine into all their glasses.

'Mary's right,' Father Lacy said. 'We can't all be great lace-makers. To one is given wisdom, to another knowledge, to

138

another the gift of prophecy, to Mary cooking, to Helen house-craft, and to Peter bachelordom.'

'That will never do for Peter,' Mary declared. 'When the right girl comes along, there'll be a change. Nora Byrne, for instance.'

'Do you want him laughed at? He's old enough to be her father!'

'Oh, Helen!' Mary and Elizabeth shouted together.

'She doesn't mean it. A slight slip of the tongue — that's all,' Father Lacy said gently, and he glanced at Peter who was trying to smile off his discomfiture. 'It would be a remarkable coincidence if I were to officiate at the daughter's wedding.'

'That could all be, Father,' Helen continued. 'But it will be to Luke Murphy, if all what I hear is true.'

'Oh, is that the way of it?' and Father Lacy looked with curiosity round the table.

No one concurred in Helen's suggestion, and the awkward silence was soothed by the sound of Johnny coming up the path singing thickly. Both Mary and Elizabeth began to speak loudly and to make unnecessary noises with their cutlery, and Father Lacy winked roguishly at Peter: 'There he goes — as full as an Infant School and just as happy.'

'I'm shocked and scandalized!' Elizabeth said.

'There's no harm in him, and why wouldn't he rejoice at this season of the year. On New Year's day he'll be coming to me and it'll put me to the pin of my collar to prevent him from taking the pledge for life. Take it to the day after St. Patrick's Day, I advise him, and we'll see about "life" after that. I needn't tell you I never see him again for another twelve months.'

'I'm shocked and scandalized, Father Lacy,' and Elizabeth closed her eyes with mock seriousness. 'Indeed I was going to ask you one of these days to give a word or two of advice to poor Johnny, but I've changed my mind after hearing you this evening.'

They all, then, spoke at once, and as the ladies drifted into a discussion on the beastliness of drink Father Lacy and Peter exchanged winks, and with solemn faces defended its use in a country like Ireland where men are cornered at every turn by overpowering women and have no place of solace except around the warm, sociable counters of a pub.

'You needn't run off with the impression that Johnny is badgered or belaboured by us,' Mary defended. 'As long as he keeps reasonable hours he can have his bit of hilarity. We both like him very much, for when we have a man noising about the place we feel secure!' They all laughed simultaneously; and Mary, for the life of her, couldn't understand what was amusing in the words she had just said; and later when they had gone off to the sitting-room and Helen had remained behind to help her to tidy up she asked her if she had noticed anything comical in her remarks about Johnny.

'There was nothing at all to laugh at, Mary. Nothing at all. You didn't catch me laughing at you. To tell you the truth, I don't know what to make of Peter or Father Lacy tonight,' and she lowered her head to brush crumbs off the plates before piling them on to the trays. All evening she had felt isolated by an angry feeling of mortification, and she began now to magnify the laughter into an insult so that Mary would share in her irritation. Mary listened to her outburst with secret impatience, and then lifting the tray of dishes she looked quizzically at Helen. 'In spite of what you say there must have been something funny in it or they wouldn't have laughed.' Much to Helen's disgust Mary began to smile, and Helen stared at her coldly and decided there was no use seeking to enlighten a woman who has as much sense in her head as an old hen. For the remainder of the evening she would keep her pride to herself and display it, not by words, but by injured silence.

On their way home in the car, Father Lacy remarked about this quietness of hers, but she just answered him dryly that she was feeling rather tired after such an enjoyable evening.

During the next few days her sullen mood hadn't lessened,

and Peter moved around pretending not to notice it. He felt that what had disturbed her was her baulked insult to him at the Devlins' — no one siding with her in her tart remark: 'old enough to be Nora's father!' He didn't intend to refer to it or ask her why she was so downcast; it was better to assume there was nothing wrong and to let her mood wear itself out without his help or hindrance. And anyway if he did bring it up she would, with her customary unreasonableness, manage to uncover some little thing that he had said or hadn't said that had caused her ill-humour.

During these days she had scarcely uttered a polite word to him, and one evening as he sat at the table correcting a pile of composition books in preparation for the reopening of the school in a few days' time, she came into the sitting-room and sat in an armchair opposite him. She had a book in her hands but he sensed she wasn't reading it. He had the advantage over her, for the work he was doing absorbed him and gave him a distinct pleasure whenever he came upon a freshly written passage or sentence. In the margins opposite these he marked 'Very Good' in red pencil. That was his customary policy in correcting books: to point out what was done well and so make each boy feel he was worthy of praise and appreciation. It was easier to condemn and be sarcastic but that, he learned years ago, drove them to subterfuge and insincerity, and only impressed upon them what to avoid. No, the best way of teaching boys to write was to encourage them by praise, and their confidence being once established, those who were feeble improved and those who were good got better.

He reviewed some of the sentences he had marked, raised his head from the books, and wondered if he read them aloud would Helen share his enjoyment. There were a few here that would surely brighten her. Or maybe it would be better to read a few compositions in their entirety: 'Our Neighbours', 'Visitors to Our House', 'Myself at Seventy', 'The Circus Arrives', 'The Boy That Sits Beside Me'. He flicked through the headings but halted at none. He returned to the marked sentences and re-read them silently to himself: 'The rain made little and big circles in the water' . . . 'As the bus raced up the hill I could see the wind rippling the tarpaulin that was covering the lorry in front of us' . . . 'Sometimes I go down to the field when I am old to watch the boys playing football and when one of the boys hits the ball over to me I would hit it back with my stick' . . . 'The boy that sits beside me is called Gerry Bailey. He got his hair cut yesterday and you can see that the white part of his head at the back isn't the same colour as his neck . . . On rainy days he wears a long loose oilskin with no belt. Yesterday he put it on over his schoolbag and you would think he had a bustle. . . .'

No, he wouldn't read those out to her, for they'd only hang in the air unattached. Better to try a full-length one. He lifted up one of his best, rattled his pencil on the table, and cleared his throat.

'Some of these little compositions are very amusing, Helen.'

'H'm, I wouldn't be surprised. Many things are amusing, these days.'

'I don't want to interrupt you at your own reading, but I'd really like you to hear this one by that little Leyden fellow. He's writing about that old Hindu that was travelling round here a few months ago. You remember him? He was selling silk scarves and perfume. Listen to what the observant little rascal wrote, and you'll laugh.'

'I'm not in the mood for laughing.'

He ignored what she said, held out the exercise book in front of him and began:

'My mammy was out and I was wishing that she would hurry for there was an Arab coming round the doors selling things. I feared he might push his way in. When the Arab was next door my mammy came down the street with the pram. When my mammy had put the pram in the corner there came a loud knock at the door. I opened it and there was the Arab with a turban on his head and an attaché case in his hand. He gently pushed me aside and walked in as if he owned the place. I liked the way he talked. My mammy gave the child to my sister to hold, while she looked in the Arab's case. She picked up a pair of stockings and asked how much they were. The Arab thought for a moment and said, "Four shillings". My mammy examined them carefully and pointed to a small ladder in the heel of one of them. The Arab took them from her, put them in the case and closed it. He took some bottles of perfume from his pocket and asked my mammy if she wanted any. My mammy took a bottle to get rid of him. But the Arab wanted her to take two bottles and she wouldn't. So he put them back in his pocket. He took the baby from my sister. But my mammy took it from him making an excuse that it had no nappy on it. He gave it his finger to lick but my mammy held the baby away from him. "Well, I must be going," he said, and when he had walked out my mammy told me to bring her the red soap and the sponge from the scullery.'

'Isn't that splendid, Helen? I don't think the lad realizes the subtlety he has achieved in writing that. Ernest Hemingway couldn't do it any better.'

'You'll have them writing insulting things about their own people next — that's what you'll have them doing. It would be better if you would teach them some manners.'

'You're in a sulky mood tonight, I must say.'

'If I am, whose fault is it?'

'Your own, I suppose; or is it that the wind is in the east? Joey O'Brien says that when the wind is in the east the women folk are apt to be cross. He didn't put it as politely as that, but that's the gist of it, anyway.'

'I'm not in the humour for listening to quotations from a half-fool the like of O'Brien.'

'What on earth is the matter with you?'

'You should know — if you let your mind rest for a minute on what happened at the Devlins'.'

He tapped his pencil gently on the table. All day he had avoided this reference, and now that he had drifted into it un-wittingly he wasn't going to withdraw.

'The thing that jumps to mind is your insult to me.'

'I'm not aware that I insulted you in any way,' she lied. 'But what has annoyed me was the way you allowed your own sister to be made a mockery of when she mentioned taking up golf.'

'Well, well, you're easily upset if that's the case. Since Father Lacy . . .'

'Let me speak!' she cried and closed her book.

He ran his fingers through his hair, and as she enlarged upon the incident he strove to shut his mind against it by watching the grains of dandruff falling from his hair on to the polished table.

'That's what has riled me — nothing else,' she concluded triumphantly.

'Well, I'm sorry' — though what he was apologizing for, he couldn't rightly say.

'If you had apologized sooner, or even had remained silent when the others were laughing I would have thought more of you . . . And now when I am on the point: when the Devlins and Father Lacy come here on Friday evening I hope you will not allow the conversation to become personal.'

'I didn't know you had asked them so soon.'

'Saturday evening doesn't suit Father Lacy. He has confessions then.'

'Wouldn't some evening of next week have suited better? You can't knock up much of a supper on a fast day like Friday.'

'If I waited until next week Miss Byrne would be back and I would have to include her in the invitation, and I don't intend to do that.'

'That wouldn't be a crime.'

'Not for you it wouldn't, or perhaps it would, if you had sense enough to see it. I don't intend to establish a friendship with that lady.'

'Why?'

'Must I give a reason?'

'I'd like to hear it, for I'm sure it is an unreasonable one.'

'I'd only sin my soul by uncharitable remarks.'

'Perhaps you've sinned it already by uncharitable thoughts.'

'It'd be better if you'd correct your books and not correct your sister on a point of conscience. You're exasperating me! But since I've exercised patience and prudence all day I'm going to continue that way in spite of all your provocation.'

'Whatever you say,' he sighed with calm irony, and as he bent his head over his books he was uncomfortably aware that she was staring grimly at him and desiring what she said she didn't desire — a real clash. Yes, he reasoned, if that would come, her discontent would be partly indemnified and she could deceive herself into believing that she really was a victim of ingratitude and mockery. But the moment had passed for that, and nothing could rouse him further.

Her attitude to Nora Byrne would have to change, he was sure of that; and it would have to change very soon if the same friendliness exists in the next school-term as in the last. It would go against the grain to be aloof or distant with her just to please a silly whim of Helen's. He would never do that — never.

He worked away at his books, and there was no sound in the room except the turning of the leaves and the slight tap of his pencil. Baffled and defeated by his deep silences Helen left her chair. She intended to say nothing to him, but at the door she turned and said: 'I hope you'll brush your disgusting dandruff from that table before you go to bed.'

'I'll do all you say, Helen girl. Good night.'

'Oh, good night; you're very pleasant company, I must say.'

He expected her to shut the door noisily but she left it open. He smiled and said to himself: 'Yes, she is exercising exemplary patience.'

✿ 11 ✿

MARY presumed that Nora would arrive by the afternoon bus, and as she yearned to meet it she avoided criticism of her intention by suggesting to Elizabeth, who had a cold, that a bottle of aspirin was badly needed and that she'd walk in to town to get it for her. The day was sharp and bright, and when she had visited the chemist she stood about in the Square awaiting the arrival of the bus. Joey O'Brien was there, too, stamping his feet against the cold, scratching his head, and eyeing Mary with darting sideways glances. She gave him a few coppers to ease her conscience, and when the bus came in and Nora stepped down with her case Mary ran forward and embraced her. Nora, she thought, looked tired and pale, but she managed to restrain herself from saying it and said instead: 'I'm glad you're back again, safe and sound. Since you left I have been thinking long.'

'And I, Mary, am glad to be back too,' and linked together they set out along the dry grey-blue road that led from the town. The air felt fresh and cold after the stale heat of the bus, and as she breathed it in deeply the memory of her first arrival came back vividly to her. There were sheep on the road then, she remembered, and blackberries on the hedges, and the leaves on the trees turning yellow. But now through the wide open hedges she could see for long distances across the bare fields, and away in front through the black trees the clean blue water of the lough.

As they walked along Nora yielded to Mary's pleasant questions and endeavoured to tell her what she had done and where she had gone during the Christmas holidays. But during the telling of it she was aware that her voice was husky and weary and she broke off abruptly and excused herself till she was in better form.

'I'm not walking too quickly for you, Mary?'

146

'Not a bit,' and she pressed Nora's arm firmly as if to protect her from the cold wind that was blowing up to them from the lough. And as they strolled along, enjoying the friendly fusion of each other's company Mary scolded her for sending such expensive gloves to them at Christmas. It was far too kind of her; and then she told her how they had missed her at the little parties they had had: first at their own house and then, last evening, at the Lynches', and how Father Lacy had talked of nothing else but the Byrnes.

'Oh, you needn't blush. Such praise he gave your father! The loss he was to the whole country, and the name he would have made for himself if God had spared him! But I'll not tell you any more for I see it embarrasses you.' She squeezed Nora's arm, and Nora forced a smile and pressed her arm firmly in return.

Yes, she must have blushed for she had felt the warm rush to her cheeks — that tell-tale colour that always gave her away, and being misinterpreted left her with a disquieting sense of guilt. She wondered what else Father Lacy had told them. Would he have told them about her mother and her sister — that they had died in a sanatorium? Is it possible he'd share that personal intimacy with them? — and if he did what will Mary and Elizabeth think of her for concealing it? Would they understand her silence on that point? Would they excuse her or accuse her? There was no answer to these vexing questions! But there'd been no need of an answer if, from the first, she had been truthful and not hidden behind half-lies. To undo it all now would be difficult, but, please God, it would come in good time, and come from herself even if Father Lacy had already mentioned it to them. Yes, she had made up her mind finally on that point. But she would take care to add that no one need fear contact with her.

She had gone, during the Christmas holidays, to see her doctor in Derry, and it seemed he was well pleased with her condition. The change to this place had improved her greatly. But she was still to keep from worry, from tension, and to get out in the air as much as possible. Better to wrap me in cotton wool, she had said to him, for to live at all was surely to meet with anxiety.

'But to avoid it, if you can,' he had countered.

'Then I am always to seek for comfort and security, Doctor?'

'Oh, Miss Byrne, like your father you've always a ready answer.'

'But, Doctor, my whole nature craves for work, for everything that a girl of my age should have. But I can't live a natural life if I am to be hedged and hemmed in by a catalogue of Don'ts. Tell me the truth,' she had asked anxiously, 'am I or am I not in full health?'

And then he had answered in a way that had dulled her confidence in him: 'Would you like to get another opinion?'

That note of dryness and impersonality; how it had annoyed her! She loathed the cowardice in it — the desire in him, she reasoned, to cast the responsibility on to someone else. That shrinking attitude had roused her anger, but she succeeded in controlling herself and had answered him boldly: 'I wouldn't like another opinion. My father, I hear, always regarded you with great confidence and why shouldn't I?'

She could see his studied, evasive smile. 'You don't seem too sure?'

'Are *you* sure?'

'Well, I'm giving you the advice I'd give, if you were my own daughter: don't overdo anything.'

'I see. I am to roam around on a short tether. But tell me this, Doctor. Was there anything disturbing in the last X-ray?'

'If there had been I'd not be advising you to go back to teach, would I? I'd be advising you to take a long rest. And I'm far from doing that.'

'Almost! But tell me this: would there be any harm in my taking up golf?'

'Golf! You wouldn't call that strenuous or worrying, except you were entering for the Ladies Open Championship! There's nothing like a nice round or two of golf when the weather turns warm. It'll get you out in the air for one thing.'

'Then you advise me to take up golf?'

'Certainly. But not to make yourself a bore over it. Take it in moderation. Golf would be better for you than bridge — and golf-conversation is less boring.'

'I see,' and she had asked no more questions; and when she was leaving his surgery he asked her to drop in again at Easter or before it if she felt that way inclined.

'Let me carry the case for a while,' Mary's voice broke in upon her.

'Not at all, Mary. It's not heavy, and we're getting along fine. Forgive me for being so quiet. I'm enjoying all the familiar places again. And look at the old coal boat still there. A stranger would think it was a permanent feature of that dock.'

'If they had a lad or two like Maguire for a while they'd know differently. That was a pant I'll never forget in a hurry.'

They laughed in recollection, and school children who were waiting to snatch up the fallen bits of coal smiled shyly as they saw Nora.

They crossed the stone bridge and presently came to the open gate where the twigs of the two birch trees hung down like bundles of fine wire.

'Look!' Mary said. 'Look there below the chestnuts — the snowdrops are coming up.' Yes, there they were, pushing bravely up through the dead leaves that covered them.

'Ring your white bells for the white death.'

'That's lovely, Nora.'

'It is, but it's not my own. It's the first line of a poem by Roy McFadden, the Irish poet.'

'There used to be McFaddens here in my mother's time. They were great pig-breeders, but they all cleared out to New Zealand. It wouldn't be one of them?'

Nora smiled at the quick memory of association, a memory not dulled by too much reading.

Elizabeth was in the sitting-room, a newspaper on her lap; and after greeting Nora and thanking her for the gloves she inquired in a weak voice if the flu was rife in her part of the country. She was sure she was in for a bad dose of it, if the aspirins didn't do their job and shift her heavy cold. She was terrified of it. It left her so depressed, so out of sorts that she couldn't even find solace in knitting or even saying her beads.

'Better not think about it. Thinking can bring it on,' Nora advised.

'I'd gladly not think about it if that would be the cure.'

'You could never do that,' Mary smiled.

With patience Nora waited till the history and origin of the cold had been tracked down. She had come home yesterday, the feeble voice went on, after a fine evening's entertainment at Helen's. Helen was so kind, and Peter played all his John McCormack records for them, and Father Lacy sang *My Dark Rosaleen* in a voice very like John's only not so sweet. It was all lovely, but when they came back they found that Johnny had let the fire go out, and she was sure it was the coldness of the house that had chilled her.

'Oh,' put in Mary, 'when we get the electric all our worries in that line will be over.'

'I don't know about that, Mary dear. Helen has all the electrical gadgets man can think of and yet she catches as many colds in a year as I do. Isn't that so?'

She turned to Nora. 'You're not subject to colds? I'm glad you're not — touch wood. I see by this paper that the flu is raging in England. It'll be our turn next — that's if it's not already here. When you go back to school you'll know what way the wind is blowing. The attendances will tell you all that.'

It wasn't the last time Nora was to hear that. For each day she arrived from the school Elizabeth fired that question at her and seemed disappointed that the attendance was normal. But at the end of a few weeks when the weather had turned to hail, the school attendance had fallen off, and the newspapers announced that influenza, a mild form, had reached Ireland. Elizabeth took to her bed.

Mary cut a few of the last snowdrops and was placing them in a tiny vase on Elizabeth's dressing-table when she was ordered to take them away, Elizabeth explaining that she had read somewhere that cut flowers exhale poisonous air during the night.

And Nora coming in from school pandered to Elizabeth's illness by going right up to the room without taking off her coat and announcing the day's bulletin: 'The attendance was wretched today, and poor Mr. Brennan is absent.' And Elizabeth, consoled that half the countryside was down with flu, marvelled that Nora, who looked so pale these days, hadn't succumbed.

'You shouldn't stay too long in this room, dear, in case you catch this dreadful infection. Was that Luke Murphy I heard you speaking to at the gate?'

'It was,' and Nora glanced at the open window and wondered if Elizabeth had heard him coaxing her to go to the golf dance and how she had refused.

'I could hear his silly laugh from here. No flu germ is likely to attack that fellow for he's too hard . . . And what kind of form is Peter in these days?'

'Mr. Lynch is always in the same form. He never changes. But I think he's a bit worried about the bad attendance. He says half the sickness is only imaginary.'

'Did he, indeed! If he had my sore back to contend with, it would cure his bright imagination in quick time. And what's Helen engaged in that she hasn't come to see me?'

'I never see her around,' Nora said, and after a pause added: 'If there came a blink of sun the first daffodils would show themselves. It may change tomorrow.'

'It's a long time making up its mind to change. Looking at that window every day and seeing the sleet slavering down it makes me more miserable than I really am. But, as you say, it may change tomorrow and take this sickness with it.'

But change it did not, for the next morning was wet and

blustery, with patches of cold blue in the sky and high flying clouds, and as Nora wheeled out her bicycle into the wet yard she heard Johnny call out to her from his little room. She opened his door and put her head into his room that was as stuffy and warm as a stable. She couldn't see him until he coughed and spoke from the bed: 'I'm afraid, Miss Byrne, this thrice accursed flu has downed me. I've all the symptoms that Elizabeth has. My throat's like sandpaper and my back is scorching like a blow-lamp.'

'Your room's like an oven and you'd be better without that little oil-stove. Wait a tick and I'll get the thermometer for you. You needn't worry, Johnny, it's only a mild form of flu.'

She hurried back with the thermometer, and after placing it below his tongue she withdrew for a few minutes to the airiness of the yard. Raindrops ran in single file from a slate above the door, a puddle shivered in the wind, and looking at them she half regretted not having accepted Murphy's invitation to the dance. It would have been something to look forward to, something to brighten these days and this eternal talk of flu. But since she didn't really care for him there was no use acting as if she did.

She knocked Johnny's door and went in. 'It should be well cooked by this time, Johnny,' and taking the thermometer to the light of the doorway she peered at it quickly, but failing to read the height of the mercury column she held it firmly in her hand and slowly followed the dark line with her index finger and saw to her amazement that it had reached its highest point.

She put her hand on his forehead. 'That's extraordinary, Johnny, you feel as cool as a frog and yet your temperature's like a raging furnace.'

'Am I very bad, Miss?' he said in a regretful tone, realizing he had held the thermometer too near the stove when her back was turned. 'I never held by them glass rods. You might as well put a twig in a man's mouth. What can the likes of them things tell what's going on in a man's insides?'

'I'll get Mary and then I'll cycle in for the doctor.'

'Go on to your school, like a good girl, before you're late. I don't want that man to be coming out here with his rubber tubes and charging Mary a guinea a peep. Tell Mary to bring me my breakfast and I'll rise after I take it. I've fowl to feed and the cows to look after.'

She went across to the house with the thermometer, and Mary bustled back with three aspirins on a saucer.

'Take these, Johnny son, till Nora gets the doctor,' she said concernedly.

'I won't have the decent girl riding in a day like that for no doctor. Put that glass rod in again for there was a sort of flame ran up my mouth when it was in the last time.'

'Take these tablets and none of your nonsense. What'd the neighbours say if I didn't get the doctor? — that I let you die of neglect, that's what they'd say.'

'And do you think I'd let any neighbour say the like about Miss Mary Devlin, the star and light of the whole country? I would not, be the holy.'

'You'd have no say in the matter, Johnny son, and you lying below six feet of thick red clay. Take these like a good man till the doctor comes.'

'Make me a glass of punch and I'll be on my feet while you'd say Jack Robinson.'

'You go on, Nora, and I'll deal with him myself. He'll not put a foot under him till I hear what the doctor says.'

Nora hurried from the room, and as she cycled out of the yard she heard Johnny's voice raised in loud protest.

The journey to the town had delayed her and it was long after ten when she arrived at the school. Peter saw her from the window and he came out and greeted her in the porch. He was glad to see her, he himself being the only teacher present.

'I hope you're not too badly soaked,' he said, helping her out of her raincoat. She had another coat under it and he fingered the sleeves of it and said she was as dry as hay. He had never seen her looking better, he told himself: her cheeks were aglow, and her black hair at the temples curled flat by the rain.

'You're very brave to come out on such a morning,' he said, as he closed the porch door against the wind.

'I would have it on my conscience not to, seeing there's nothing wrong with me.'

He was sure no more children would turn up, and after correcting the rolls he herded the few in the lower standards into one room where Nora could keep them employed. And into his own room he collected all the biggest boys and asked them to write a composition on 'A Wet Day', or 'The Flu Comes to Our House', and offered a shilling for the best in each section. 'Think of nothing else and you'll write well. Give us the feel of the day — the wetness of it. Think of puddles and pot-holes, wet fields and wet hedges, wet yards and wet roofs, splashes of oil on the wet roads — rain and rain, and not a bird in sight. Feel it — become a sponge, a bog, a piece of blotting paper . . . And for the flu, boys — what will you write?: the upset in the house, the talk, the doctor, the visitors, the sounds at night and the lights in the bedroom. Hear and see everything in the house connected with the sickness and write it down.' He clapped his hands. 'Silence now, and take plenty of time.'

He went into Nora's room and helped to set work for the boys with whom she had no experience in teaching. 'You've great big sturdy men here, Miss Byrne. Fellows that are not afraid of a bit of wind or a few hailstones.' They smiled up at him with a chill of pleasure, and when the sleety wind whined under the doors and thunder rumbled somewhere in the distance their pride overflowed into a courage that had conquered fear, and school became, for the moment, a place of wonder and magical splendour.

At lunch-hour the rain and wind had increased, and the children lay against the radiators in the room, enjoying the heat and swopping pieces of bread with one another. But when two o'clock struck, a break had come in the clouds and Peter dismissed the school and told them to hurry home for he feared there'd be more thunder soon. And from the window after he had seen them scamper across the playground to the gate and run off along the roads he suggested to Nora that they both remain on until three-thirty in case some inspector would happen to be moving around the district.

He stayed in his own room for a while correcting books, but when lightning squiggled on the window like a crack and thunder rolled overhead he came down to her room and found her seated at the table, a pile of exercise books in front of her. As he sat on top of one of the desks and lit his pipe another flash of lightning branched against the pane and he saw her bless herself in fear.

'Don't be frightened,' he said, holding the match above the bowl of his pipe. 'It'll pass over in a few minutes. I only wish the flu would pass just as quickly,' and as he was speaking, the thunder broke in fragments and heavy rain struck the roof like a thousand bird-pecks. 'If any of the youngsters are caught out in that downpour, I'll be blamed for it.'

'They'll all be at home long ago,' she said, tapping on the table with her red marking-pencil.

As she bent her head he noticed in the grey parting of her hair a few dots of red where she had unwittingly pressed the pencil. The red spots held his eye, but when she suddenly raised her head and caught his intent look he was forced to say: 'I'm looking at a few red pencil marks on your hair.'

'Where?' and she moved her index finger along the parting of her hair.

'A little further back . . . Further still. Now you're covering them.'

She took her handkerchief, wet a corner with her tongue, and began manœuvring it towards the spots.

'Wait,' he said, rising to his feet; and taking the handkerchief he rubbed off the spots and showed her the pink stain on the handkerchief.

'Thanks,' she said, tucking the handkerchief in her sleeve. 'I suppose my grey patch now looks as if it were dyed?'

'It was never grey. It always looked a kind of blue colour to me. I must say there's a bit of distinction about it.'

'It's a distinction I'd gladly surrender — if I could.'

'You'd look odd without it.'

'I'm sure I look odd with it.'

He relit his pipe, and she saw his eyes twinkle in the light from the match.

'I often wonder why you took up teaching as a career. Somehow I'd never associate you with it.'

'Is that meant to be a compliment, Mr. Lynch?'

'It could be, I suppose. We are always represented as a grim bunch. But that could be true of every profession if we only took the trouble to test it. All the same, schoolteaching is hard work, and when a girl is ten or twelve years at it she loses — what will I call it? — much of her charm.'

'And what would I turn to, pray?'

'Marriage.'

'So you'd like to get rid of me already — is that it?' and she swayed back in her chair and laughed pleasantly.

'I'd be sore sorry to lose you; I would indeed.'

'Then I should remain single — is that it?'

He laughed and blew smoke rings towards the ceiling, but on hearing the clock strike three he strode over to the window, swept the mist off it, and gazed out at the deserted playground and at the thinnings of rain dancing like midges in the puddles. Low ragged clouds hung over the trees, but beyond them there was a gap of washed blue and he guessed that the bulk of the rain had passed. Her pencil fell on the floor, and turning round he saw her grope for it without getting off the chair.

She was conscious of his eyes upon her, and she rejoiced in her power to attract him. She sensed he wanted to say something but was afraid to say it. She was nearer to him than he imagined — so near, in fact, that she was not conscious of the markings she was making with her pencil, but was listening to the slow puffs of his pipe and knew that his back was to the window.

At last she sighed, put down her pencil, and leaned back with her head resting on her arms. 'That will do for the day,' she said, and swayed back on her chair.

And then suddenly he said: 'Would you by any chance come to the Golf Dance with me?'

'I have already been asked, but I haven't decided yet,' she answered quickly.

His face reddened, and she realized that the quickness of her answer had hurt him. There was silence for a moment, and she felt a twinge of self-contempt, and knew that her half-lie, pleasant as it was to her vanity, would give her no peace. He stood, expecting her to speak.

'It was Luke Murphy who asked me,' she said, and she lifted her pile of books and pushed in her chair. 'And, to tell you the truth, I did decide when he asked me. I told him I didn't want to go. And now if I agreed to go with you he'd feel piqued over it — that's the fix I'm in.'

'I wouldn't want you to do that,' and he tapped out his pipe against the desk. 'But would you do this for me? Would you come to a Beethoven recital in Belfast next Friday fortnight?'

'Thank you very much. I'd love to go.'

'I'll keep you to that promise.'

'But if Mr. Murphy asks me again to go to the dance I might go . . . seeing it was he who asked first.'

'First come, first served. But you really should go, for I feel you'd enjoy one of the local hops.'

He took his ring of keys from his pocket, and as he went off to lock up she stowed away her books, combed her hair at the mirror hooked to the inside of the press-door, and was waiting for him when he came back twirling his ring of keys. He wheeled out her bicycle from the shelter in the yard, but the back wheel was flat, and the air escaped as quickly as he pumped it up.

'Come on up to the house and I'll mend it for you in a few minutes,' he suggested.

She tried to insist on walking home, but he wouldn't hear of it; and as they stood laughing and arguing in the drizzle of rain he pleaded with her to come up, and reminded her of her promise before Christmas.

'And anyway,' he added finally, 'I'd like you to get to know Helen better.'

She'd like that herself, she said to her own mind; but, to tell the truth, she always found Helen a bit distant. But, perhaps, she was just as much to blame as Helen for that. Wasn't she always somewhat aloof herself on meeting someone whom she immediately disliked for some flimsy reason of voice or appearance? She must try to get rid of that! Indeed there was more good in people than bad, if one took a little trouble to find it. Look at the Maguire boy, for instance: sure he'd do any mortal thing for her since his night excursion to Scotland!

She went with him, and after he had wheeled her bicycle into the garage he ushered her into his sitting-room, flung wide the glass panels of his largest book-case and told her to take what she liked.

'Make yourself at home, Nora. I won't be a jiffy mending the puncture.'

He found Helen in the kitchen, ironing clothes.

'Did you know that Nora Byrne was in?'

'I did, but I've this work to attend to. The iron's hot and I'm not going to switch it off.'

'Go in for a minute or two. You needn't stay long.'

'I'm not going.'

'There's such a thing as hospitality — hospitality without murmuring.'

'I hope I make myself clear: I'm not stirring hand or foot out of this kitchen till she's gone. And you know the reason.'

'There's nothing between us, if that's what you're hinting at.'

'You'd no call to bring her up here on a day like this; and the two of you stumping through the house in wet shoes.'

He explained about the punctured bicycle.

'A fine excuse! That girl, in spite of her youth, has too much guile for the likes of you.'

'You shouldn't allow yourself to jump so quickly to conclusions.'

'You're in love with that girl — and you know it.'

'I don't know it!'

'Then I have a pretty poor understanding of men and women.'

'It's inexperience.'

She rested the smoothing-iron on its end and turned on him: 'That's hard! But, perhaps, if I hadn't looked after your interests and comforts so conscientiously I could have had my chance of marriage like many another.'

'I'm sorry, Helen. I didn't mean that.'

'You meant it all right! You don't throw off words unthinkingly.'

'I didn't mean it, in that way. As God's my judge, I didn't.'

She turned her back on him, gripped the smoothing-iron, and went on with her work.

'I'm sorry, Helen,' and he rested his arm on her shoulder.

She shrugged away from him and told him to leave her alone for pity's sake.

He went out to the garage, discovered a nail in the tyre, chalk-marked the place, and levered it off. He mended the puncture quickly, and hurried back to Nora.

She was standing at the book-case where he had left her, and was flicking through a volume of Yeats's poetry.

'Helen didn't come in?'

'No, not yet. But don't take her from her work, please. I'd really like to slip away now, for Mary will be wondering what has kept me.'

'Pity you couldn't stay for a little while — till you had got a cup of tea, at least.'

'I would if I could. But with Elizabeth sick and Johnny sick, everything will be at sixes and sevens.'

'You'll have to take something, Nora,' and as she was pushing the book back into its place he took it from her and wrote her name and the date on the flyleaf. He flivelled the pages with his thumb, and his eye resting on a few lines he had marked with pencil he said them over to his own mind:

> We had fed the heart on fantasies,
> The heart's grown brutal from the fare;
> More substance in our enmities
> Than in our love. . . .

He smiled and wondered to himself why he had ever marked such bitter brooding lines.

'Take this, Nora,' he said, handing the book to her. 'It will remind you of the — the Great Flu!'

'It will remind me of something more pleasant than that, I hope.'

'We'll have no more rain this evening,' he remarked, going to the window and watching the clean swept sky and the life-belts of water around his standard roses. He was trying to delay her, in the hope that Helen would come in.

'That poor garden of mine is pretty miserable-looking — and so is the whole countryside for that matter. But it won't be long now till everything comes into leaf again. And then, of course, we've the concert to look forward to.'

'I trust the flu won't bowl any of us over before then,' and she placed the book on the table and fastened the top buttons of her waterproof. 'With two coats on I must look like a wife of Joey O'Brien's if he happens to have one.'

'In the country you can wear anything and no one will criticize you — that's one freedom you can enjoy here.'

She plucked the creases from her coat and put her book under her arm. He didn't move from the window, not wishing her to go. He felt somehow that his vexation with Helen was registered in his voice and manner, and he strove to say something that would slacken the stiff atmosphere of unfriendliness.

'If there's any other book you'd like to take, don't hesitate to ask me. They're only gathering dust sitting there, and you might be able to make better use of them than I have done. Believe it or not I haven't read a quarter of them. I buy them, read a few pages, and leave them aside hoping I'll have time to read them later on. But the books accumulate, the years pile up, and my time for reading seems to shrink instead of lengthen. It's well I have no Ex Libris plate decorating the inside cover, otherwise a myth could grow up round my name: the great reader I was, or, mercy on us, the great scholar! It's easy in a provincial place to get the name of being a brilliant man — the passing of an examination can start that ball rolling, or the collection of an unread library like my own, or even the publication of a poem on spring or an article on the rearing of poultry.'

She smiled: 'You talk like a disappointed man on the verge of his retirement.'

'I've a good twenty-five years to do before that closure.'

'A quarter of a century! It seems a lifetime,' and she walked towards the door.'

'I wish you could stay for a while.'

'I really must go. Go like the beggar when everything has been done for him: the bike mended and a gift in my hand. You forget I've Mary to face yet.'

'You couldn't face anything milder than Mary Devlin. You can tell her I kept you late.'

He lingered in the hall, speaking loudly and wishing that Helen would appear. But there was no sound about the house except the leisurely tick-tock of the grandfather clock, and from the open door of the kitchen the buzz of the kettle on the stove, and the warm smell of smoothed clothes.

'Are you there, Helen?' he shouted. There was no answer, and he shook his head and said casually: 'She must have gone out.'

He walked with Nora as far as the gate, and as she hopped on her bicycle she waved to him gaily. But she was glad to get away, glad to feel the cold wind on her face, and glad to be rid of a stifling constriction that had closed in on her all the time she had been alone in the sitting-room and could hear a thudding sound as of Helen scrubbing a floor in the rear of the house. And, then, when Peter had returned after mending the bicycle he seemed to have lost his usual serenity; and, she reasoned, that all his talk about books was forced and unnatural, a defence to hide some disappointment. Perhaps it was her refusal to go to the dance that had caused it or, maybe, it was of something Helen had said to him. Helen, at least, should have had the politeness to speak to her, if only for a minute. She couldn't recall having said anything that could have annoyed Helen. Indeed, now that she came to think of it Helen and herself had exchanged few words at any time. It would be a long time before she'd allow herself to be inveigled up there again!

A feeling of self-contempt swept over her, and she realized that if she brooded any longer on Helen's unfriendliness a depressed feeling would creep in with it. Hadn't she gone out of her way to meet Helen? — had fought with the inclination to avoid her, and having conquered it this is what she got for her trouble. There was one thing to be said for Peter: he didn't resort to polite lying to excuse his sister's non-appearance. He was loyal to her, and though he didn't face the truth boldly, at least he didn't try to choke it.

The bicycle jolted into a puddle, and for a moment her eyes followed the thin rib of water that hissed round on the tyre on the wet road. At the foot of the hill the road was completely flooded and she had to lift her feet high above the pedals and allow the bicycle to swish through it like the bow of a boat. She sped through the gate and up into the yard where she was surprised to see Johnny back out from the fowl-house with two buckets, one inside the other. And before she had time to ask him how he was feeling he was already announcing that he was as right as the mail and how he happened to be milking the cows when the doctor had come and how he had hidden in the hay shed till the doctor had driven off again on his rounds. He wasn't going to lie up in bed for any doctor and have poor Mary run off her feet with dancing attendance on him!

He took her bicycle from her, and shortly afterwards as she was washing her hands in the bathroom she could see him through the open window cleaning the bicycle and whistling to himself with increasing contentment.

That evening, noticing that Mary was fagged out and in no mood for conversation, Nora slipped off to read the book of poems in her own room. She read first the pencil-marked passages and endeavoured, by piecing them together, to form some aspect of Peter's nature that had lain hidden from her. Marked with double lines was:

Does a man brood most upon a woman lost or a woman won

and with a single line:

> O may she live like some green laurel
> Rooted in one dear perpetual place.

There were other passages with question marks scribbled in the margins, but these she did not dwell upon, conscious that they hadn't Peter's full approval. And she reread with serious attention:

> I am content to live it all again
> And yet again. . . .

and smiled with secret pleasure on reading, marked with blue pencil,

> The folly that man does
> Or must suffer, if he woos
> A proud woman not kindred of his soul.

And then suddenly she snapped the book shut and leant back in the armchair with her eyes closed. She had done wrong, she told herself; her whole action was dishonourable and ugly, like read-

163

ing a secret diary not addressed to her. She would tell him what she had done when discussing the book with him — in that way only could she excuse herself and rid herself of this feeling of guilt. And she would smile and wag her finger and say: 'I read each of the poems once except the marked passages, and these I read two or three times over'; and should he ask her why, she'd toss her head and say: 'A marked book tells tales.'

It was strange that a few minutes ago she felt so depressed, and now as she opened out her hair and brushed it vigorously she felt like singing. She restrained herself and indulged in gentle humming, not loud enough to disturb Elizabeth in the next room. She combed the hairs off the brush and drawing the edge of the blind aside she let them float into the night wind. She knelt by her bedside and said her prayers, and after quenching the lamp and letting up the blind she stood in her nightdress at the window looking out into the dark night. Through the shaking trees she saw a light in the direction of the school, and reasoning it was the light in Peter's sitting-room she pictured him in an armchair smoking his pipe, listening to the radio or reading a book. She thought keenly of him and hoped that her concentrated thinking would stir his own thoughts towards her. He was kind, and he wanted to be kind to her; and she in turn, despite Helen, would return kindness for kindness.

In bed, without raising her head from the pillow, she could still see the light shine down from the hill, and could see it glimmer and break when the wind swayed the branches of the trees outside.

'I love him,' she whispered to herself, 'but why I do not know.' Though he was older than she was, yet, at times, she underwent the feeling that she was the elder. Was it that her life with its share of sorrow, her lack of friends, her isolation had done this for her? — had aged her feelings ahead of her age in years. To have been in love once is to know life at a deeper level than not to have been in love at all. The deepest knowledge comes from experience and not from what you read in books.

She had done nothing to attract him — and hadn't she every reason to be timid and withdrawn in that connection? She hadn't sought after him, hadn't gone out of her way to please him, and now, in spite of all her vigilance, this is where she had drifted. At present she'd suppress her affection for him, wouldn't outwardly show it until she had made known to him all about her family. Till that was done she'd have to efface herself and play the hypocrite to her own heart. There was no other way open for her: no other way except to turn aside from the voice of her own conscience, to lie to him or to keep a cowardly silence about her family — that, with God's help, she'd never do! Never! — even if it meant the breaking up of her desire.

✿ 12 ✿

A FEW days later Elizabeth, being able to be up again, was standing at the sitting-room window admiring the tight varnished buds of the chestnut trees when she saw Nora and Murphy arriving at the gate together on their way from school. From the edge of the curtain she watched them for a moment, and then sat down wearily in an armchair, her nerves not strong enough to endure Murphy's swaggering, confident pose. Nora saw her as she entered the hall, and going in she said with bold recklessness: 'I'm after agreeing to the maddest thing in my life. Murphy has asked me to go to the Golf Dance with him and, lo and behold, I said yes. I suppose I'll regret it,' and she took off her hat, jabbed the hat-pin into its place, and twirled the hat round on the tip of her finger. 'Wasn't that a crazy notion to take?' she added smilingly, expecting that her playful manner would lessen Elizabeth's displeasure.

'Well, well, it certainly is a mad notion to take. Mad, indeed, to go off to a dance with a mad-hatter the like of him.'

'I did it, more or less, to get peace. He has plagued and pestered me for the past fortnight. Mr. Lynch also asked me, but I couldn't very well go with him, seeing it was Murphy who asked first. That's the fix I was in. But Mr. Lynch has asked me to go to an orchestral concert in Belfast, the week after next, and that's something I'm looking forward to.'

'You're in great demand this weather. And with plenty of outings it's no wonder you're in great form. I wish it were warm enough for me to take a turn outside. Nobody cares a straw about you when you get up in years. Look at Helen — not a visit from her, and me lying day after day in my lonely bed.'

'Perhaps she didn't wish to catch the flu.'

'You didn't catch it, nor Mary, and both of you in and out of the room every day. And Father Lacy visited me twice and he wasn't laid low. The same lady will get a cool reception from me when she does decide to call.'

When Nora went upstairs Elizabeth sought out Mary in the kitchen and bemoaned, with peevish concern and cold disdain, that Nora should decide to go to a dance without first consulting them.

'Say nothing to her, Elizabeth. She'll have to be allowed to make up her own mind without interference from us. Murphy might be nice in her eyes.'

'Nice! How could an unmannerly stick like him be nice to anyone? And in all probability he'll be drunk before the night's half out. I'll not be here to receive him should he decide to call for her on the night of the dance. I will not!'

'There's little enough jollity about here for any young girl. Nora has been very good, and not once has she kept us out of our beds beyond our time of going. She has given us no trouble in that way.'

'Well, if this is the beginning of a randybooze and late nights it'll be the end of her stay in this house.'

'Elizabeth, how could you say the like! When the weather mends you'll mend with it, and you'll look at all this in the way you should.'

'I've a good mind to go up and give her a solemn warning in time.'

'Elizabeth dear, you wouldn't do the like of that! It would destroy the blessed peace of our home and make the girl feel she wasn't wanted. You would hurt her to the quick . . . Maybe you should lie down for a while and I'll bring a nice warm meal up to you on a tray.'

'I'll do nothing of the sort! You think I'll not be able to control myself at the dinner-table. But I will show you and her that I am a lady to my finger-tips. She knows I dislike Murphy and dislike this dancing expedition with the likes of him; and she'll also understand before very long how, like a lady, I can keep a charitable silence.'

'We all know that,' Mary lied soothingly and was relieved to see her stretch out on the kitchen sofa and prop a cushion under her head.

At the dinner-table Elizabeth held firmly to her ladylike aspiration and resisted the ugly impulses that struggled for expression; and later, when they were all in the sitting-room and the lamps lighted, she took up her knitting with her usual alacrity and to Mary's amazement asked Nora, as a special favour, to play her some of Moore's Irish melodies. At the end of the week she was reconciled to Nora's going to the dance but unrelenting in her intention not to receive Murphy in her house — she would never stoop to that!

Nora spent Saturday in Belfast buying her frock, and though she was tired on arriving back Elizabeth insisted that the frock should be tried on after supper. She spent a long time dressing, and on coming down she was arrayed as she would be on the night of the dance. The frock was black net, a pink artificial rose was pinned near her left shoulder, and silver shoes were on her feet. Mary spread a newspaper on top of the sitting-room table and made her stand on it so that she could get a full view of herself in the pier-glass above the mantelpiece.

'It's too low about the neck,' Elizabeth said, peering at her over her spectacles. 'It could do with a little modesty vest.'

'It's in the height of fashion,' Nora said, smiling.

'I don't think much of the height of fashion if that's an example of it.'

'Neither do I,' Mary agreed, 'but wouldn't she be odd if she dressed in something that was out of date?'

'You're not a bold girl, but yet that dress makes you look bold,' Elizabeth went on, surveying her from head to toe, from bare shoulder to bare shoulder.

'It's beautiful, Nora, and you look beautiful. And that little grey patch in your black hair is like . . . is like . . . a grey ornamental butterfly! It tones in with everything, doesn't it, Elizabeth?'

'All I hope is that Father Lacy won't turn up at the dance and see you in that.'

'And your gold cross round your neck is also lovely. I wish I were young enough to go with you,' and Mary held out the frock at each side and was amazed at the width of material in it. She asked her to give it a swirl or two, and as Nora did so the paper on which she stood rose up at the corners and a pleasant perfume drifted about the room.

'You'll be the loveliest girl at the dance. There's nothing surer than that. Isn't that so, Elizabeth?'

'It could all be. But she'll not have the handsomest partner — I am sure of that.'

Not wishing to hear a harangue on poor Murphy Mary hurried her off the table and went upstairs with her to help her out of her frock.

'I'm sorry now that I've agreed to go to this dance,' Nora declared when they were alone in her bedroom.

'Nonsense, girl. Don't pay any heed to Elizabeth in her present mood. She just thinks Murphy isn't good enough for you, and that's why she says these hurtful things. She shouldn't say them, but don't let them worry you. By and by she'll come to like Mr. Murphy.'

But Elizabeth's disfavour was the least of Nora's annoyances. What disheartened her was her own self, her wild decision to go out with a partner for whom she had little respect.

On the day of the dance her depression had not lessened. Mary had anticipated a display of gaiety and enthusiasm, of song and hurry and fuss, and since there was none she accused Elizabeth, in the silent dismay of her own mind, of breaking the girl's happiness. In the evening Murphy was to call for her in a car, but instead of driving up to the front door he stopped on the road outside the gate and sounded the horn in one prolonged blast like the collier's whistle.

'Man alive, but that's the impatient fellow,' Mary said, taking a pin out of her mouth and helping Nora to affix the pink rose to her frock. 'Let him drive up the path like a gentleman, and not have you walking down to the gate in the rain.'

With a few rapid blasts he again sounded the horn and it disturbed Elizabeth, who was resting in the darkness of her own room, determined not to have any hand or part in welcoming him to her house. Out of curiosity she went to the edge of the window, and peering out into the wet darkness she saw the head-lights of his car shine on the bare hedges. There was no move-ment or noise from the house, and they fancied him gazing sternly at the lighted bedroom window. They heard him get out of the car and bang its door as if trying to test the strength of the hinges.

Nora started laughing, and Mary encouraged by this sudden playfulness laughed too; and then unexpectedly Nora whisked away from her round the room, turning and twisting till her wide skirts swirled about her like a Spanish dancer.

'Nora, Nora, you don't care one bit for him. You wouldn't mind if he drove off without you. Am I right?'

'Yes, Mary, you are. But now that I'm decked out in all my finery I wouldn't like to miss it,' and she skipped round the room again, stopping abruptly when the front door was loudly knocked. She put a finger on her lips and raised her eyebrows impishly.

'Mercy on us, he'll put the door in, if I don't go down,' Mary exclaimed, and was hurrying from the room when Elizabeth entered with her hand raised.

'Just let him cool his heels for a few minutes,' she ordered, and sticking out her head from the landing window she said with cool dignity: 'Is there anybody there?'

'It's only me, Miss Devlin,' came Murphy's voice. 'I've been knocking for the past half-hour.'

Mary ran downstairs to usher him into the sitting-room, and Elizabeth going into Nora's room delayed her intentionally by fingering out a crushed petal of her rose and giving the bust of her frock a few upward plucks. 'I'll not go down to him for fear

I might say something out of place. But I know you'll behave yourself and come home at a reasonable hour,' and after Nora had descended the stairs Elizabeth leaned over the banisters and saw the top of Murphy's hair stiff with oil, his coat collar turned up, and the fingers of his kid gloves portruding from his pocket.

Nora gathered her skirts about her while Mary escorted her down the path, holding an umbrella over her. The sight of the ramshackle car appalled her, and she was sure Nora's frock would surely be crushed or even stained with oil. The engine had been kept running because, as he explained with a laugh, he had difficulty in getting the old bus started; but with careful nursing it would do the job. As the car drove off, the wind blew cold through the window that wouldn't shut and he suggested that she snuggle close to him and keep herself warm.

'Oh, I'm quite comfortable, thank you,' she said, sitting back in the spring-broken seat.

'Did you not hear me honking the damned horn for you?'

'We did, but we thought it was someone passing on the road.'

'I didn't want to go up to the house. Those two old women give me a pain in the cranium every time I look at them.'

'Look out, you nearly ran over that cat.'

He began to laugh — a laugh that made her uncomfortable, for she wondered had he drink taken.

'Did I ever tell you the one about the old tomcat with three legs?'

'You didn't, and you needn't trouble yourself.'

'It'd be no trouble; it'd be a pleasure.'

'It's a pleasure I can forgo, for I am not greatly interested in cats.' He was in one of his moods that always disconcerted her, and she feared, if she didn't curb him, that he would begin to tell her a few bawdy stories. He began to hum to himself, not in the least affected by the dryness of her mood.

'Here we are, and done in record time!' he said, swinging up to the club-house, whose lighted windows shone out on the roofs of cars already parked around it. 'We're at the tail-end of the queue and can make a quick get away after the ball is over.'

Coming out of the cloakroom she stood about with him watching a dance in progress, and then made their way to two vacant chairs near the small orchestra. Her eye ranged quickly round the hall: it was cheerless-looking in spite of the balloons and bunting strung across the ceiling, and when a door opened behind them a cold draught rushed in and she gave a slight shiver.

'It'll be warmer dancing than sitting,' he said as they stood for their first dance.

He danced without rhythm; he held her too close, and time and again his toe caught on the hem of her frock.

'Is Mr. Lynch here?' she asked, trying to appear at her ease as they waltzed clumsily among the other couples.

'I don't see his nibs anywhere, and I don't suppose he'll be here now. He's come-early, go-early; daren't disturb Helen's sleep, you know. If you look under that billiard-marker on the wall at our right you'll see a few photographs. He's in one of them, driving off from the first tee.'

She was glad when the first dance had ended and only wished that it had been the last. She tried to smile but felt that her unenjoyment was apparent even in that. It was her own fault and not his.

'Would you like a drink?' he asked her after their fourth dance. 'The room's got terribly close.'

'Not just yet. Anyway I take nothing stronger than orange crush.'

'Would you like to step out in the air for a breather?'

'It's still raining, I think,' and she spread out her dress at each side of her and joined her hands on her lap. His arm was drooped over the back of her chair and she shuddered as her bare shoulder leaned against it.

'If you're not coming for a drink or fresh air you'll not mind if I go alone?'

'Not in the least.'

Though her refusals harassed her she was glad that her aloof attitude had not dampened him; he had come to enjoy the dance and she only wished that she could help him to enjoy it. But his ways were not hers, and she was already worrying how she would get home if he took any more drinks. While he was away one of the local bank clerks gave her a dance, and as they glided off at their ease he condemned the state of the floor and declared it was unfit for dancing and that in his opinion the golf committee should have applied to Father Lacy for the loan of the Parochial Hall. But that wouldn't have suited Mr. Murphy, he added with a sly smile — no wine, beer, or spirits would be consumed on or off the parochial premises.

'If Mr. Murphy takes a drink, surely that's his affair,' she defended.

His face reddened at her retort and he answered nervously: 'Oh, Miss Byrne, I'm not criticizing Mr. Murphy. I wouldn't for the world do a thing like that. I was only making a little joke — that was all.'

Nothing was going right for her; and in everything she said or did she was left with a feeling of guilt. Murphy rejoined her after twenty minutes and apologized for being so late; the bar was crammed and he was a long time in being served. His face was red and he kept brushing back a lock of hair that fell over his brow.

'We'll dance again the whole night through,' he said, rising heavily to his feet.

'I'm not too sure of the fox-trot,' she said, remaining on her chair.

'Leave it to me. I'll pilot you through this stormy sea of dancing dancers,' and he flung out his arm like an orator, and to avoid notice she rose to her feet. He held his head close to hers and all the time he kept humming the tune a few bars behind the orchestra. Time and again he would bump into other couples, and detaching his arm from around Nora's waist he would give an over-polite bow and say 'Excuse me!'

She tried to induce him to leave before the last dance, but he wouldn't listen to her; they had paid their money and he would see that they got full value for it. She remained close to him for the rest of the long night and maintained that she would go off to the Miss Devlins' without him should he dare to take another drink.

At three o'clock the dance came to an end, and as they were moving towards the car she asked him if he were sure he was all right.

'If the old bus is all right, I'm all right.' He tried to start it but not a whimper came from the engine. 'She's stone cold. She needs warming up.' He got out, and in the lights from the headlamps she saw him try to crank up the engine and fall exhausted over the radiator.

In panic she got out, and gazing at the few remaining cars, she implored him to ask someone for a lift before it was too late. He shoved in the starting-handle again, failed to turn it, and in anger with himself and with everything he flung it into the darkness.

'We'll get somebody to tow us or else we'll sit in her till the dawn breaks.'

'We can't do the like of that!' she cried, and in desperation ran to a car that was pulling out. It was the captain of the Golf Club and with him was his wife. They'd plenty of room and would only be too pleased to give them a lift.

As they settled themselves in the back of the car Nora whispered to Murphy that he should get off at the Square and not go tramping home all the way from the Devlins'. No, he wouldn't agree to that, he announced loudly; he brought her to the dance and, like a man, he'd see her safely back to her house again. There was no call for him to put such a journey on himself and it raining, she explained. He didn't give a damn if it were snowing — he was going back with her; and he didn't care a twopenny ticket who knew it or who didn't know it.

She sat back and saw in the headlights how heavily the rain

was falling. She didn't know what to say or what to do. She certainly couldn't bring him into the Devlins'! Suddenly she felt his arm around her, and she detached it without a word and edged away from him. He leaned towards her, but the smell of whiskey disgusted her and she shot up and sat on the other side of him. She peered between the two heads in the front seat and saw that the car was swinging past the collier's quay. She gathered her wrap tightly around her, and immediately the car stopped on the road outside the Devlins' gate she said, 'Thank you! Thank you!' and swung open the door, and in a flash shut it behind her and fled up the path to the house. The key was in the door and she let herself in quickly. Her oil lamp with the wick lowered was on the hall table and she blew down the globe and stood listening in the darkness. She could hear the pat-pat of the rain on the pebbles on the path but no sound of a footstep. He hadn't followed her for she'd surely hear him stumbling about on the path or leaning his weight against the door. She stood where she was for some minutes, and when her fear had subsided in the warm stillness of the house she groped about for the handle of the lamp and tiptoed upstairs to her room.

She sat on the edge of the bed before taking off her things. She was weary — weary with self-contempt and fagged out by the tensions of the whole evening. She deserved what she got. What else could one expect for being false? She had betrayed her own conscience and that betrayal had brought its deserts. Under the impulse of some hidden perversity she had agreed to go, so why should she expect anything else but unhappiness and soured dissatisfaction? Better not to think about it now — forget about it till she had some sleep.

But in bed sleep, she knew, was far away from her. Her head was throbbing, and the beat of her heart was loud and quick. What did it matter if sleep didn't come! She was resting all her limbs, and she really believed that the worrying about not sleeping causes more harm than the sleeplessness itself. She was lucky to be in bed at all and not sheltering in the old car with

Murphy at the edge of the golf course — that indeed would have been a lovely scandalous story! If she'd known that Murphy would have been drunk she wouldn't have gone with him to any dance. And if that were the reason for Elizabeth being so dead-set against her going she needn't thank her now for being so indirect. Why didn't she give her a clear warning instead of the few surly glances that always missed their mark? Elizabeth would hear precious little about the dance from her. Indeed it would be better if she didn't speak about it to anyone — her whole behaviour was nothing to brag about. And this bitter remorseful mood, she confessed to herself, would have been the same if Murphy had been sober. It was useless to hide that fact or to blame Elizabeth in any way for what did happen. The fault lay with herself and in herself — there was no escaping the stubborn reality of that. She was proud; she had no humility, no strength to confront her difficulties boldly. Why did she go with him? Was it all calculated or was it impulsive? Better for her to waylay that now and drag it into the clear spaces of truth. Had Peter anything to do with her going out with Murphy? No, no, he hadn't — that was the truth. He hadn't! But — but Helen had — it was she that drove her to it. Helen was the reason for her going, and with it her own silly pride. Yes, she had played the hypocrite to her own heart and had got her just reward.

She closed her eyes, but they felt hard as marbles and she opened them again and stared with relief at the dark window on which the rain was rattling. She lay limp and forced her mind back to her childhood days. She thought of the summer father had brought Eileen and herself to France — that was a happy holiday and few of its memories had blurred in the rush of years since then. She recalled the hot, hot sand on the beach and the green waves sweeping in and the dry grains floating like meal on the thinning surface of the water; and near where they had been digging and making sand-pies lay their father, his body brown as chocolate and his sun-glasses sticking out of a book he had been reading. And she remembered, too, the women in black and the wings of their coifs swaying as they trundled barrows of damp clothes up from the washing-streams. And then there was that strange port that stank as the tide went out, and it was there that she had seen a dead sardine floating with confetti circles of oil around it and a gull snatching it up and swallowing it in the air in one gulp. It was in the evening that had happened, for it was on the same evening she had sipped her father's red wine when his back was turned and was surprised that it tasted like sour vinegar and not like raspberry jam as she had hoped; and it was on the same evening too she had seen in a side altar of a church a dead bishop with buckled shoes on his feet, his eyes open, his beard red, and his hands holding a chalice on his outstretched body. That was the first thing she told mother on arriving home and mother immediately scolded father for bringing little children to see the like of that; and later when her hair was being washed mother noticed her raw sunburnt back and began to scold father again for having such little sense and he a doctor. Her father had laughed. 'You should have seen it before I had put the oil on it!' The following summer they were to go again and mother was to come should she feel fit for the journey. But that summer never came for any of them. . . .

She opened her eyes and repelled that siege of memory, and her gaze sought in the darkness for some friendly object — the white knob of the door or the gleam of the brass bedrail — to tell her that dawn was not far off. But she could distinguish nothing; all was drowned in darkness; and with a sigh she turned on her side, and listening to the rain scampering on the pebbles like mice, she fell asleep.

She awoke when the low sun was glancing into her room and glistening coldly on the heavy drops that drooped from the chestnut trees. Her black frock was thrown carelessly over a chair, her silver slippers lying on their sides, and her stockings showing the little blobs where the suspenders had held them.

'Make a nice subject for a painter!' she said with careless irony, and decided, before Mary would come in, to place everything in order. She was too weary to move, and placing her arms under her head she closed her eyes from the annoying sunlight. She intended to doze for a few minutes but fell asleep again, and it was Mary carrying her breakfast on a tray that wakened her.

'You'll just be in nice time to take your breakfast and be ready for second Mass. I didn't call you earlier for I knew you'd be dog tired,' and she placed the frock carefully on a hanger and hung it in the wardrobe. 'I hope you enjoyed the dance.'

'I did and I didn't.'

'We'll have a good talk about it later. Any minute now you'll be hearing the first bell,' and she poured out a cup of tea for her and arranged the pillows at her back.

'Thanks, Mary. You're very kind, but you're a great encourager of sloth.'

She stirred her cup and smiled to Mary as she went out of the room. She shook her head and said to herself: 'There's very little I can say to her about the dance. I can't very well tell her that Murphy was drunk for most of the evening. After the disappointment I must have been to him I can at least spare him that and keep silent.'

Within a few days she discovered that her silence was unnecessary. A rumour spread around the countryside that Murphy had tried to lock her in his old car outside the golf club and that she escaped through an open window and that only for the captain she would have had to run home in the rain and the dark. Another rumour had it that he had tried to follow her into the captain's car, that she nearly snipped the fingers off him in the door, and that the poor fellow wandered about the course all night searching for the handle of his radiator that somebody had stolen. As Elizabeth recounted these stories Nora smiled and told her there wasn't a grain of truth in them and that Mr. Murphy wasn't as drunk as the rumours made him out to be. 'It was true,' she admitted, 'that he couldn't get his car started after the dance, but that was the car's fault and not his. And as to his wandering about the golf course or sleeping out in the car all night — I just don't believe that.'

'That'd been the proper medicine for him — I'm sure it's true!' Elizabeth interjected with emphatic nods. 'Stories like that just don't grow on the hedges. I knew he drank, but I thought he'd behave himself when he was out with a lady from this house. Allow me to say he's not the right class of company for a doctor's daughter.'

'We're certainly not suitable as dancing partners: I know that now and so does he. On our way from school today we both had a good laugh over the whole affair.'

'When a man makes a fool of himself I don't see what there is to laugh at. Anyway I am glad, for your sake and for ours, that you behaved in a ladylike manner and that no one has accused you in my hearing — and there are many would if they could — of being brazen. Of course I still hold that your frock was not to my pleasement. I am surprised you didn't get a founder from wearing such an article as that. You'll not be wearing it, I hope, at this concert Peter's bringing you to?'

'No, Elizabeth,' and she could barely keep from smiling. 'I'll probably wear my grey costume.'

'That's sensible. With all this running about I wouldn't like you to catch cold. Yesterday Father Lacy complimented me and Mary on the great care we were taking of you. I'm anxious that that will continue and that you may consider yourself one of the family now. I told Father Lacy that Peter and you were going to this recital together and he was delighted to hear it — delighted to hear that you were settling down well in your new surroundings.'

✿ 13 ✿

DRIVING out from the city after the concert the moon shone ahead of them, shining so hard and clear that the stars were almost blotted out under its wide-spreading radiance. The shadows of the tree trunks lay as solid as planks on the tarred road, and in the pockets of the hills the gables of the houses shone white and the roof slates glistened coldly like the skin of a salmon. Freshly ploughed furrows lay like steel rails upon the fields and the wire fences gleamed like columns of mercury.

'It's so bright, Nora, we could almost do without the head-lights.'

'It's a beautiful night. I just want to sit still, look out at it and try to relive that Fourth Piano Concerto again. For me it's Beethoven at his greatest.'

'I'll just drive leisurely. There's no need for us to hurry.' And as they drove on, mile after mile without speaking, at rest and at ease in each other's company, the slow movement of the concerto came back to Nora in all its final peace: the feminine pleading of the piano confronting the masculine stride of the orchestra, and gently swaying it to give way and listen to a lovelier strength.

And as the car wheeled on to the road that led to the collier's quay the estuary opened out in front of them; the tide had long since ebbed, and the tall stakes that marked the channel reflected in the still water like the ribs of some old galleon. He stopped the car and they stepped out into the cold echoing air from the water. There was not a soul to be seen; dark lines marked out the unlevel flagstones at their feet, and from the stone wall of the coal-store a lifebelt stared at them like the frame of an old clock. They stood quite still, and as they caught the sound of the stream dabbling its unseen way between mounds of shining mud Peter recalled the snowy night they had come here searching for

Maguire and he wondered if the same thought were now stirring in Nora's mind. He was about to ask her when suddenly she said in a whisper: 'I never saw it so still before — not even on the snowy night we came here looking for Malachy Maguire.'

He held his breath but the words he meant to say didn't come and instead he found himself saying in a low tone: 'It's so bright you could read a book in that light.'

'Your Yeats' book?'

'Any book, Nora.'

She laughed timidly and told him of some of the poems he had marked in pencil.

'Of course I only mark what I think is beautiful,' and his friendly eyes smiled back at her.

'That's just what I thought.'

'But I must examine it if you let me have it for a day or two. God knows what secrets I've been telling.'

She turned towards the car but a rat scampered across the road and she gave a little scream and caught his arm.

'I hate the sight of them!' and she shuddered as if with cold.

He locked her arm firmly in his as they stepped across the road and entered the car with its warm smell of leather. He was reluctant to start. She said nothing, and sat staring at the illuminated hands of the clock on the dash-board.

'Everything's changed since the day you took the singing class for me.'

'In what way?'

'For one thing, you're content in the school, aren't you?'

'I am. Indeed I am.'

'And, then, I don't know how to say it — but you mean much to me, Nora. Since you came the school's been different. You've made it a very happy place for me.'

'It's nice of you to say that' — and she smoothed the polished steering wheel with her hand. He grasped her forefinger and she made no attempt to withdraw it. She half shut her eyes and gave her melancholic smile. He put his arm around her and drew her close to him. She did not resist him; and as he felt the coldness of her brow upon his cheek he bent down and kissed her.

'I love you, Nora,' he said, 'I do indeed!'

She closed her eyes and when she looked at him again he saw they were wet with tears.

'I love you,' he said again.

She smoothed the back of his hand and slowly shook her head. 'But you don't know me well enough. If you did, Peter, you might regret what you've said. And, then, the school would be an awkward place for you and for me.'

'You're not annoyed with me?'

'No, Peter, I'm not. The whole night has been lovely. You're very kind. But we'll have to go now. Look how late it is.'

'Look up at me,' he said and he turned her head towards him. She gave a tearful smile and looked away from him. He kissed her again, feeling her tears upon his lips and believing they were tears of joy.

He sent the car forward, and on reaching the Devlins' gate Nora got out quickly.

'Good night, Peter,' she said. 'Good night.'

'I hope we'll have many another evening together. And after Easter when the ground dries you must really take up the golf. No perhapsing about it — you've the height for it.'

'I'm sure that's not everything.'

'Well, you've the slimness too.'

'That'll do you,' and she stood back and waved him off.

For some minutes after the car had gone and she could still hear its drone shrinking among the hills she stood in the sharp shadow of the gable of the house where no one could see her; and alone now with the moonbright night and the dark trees she felt the happiness of her evening edge away from her under the pressure of a rising remorse.

It was she, and she alone, that had led them into this tangle of ifs and buts — a tangle that time would ravel up more and more.

If only she had told him everything long ago without waiting for this to happen. But she was weak, and deception seemed easier and pleasanter than the cold truth. If only she had known that he cared so much for her! But there was no way of finding that out convincingly until this evening. As yet, he wasn't sure of her love for him. How could he be sure when deep within her there was always the hidden pull, holding her from expressing and showing all she thought? She loved him. She could say that aloud to herself but to no one else. And where there was love there should be no deceit. She'd never deceive him. She'd pray for the strength to reveal everything — no matter what would follow from it. But when or where or how? — that was the difficulty. If she were once aware that he possessed the truth about her family it would test the strength of his love; and she could watch for the first tentative withdrawals and the sparse words of his disillusionment. And with her own dignity intact she could aid him and ease his regret. Dignity! — she was always kind to herself! Why didn't she say Pride and have done with it?

As she stepped out from the shadow of the gable on to the path she saw a light glide into the dining-room. It was Mary; and through the window she watched her put the lamp on the sideboard, take out the cutlery and lay the table for the morning. Her actions were quiet yet studied, moving always so that the light fell on the table. Nora searched her mind for some line of a poem or some piece of music that she could always associate with Mary and with this evening, but nothing came to her bidding, not even the final phrase of the slow movement of the concerto, and so she ceased her quest and continued to watch until the table was laid. Then Mary lifted the lamp and held it above her head, her eye ranging over her work with loving care. She touched a spoon, a napkin, rearranged a few of the daffodils in their vase, and with a last look at the table she ambled from the room.

In bed that night, with the lace curtains hanging quiet at the open window, that scene of Mary laying the table came back to her unwittingly and she knew that it would come again on nights like these when the moon would be whitening the gables of the houses and shining like dew upon the fields. She had no need to search for any other image to recall it. Quietness and whiteness — that was Mary: a woman without guile.

On the following days she sought, during school hours, for a natural opportunity in which she could speak about her childhood with apparent casualness and so tell Peter about her mother and sister. But the opportunity did not come. His manner, so free and joyous, troubled her with a sense of guilt and silenced the voice of her heart. His mood was not the mood she wished for her revelation, and on days that she wished he would come into her room he didn't come.

Spring was all around them. It showed in the well-washed faces of the younger boys as they came into her room in the morning, dressed in lighter clothing, and carrying bunches of daffodils for her. And it showed in the access of joy that came into her singing class. And from her own window she witnessed the afternoon sun coaxing out to the playground, class after class, for games or physical training.

And one day, the sun being unusually bright, she heard Peter assemble his own boys in the playground; she looked out and saw them arranged two deep, spades and rakes over their shoulders, and Peter with a bundle of white stakes in his hand and cord hanging out of his pocket. He saw her and with a roguish smile gave her a soldier's salute. He marched them past her window and she saw last year's clay on their spades and dabs of rust on the teeth of their rakes. And as they broke into the Dwarfs' Song from Walt Disney's *Snow White*:

> Dig, dig, dig; dig, dig, dig; . . .
> All the whole day through. . . .

her own class stopped working, and their eyes, wide with contemplating the joy of being grown up, stared at her. Some hands were raised, making a polite excuse to get outside, but she ignored them and continued to cast a glance out of the window to see the army of boys halt in a sloping patch of ground opposite the school. Peter drove the white stakes into the ground, marked out rectangular sections with the cord, and blew his whistle to start the breaking of the soil.

Within an hour she heard them troop back again, singing *The Minstrel Boy*, their spades glinting in the sun, and the upturned soil white with gulls.

On her way home from the school Murphy joined her and asked what she thought of the Walt Disney performance.

'I only wished I were a boy!' she said.

'I only wished I had a machine gun!' and he nodded his head hopelessly. 'He has his damned class ruined; and their noisy antics so razzle-dazzled my own I couldn't get a bit of sense out of them the whole afternoon. Lynch and his horticulture — it's a damned useless pastime in a place like this.'

He began to laugh. 'He didn't tell you what happened to his horticultural display last year? It's a damned good one: the lads had their patches in grand botanical order for the inspector's visit. They had cabbages as green and as hard as their own heads, lettuce with hearts in them as cold as some people I brought to a dance, and they had parsley, and parsnips and beetroot and carrots and the God-knows-what-else. Lynch expected to get high commendation for his work — I should say for his supervision of the free labour — but, lo and behold you, what do you think happened? Three sacerdotal cows broke in with malicious intent, and what they didn't eat they trampled, and what they didn't trample they fouled, and in the morning the earth was scorched. Lynch mourned his dead vegetation, and the army without banners had departed to the quieter precincts of parochial property where they lay and chewed the mixture of their cud with sad-eyed stupidity. But they'll not break in this year. He's erecting a fence that'd repel a bulldozer! Spring's coursing through him like a greyhound these days, and so you may bring your knitting for the afternoons, for you'll not get your class to do a hand's turn once his army clatters on to the yard. Either that or pray for rain! If this horticultural carry-on was educational, I wouldn't mind putting up with a bit of noise now and again.'

'But surely, Mr. Murphy, it gives them a taste for gardening.'

'Do you know what I'm going to tell you? There's not one of those big fellas would lift a spade in their own homes except they're driven to it.'

'Maybe when they get married and have homes of their own they'll change for the better. Marriage brings changes.'

'It does,' he said dryly, 'but not in the gardening department.'

To change the subject she halted at a roadside bush that was already white with blossom and asked him the name of it.

'That's blackthorn. For some crooked reason its blossom comes first and its leaf afterwards. It does things backwards — but that's nothing unusual in this part of the country. I have a fella in my own class and he writes simple words like "for" and "of" backwards: there are times when I think he was born with his head back to front. And there are times, Miss Byrne, when I look at old Brennan I believe in my granny's yarn that some of us were found in a cabbage and others in a bag of spuds. Brennan could have been found in a wreath in the graveyard!'

'I'm afraid the spring's affecting us all,' she laughed, and looking ahead of her she saw a patch of the lough and remarked that she'd never seen it so blue before.

'I must get the loan of a boat some day and take you for a cruise. Would you come?'

'I might,' she said doubtfully.

He assured her that she needn't be afraid; and he'd promise on his solemn oath he'd take nothing aboard except a bottle of water, a few sandwiches, and two guaranteed lifejackets. She'd decide after Easter, she said, and with that she parted from him. Going up to the house she was smiling to herself but, on seeing Elizabeth sitting in the sun in front of the house, she put on a graver face. Elizabeth had her eyes closed, and two kittens were playing at her feet around the bench. Her face was yellow and shrivelled, and her hands lay loose on her lap. Nora stepped lightly, intending to go in without disturbing her, but Elizabeth heard her.

'I'm just dozing, girl. I had Helen here for an hour or two and she brought me a warm bed jacket as a little present. It's good to have kind and thoughtful neighbours near you. I couldn't say a word to her about her scarcity of visits since Christmas. However, she's very kind.'

She attempted to get up and Nora held out a hand and helped her.

'I get stiff now when I sit any length of time. I'm not as supple as I used to be. And Father Lacy forbids me to go to Mass till the dregs of the old flu have fled from me.'

Resting on Nora's arm she guided her round to the orchard where the sun shone through the trees in stilts of light. Johnny was digging at the far end, the soil brown and dry, and a robin hopping close to his spade.

'When you come back after Easter you'll see great changes in everything. Everything will grow with a rush. Thanks be to God for the spring!' and she gave Nora's arm a friendly squeeze and asked her why she was so quiet.

'I suppose I'm a bit tired after my day in school.'

'If it's anything to do with Murphy, as Helen has hinted, put him out of your head. He's not much good — at least he wouldn't suit you.'

'There's really nothing between us except that we teach in the same school.'

'I'm glad to have your word for it.'

Mary tapped the back window and called them for their dinner.

And that evening as Nora was going out for a walk, before the sun had set, Elizabeth suggested that Mary should go with her: Mary was too much stuck in the house all day and a walk in the air would do her a world of good. Nora sat down at the piano to wait for her to get ready, and as she played a few pieces, more to appease Elizabeth than to please herself, it suddenly occurred to her that this evening she should take Mary into her confidence. If she told her it would surely reach Helen and Peter before she had returned from the holidays. She would tell it easily, and as it were casually, without the semblance of secrecy.

Her fingers rippled over the keyboard as she sped through Debussy's First Arabesque, and when she had finished she sat back and closed the piano, blending that gesture into the mood of the piece.

'I never heard you play better,' Elizabeth said.

'Nor did I,' sided Mary, who had been standing unnoticed at the open door.

'I'm sorry I didn't keep up my music after I left the boarding school, Elizabeth said.' 'The nuns used always to be writing to mother and telling her I had a natural gift for it. Isn't that so, Mary?'

Mary was gently tracing the design of the carpet with her walking-stick and pretended not to hear her. She raised her head and looked at Nora: 'We'd better go before the daylight leaves the roads.'

'If I go to bed before you're back I'll leave the key in the door.'

They walked to a rise on the road where they could see the open lough below them, one lone collier on it like a child's boat, and a few round islands fringed with trees like candles on a birthday cake. The sun had set and a frosty mist covered the horizon.

'I suppose on many a summer day you sailed down there with your father?' Nora said.

'I was only on the lough once, but it wasn't with my father,' and she embarked on a long story of a motor-boat excursion which Father Lacy had organized only a few years back. 'That's the only time I was on the water in my life. It's hard to believe it, but it's true — and I was over sixty years of age at the time. Elizabeth was further afield than that — she was in Lourdes.'

'When I was only nine my father brought me and my sister

188

Eileen to France. That was a long, long journey for two little girls.'

'I didn't know you had a sister till now. And what does she do, Nora?'

'Oh, she's dead. She was only sixteen when she died in a sanatorium.'

'Dear, oh, dear! She hadn't begun to live you may say, before she was taken from you. You've had more than your share of trouble, Nora. Your mother and your father. . . .'

'Mother died in the same sanatorium as Eileen. But I suppose you know all about that from Father Lacy.'

'No, Nora, we didn't. He never gossips — not in that way,' and she hugged Nora's arm tightly to her side. Mary didn't know what else she should say or what to do: and she sensed, without being told, that a heart's secret had been revealed to her.

'I'll remember them always in my prayers, Nora. I will indeed.'

Nora avoided her warm and candid look — a look that was like a reproach to her own cold and calculated honesty. She was only using her to spread abroad what she herself hadn't the courage to do. And instead of relief and ease a dry, joyless sensation began to oppress her.

They fell silent as they strolled back along the road that was already losing its greyness under the edge of dark. Lights from the scattered homes were beginning to glimmer over the ploughed fields and a few tiny stars were wrestling with their own light.

Nora tried to rouse herself, tried to hum but the tune died on her lips.

'God love you, but you've the light step,' Mary exclaimed. 'For myself I haven't a tint of breath left in me.'

They walked more slowly as they neared the house. A light from Elizabeth's bedroom shone out upon the chestnut trees, their hard buds gleaming like polished acorns.

'I'm done out,' Mary sighed and plumped down on the bench

in front of the house. Nora sat down beside her and Mary grasped her hand. She poked at the pebbles on the path with her walking-stick and gazed at the patch of lawn illuminated by the light from the room above her.

'In two days' time you'll have gone from us again, Nora.'

'I will. This term has flown in.'

'Bad and all as the winter was you braved it well'; and she sat so close to her that Nora could feel her warm breath upon her cheek. 'You didn't take the flu and you weren't a day absent from the school. This place agrees with you.'

'It does, Mary. I'm very happy here.'

'And we're happy to have you. Indeed we are.'

The light was extinguished in the room above them and they were suddenly surprised at the darkness and at the handful of stars sparkling like a child's firework among the chestnut trees.

'We'll go in. It's foolish for an old woman like me to be sitting out here.'

✿ 14 ✿

THAT night, after Nora had gone to bed, Mary sat alone in the firelight of the kitchen. She had just finished her prayers, and her beads lay on her lap. She didn't hear Johnny clatter across the yard or see the light from his window go out or hear the clock in the sitting-room chime out its hours. There had settled on her mind a chilling dread, a dread to which she could give no name. What lay ahead she did not know, could not even guess at. She wasn't frightened of what Nora had told her or afraid that the girl was ill in any unseen way. No, she had no fear of that, thanks to the good God. And there was no reason why she should ever have — a woman of her time of day who had lived out most of her span of life; and would live it all over again, but in a different way, if such a thing as a second chance were given to her. Nora's presence had shown to them what she and Elizabeth had missed: they should have married; and even if their children were grown up and left the nest they would still have their days and nights filled with talk of them, with letters from them, and their children's children coming to stay with them in the long days of summer. As it was, Nora was like an adopted daughter and she felt towards her what a mother must feel when the love between them is being gnawed by some force which they can't control or foresee.

She sighed deeply, poked up the remains of the fire, and sat quite still. Yes, the love that held them would be snapped as soon as she'd confess to Elizabeth what she had just heard. She recalled the autumn day Nora had first arrived in the house: her pale face, her unaired look, and how Elizabeth had forewarned that they had brought a delicate girl amongst them. But since then her looks had undergone a change for the better: and at no time did Nora ever complain of being ill except when that rascal Maguire had tortured her — a rascal that'd have worried heart and soul out of any teacher. And tonight she never looked better — so tall and slim, and the fine strike of her shoe on the road. But would Elizabeth notice these things if the truth were told to her? She would not indeed! She'd only notice what would feed her doubts: she'd be alarmed if Nora coughed, and she'd be pleading with her to rest more, to visit the doctor often, and to open her windows wide at night. But what was worse she might, without hinting at her trouble, ask her to seek accommodation elsewhere. Yes, that's what Elizabeth would do! It'd be wiser not to tell her anything, and so allow the life and peace of the house to go on as usual. And, then, some day she could mention to Nora she hadn't spoken to anyone about the heart-to-heart talks they'd had together: Nora would know rightly what she meant by that.

She got up from her chair. The fire had burned down in the grate, and in the sharp frame of the window a few stars glittered like frost. She lit her lamp and quietly climbed the stairs. On the landing she halted and inclined her ear towards Nora's room and then to Elizabeth's: there wasn't a sound. The whole house was at rest.

For the first few days after Easter she held firm to her intention. She avoided Elizabeth's company as much as possible. She overstayed her time in the kitchen, worked in the garden, and in the evenings, because Helen dropped in now to see Elizabeth, she made off to the chapel to do the Stations of the Cross. She hoped to continue like this till Nora's vacation was at an end. But one evening on her return from the chapel she was surprised to see Elizabeth sitting alone in the sitting-room and the fire almost gone out. She hadn't time to take off her hat and coat before Elizabeth was scolding her for scampering out of the house at every opportunity.

'It's Easter week and I've my devotions to attend to.'

'You've suddenly grown very pious. Piety should increase your kindness, but I don't see much of that with you. I'm a very lonely woman and, at the moment, a semi-invalid.

You've forgotten some of the corporal works of mercy.'

'I thought Helen was company enough for you these evenings.'

'She didn't drop in this evening, and I've been sitting all alone shivering in this cold room.'

'Why didn't you put some coal on the fire? There's no sense nor grace in trying to martyr yourself unnecessarily.'

'In my present condition the coal-bucket is too heavy for me to carry in from the kitchen. You should have filled that coal-scuttle there, before gallivanting out of the house.'

'I'm sorry, Elizabeth.'

'Your sorrow won't be of much help if my cold is renewed. You never give a thought these days to your own sister. You think of no one only your own self. Even since Nora left I haven't heard you speak of her once. And yet her name is never out of Helen's mouth — but not in a way that pleases me.'

'What has she got to say, pray?'

'From all sides she has heard that Murphy and Nora are as thick as thieves. Now, isn't it a great wonder you haven't heard it and you frisking about these days like a stray goat?'

'I never heard it from anyone. And what's more I don't believe one word of it!'

'There's no smoke without fire. Maybe I shouldn't say that and me staring at that smoky grate all the evening,' and she shrugged her shoulders and sniffed loudly.

'It's Helen herself that's spreading that silly rumour.'

'Mary, you've no right to say that! Nora hasn't told you anything about it, has she?'

'No.'

'I thought so. I asked her about it and she denied it.'

'That should be enough for you.'

'It isn't enough. There's a darkness about that girl that sometimes puzzles me. There are days when you'd hardly get a word out of her. You'd think a doctor's daughter would have more to say for herself.'

193

'We can't go probing into her mind like a lawyer. We must have reverence for the differences in people.'

'Are you standing up there trying to lecture me, Miss Mary Devlin? I won't have it, I tell you!'

'I'll go and make something warm — that's what we both need,' and she hastened from the room to escape any more unpleasantness.

She raked up the fire in the range, prepared a tray with cake and sandwiches, and made the tea in Elizabeth's favourite silver teapot. As she carried the tray down the hall she called out cheerily: 'Here's the tea at last!' but when she pushed open the door with her toe she found the room in darkness and Elizabeth gone to bed. She brought it up to her, and without a word of protest she said gently: 'Sit up, Elizabeth dear, and take this. It will help to ward off the cold.' She fixed the pillows at her back and praised the softness of Helen's bedjacket which she was wearing. 'And now while you're taking the tea, hand me your hot water bottle and I'll heat it up again.'

'There's no hot jar in the bed!'

'How on earth did I forget to leave it up?'

'Like everything else of late! You've no head or heart for my poor needs. You're all bound up with your own selfish concerns. Selfishness — that's your besetting vice. Pure, downright selfishness!'

Without one word of defence Mary withdrew from the room. She filled up the hot water bottle, but Elizabeth didn't thank her or look at her when it was brought to her.

'Your tea all right, Elizabeth?'

'A bit on the strong side. I hope it won't keep me awake.'

'Like a little hot water in it?'

'Well, no. The harm's already done and I feel very wakeful. You needn't bother waiting for this tray, I'll leave it out on the landing when I'm finished. I'm sorry I give so much trouble. Good night.' And she did not raise her eyes to look at Mary standing so penitently beside her.

That night as she lay in bed Mary asked herself over and over again if she had neglected Elizabeth of late. She dwelt on the accusation that was darted at her: Selfishness! — and the word rose before her in letters as big as those on a hoarding. She tried to wrest it from her mind but it pressed itself all the more blackly forward, and with it jogged the words: Disloyal and Deceitful. She created a hideous picture of herself — a picture of a lost and wretched soul. Was she seeking her own selfish ends in not telling Elizabeth everything? Could she truthfully say it was really Nora she was concerned with and not herself? Was it fear of losing Nora's company that kept her silent? The questions danced in front of her, and skipped off, before she had time to answer them. If Nora had only pledged her to secrecy she'd be at peace and wouldn't be tossing and twisting with this jagged load upon her mind. And there was no one she could bring her trouble to — no one. Her mind swept from the house and followed the familiar and friendly roads outside; it halted for a moment with Peter, said nothing, and went further along, past the school-house to Father Lacy. There was no need to go further. She'd ask him. Yes, that's what she'd do: she'd ask his advice and act on it. And she wouldn't rehearse her words. She'd just call on him and say her say without any quibblings or nibblings.

'In God's name,' she said aloud to herself in the darkness, 'put it out of your mind till you see him.' The decision eased her and she turned to sleep.

The following evening Helen came over, and Mary dressed herself quietly and slipped off without a word to Elizabeth where she was going. After visiting the chapel she went round to the priest's house. The place was in darkness, but as soon as she rang the bell the electric light was switched on above her head and the housekeeper led her into the sitting-room where Father Lacy was bent over a chess-board solving a problem.

'Well, well, Mary, this is a pleasant surprise. You're just in time to join me in a nice cup of coffee.'

'No, no, Father, I wouldn't have time for that — thanks all the same. I have to hurry back,' and her eyes flickered from the brilliant light on the wall to the black kid gloves on her lap. 'I've a bit of worry on my mind, Father,' and she placed one glove on top of the other and tapped them on her lap.

'Is Elizabeth's health worrying you — is that it?'

'No, Father; it's about Nora — I mean Miss Byrne.'

'And what's she been doing on you?'

'Oh, nothing! She's a good, kind, lovable girl.'

'Yes, Mary.'

'I'm afraid I'm making a fool of myself. You see — at least it's this way. She told me just the other evening; she told me that her mother and sister died in a sanatorium.'

'I see; and you're worried that she may have . . .'

'Oh, no, Father, it's not that at all. It's because I haven't told Elizabeth — and it's that that's worrying me.'

He didn't interrupt her; he joined the tips of his fingers together and gazed at the fire; if he waited patiently he'd get to understand, sooner than later, what her trouble really was.

'It's this way, Father: Nora hasn't told Elizabeth and I want to know if I should tell her.'

'Has Nora Byrne asked you to keep it secret?'

'I wish she had, Father. I'd have no worry on my mind if she had done that.'

'But why do you wish to keep it from Elizabeth?' — and he ran his hand over his face to hide his smile.

'Because . . . because Elizabeth would ask her to leave the house. I'm sure of that, Father — I am indeed.'

'It's a bit of a teaser, Mary, no mistake about that. It's mixed up with your affection for Nora Byrne and with your love for your sister Elizabeth.'

He joined the tips of his fingers together, glanced at the chess-board and thought it easier to solve a problem in chess than one in ethics — in many ways they were similar, each having to be approached as a new and individual case. He smiled and looked at her with friendly solicitude. 'You shouldn't worry yourself unduly about this matter, Mary. It will all work out smoothly.'

'I'm to tell Elizabeth?' and she shook her head sadly. 'No sooner will I have told her than she'll reel it off to Helen Lynch, and everything will be broken off.'

'What'll be broken off?'

'Peter, I think, is in love with Nora. I'm not too sure, but I feel he is. They're very great with one another.'

'The problem deepens; there are more moves in it than I thought. Have you any reason for supposing that they don't already know about Miss Byrne's mother and sister?'

'I have, Father. Elizabeth and myself would have heard the blunt truth from Helen ages ago.'

'I see,' he said, staring at the chess-board: not much use in calling in a bishop to solve this problem. He moved a knight on the board. He joined his hands on the table. 'Most of what you told me concerns Miss Byrne, and I'd cease worrying and let things rest for a while. Wait till Miss Byrne comes back after the holidays: she'll know what to do.'

'So I'll not tell Elizabeth?'

'If it would cause her any anxiety or cause any unpleasantness, it would be better not to. Just let the hen sit. When Elizabeth has regained her health she'll be in a healthier frame of mind to listen to you without alarm.'

'Thank you, Father; that's a load off my mind.'

'Off yours on to mine — is that it, you old heathen?'

'The poor girl didn't know what she was doing on me, or she'd have kept quiet. I'm to wait a month?'

'We needn't be too exact about the time. The time for it will come without our measuring it. In your attitude towards Elizabeth just try to forget what Miss Byrne has told you. And, Mary, don't be busy about too many things — especially about people's love affairs.'

'You're very kind, Father.'

'I hope I'm very wise,' and he replaced the knight in its former position.

'I'll go now, for I've a whole lot of things to do before bed-time.'

He went out of the room with her and switched on the light above the hall door, and as she walked down the path her shadow walked in front of her. She waved to him from the gate, and as she strode off she thought of the comfort there'd be in their own house when they had the electric installed.

✿ 15 ✿

At the end of a fortnight, on a Saturday afternoon, Nora was back again after her Easter vacation. It was like coming home, she told herself, as she walked out from the little town, having left her bag in the grocer's for Johnny to collect. In front of her the road stretched blue, the hedges were turning green, and in the fields the cattle walked stiffly, their hides dry and dishevelled after their long enclosure in the unsunned byres. At the estuary the tide was full in, a gentle breeze leaving its fingerprints on the water, and two men red-leading an upturned boat at the water's edge.

Elizabeth and Mary were sitting on the bench in the sun as she entered the gate, and she was half-way up the path before they heard the sound of her step, both turning their heads simultaneously and shading their eyes at her approach.

'It's Nora! Welcome back!' Mary exclaimed, putting her arms round her and planting her on the bench between the two of them.

'We didn't expect you till the evening or till tomorrow,' Elizabeth said, prodding her stick at the pebbles in front of her.

'There's only one train on Sundays from Strabane and it didn't suit.'

'It wouldn't have mattered one snap if you'd come a week earlier. We're always glad to see you and sorry when you go. Your room's aired and ready for you,' Mary said, involuntarily screwing up her eyes towards the window that was wide open to get its fill of the blessed sun.

'You're both looking well,' Nora said, doubtful of Elizabeth's welcome.

'I'm afraid the only thing that looks well is the fresh greenery of the fields,' Elizabeth complained, and launched into a tedious account of her long sleepless nights and the shuttling pains in

199

her legs. 'And into the bargain, I've no energy left in me for my crocheting and knitting or helping poor Mary with the housework.'

She's gradually preparing a polite way to get rid of me, Nora thought. But the next moment, as Elizabeth took her hand in hers and admired the healthy pink of her nails and their large half-moons, she resolved not to be so sensitive and boldly decided to pass on to Elizabeth some advice her own doctor had given to her on a recent visit.

'You should try to change your attitude towards your sleeplessness, Elizabeth. Don't worry over it, for worrying can do you more harm than the countless sleepless nights. Just say to yourself when you're in bed: "I'm resting all my limbs; my heart's at rest, and as the days improve I'll improve with them." '

'God help your wit, child. If you'd a mob of pains flying helter-skelter through your legs you just can't say to them: "Behave yourselves, I'm going to sleep." '

'You sleep far more than you imagine,' Mary said, impatient to change to a healthier subject.

'You've no right to say that to me!'

Elizabeth was irritable these days without reason; she'd blaze up at a harmless remark, and Mary was afraid that she'd fly into a tantrum and lose her dignity in front of Nora.

A silence fell; Elizabeth jabbed at the pebbles on the path, Mary squeezed at a green paint-bubble on the bench, and Nora stared at the chestnut trees with their clusters of green leaves pointing upwards like toy umbrellas.

'The trees have come on well since you left,' Mary said. 'It'll not be long till the spiders are swinging their hammocks from branch to branch, and it won't be long now till you'll hear the blackbirds and the thrushes testing their voices in the early morning and in the evening. It gives me great heart listening to them.'

'They wouldn't be in much fettle for musical caperings if they had one of my pains.'

Mary cleared her throat and raised her eyes to the sky where a pure white cloud, overfed and lazy, was shouldering its way towards the sun. In a few minutes it had swept the sunlight away from their lawn, Elizabeth sneezed, and without a word they all rose and went into the house.

And as day followed day Nora, always prepared for a subtle change of affection, could perceive no alteration in their hospitality or their friendliness towards her, and she herself felt less constrained with them. It was true that Elizabeth was touchy but it was always with Mary that she quarrelled; and in the evenings after she had gone to bed Mary and Nora used to whisper together like conspirators and arrange the best methods of humouring her. And in those evenings with their heads close together and their breaths mingling, as they laughed over their manœuvres, Nora realized with conviction that Mary never gave a thought to herself or her health.

And in Peter, too, she perceived no change; he often dropped in to see the Devlins, bringing with him a piece of music which he would like Nora to play for him. And during school hours he was often in and out of her room on the slightest of excuses: inquiring about absentees or about clever boys that should be promoted rapidly, or to hand her the latest catalogue of new books for the infant department. She always listened to him keenly, seeking for a hint or clue that would show her how much he knew now about her family. Did the Devlins tell him all, during the Easter holidays? she wondered; and time and again she was on the point of asking Mary, but, for some reason, either of upbringing or timidity, she held back. She would sense his knowledge of it soon enough, without her stirring to meet it or raise it.

She had a few rounds of golf with him but displayed no progress in it or enthusiasm for it. She went because he coaxed her, and because she enjoyed his company and felt refreshed and rested when out in the clean air that blew over the smooth turf.

One Saturday as she sent the turf flying and felt a flush of annoyance at her awkwardness he said smilingly: 'Bleed, bleed, poor country,' and with amiable patience demonstrated how to swing the club sweetly, to keep her eye on the ball, and not to give a tinker's curse for any straggler that might be eyeing them from a window in the club-house.

'You did well this evening,' he said with pride as they strolled back from the links by the long road near the coal-quay. 'And do you know why? — because you did what I told you.'

'But I always do what you tell me.'

'Except one thing.'

'And what's that?'

'Come and finish off the evening with me and Helen.'

'If I started that, I may as well shift my digs and live with both of you entirely.'

'That'd be the very thing that we'd want.'

'I wonder, would it?' she laughed, and called his attention to a yacht that was passing up the channel.

'To blazes with yachts! Do you remember what I said to you here on the night of the concert?'

'I'm not likely to forget it.'

'You don't regret it, Nora — honestly?'

'No, Peter, I do not.'

Two women with baskets of groceries covered with brown paper passed them and bid them good evening, and Nora quickened her pace and led the conversation away from that which disturbed her. She talked without ceasing till she reached the gate where Elizabeth was superintending Johnny as he painted the bars in fresh green. They stood to watch him. He was nearly finished, and he was maintaining that he didn't believe in having metal gates near the sea: they were a botheration and were always falling in rusty flakes at the first touch of sea air. He'd prefer no gate at all, Elizabeth was countering: a wooden gate would grow soft with rain if it weren't painted regularly. If there were any brains in the country they should be able to make a gate with concrete rods, Johnny contended, and appealed to Peter for support. Peter smiled and nodded, and Nora knew he wasn't listening.

He resisted Elizabeth's invitation to tea and stood on, wishing she would go away and leave them. But Nora stood close to her, and as he parted from them his sad and reproachful look confronted her with piteous accusation, and remained with her throughout the evening like an echo of her own conscience.

And late that night, discovering that Mary was still moving around the kitchen, she hastened down to her and confessed her love for Peter and his love for her.

'That's great news. May God direct and spare both of you. It's what I've been praying for all along.'

'You needn't tell Elizabeth for a while yet,' she whispered. 'She knows, of course, about my mother and sister?'

'No, Nora, she doesn't. I didn't tell her. I thought, perhaps, it was ... Och, I don't know what I thought.'

'Do tell her. It would be easier for you, than for me, to speak of it. Later on we can let her in on this other matter. Good night, Mary; and thanks and thanks for all you've done for me.'

Next morning, Sunday, Nora rose for the early Mass. She went to Holy Communion, spent a long time in thanksgiving, and on coming out from the chapel found that the usual groups of gossipers had gone from the gate and that there was no one there except Peter, smoking his pipe and waiting for her.

'Dammit all, I thought you were never going to come out. I hope you included me in your litanies for I'm not much of a craw-thumper even at the worst of times. But here's what I want to say — would you come for a drive after dinner?' and he began to describe the loveliest bay in Ireland that he'd bring her to. They could have the whole warm day to themselves. She could have a swim, if she liked, and a bit of golf on the sheep-lands above the bay — a place where they could hack up the whole countryside without a critical word from anyone. She'd go, of course she would; and he spoke with a quick enthusiasm that, for some reason, seemed to foreshorten the disparity in their years, and made her feel that she was the elder of the two. They walked slowly, stopping to admire the growth in his schoolboys' plots, and halting at his own garden where the tulips were opening their moist lips to the warm sun. The windows in the house were flung wide and the curtains hanging still. As he stooped to cut some tulips with his penknife he hoped Helen would appear at a window and wave out to them. But there was no movement at all about the house except the black smoke from the chimney. He held the bunch of tulips in his hand, and shook the dew from their heavy heads before giving them to her. She held them in her arms and smelt their damp fragrance.

'If I had known they were for me I wouldn't have let you cut so many.'

'They're not for you,' he smiled. 'They're for the Miss Devlins, and you can give them my best love along with them.'

'I'll be able to manage part of that.'

'I'll call over for you at two,' and he raised his eyes to the blue sky. 'That day will turn out a real scorcher. Goodbye till two o'clock.' He walked up the path, smiling to himself as if recalling something very pleasant.

At the breakfast table Helen tackled him about hanging around with Miss Byrne so much that he'd be sure to get himself talked about. 'I don't mind who talks about us,' he answered, with a shrug.

'All I have to say is: you can't play around with her as if you were an engaged pair.'

'You told me yourself it was Luke Murphy her name was linked with.'

'I've only related what I've heard. And I hope you'll tell me frankly if there's anything between you and this girl.'

'I enjoy her company.'

'Isn't that the prelude to something more serious? A man of your years is not so innocent as to think otherwise. She'll think it if you don't. For the life of me, I don't know what you see in her. For one thing she hasn't the bloom of health about her. And she thinks of nothing but dress.'

'I like to see a girl well dressed,' he said quietly, and poured out a cup of tea for himself. 'And anyway, you should be the last to sit in judgment on her: you've avoided meeting her at every turn and you only visit the Devlins when she's not there.'

'I don't deny it.'

'Then you shouldn't be critical of her till you know her.'

'I don't intend to give myself the displeasure of knowing her.'

'Some day you might have to.'

'So there is something serious going on between you!'

'I tell you there's nothing — yet.'

'I'm glad you're honest enough to add the *yet*. And when do you expect there will be?' she asked with polite scorn.

'I'm driving her over to Benderg, this afternoon.'

'You're a refined shifter and I can't fathom you,' she added crossly. 'If my life is to be ruined I'd better know now.'

'How ruined? Sure if Nora Byrne happened to marry me, the house is big enough for us all.'

'So you have everything planned!'

'There's nothing planned, I tell you.'

'I've given the best part of my life to make you comfortable — and this is how I'm to be rewarded: bringing a stranger into the house I made.'

'Many a one has to live with three or four of their in-laws, and are glad of it.'

'I'm not that kind!'

'You should try to be. Fling off this stupid selfish attitude: receive the girl with open arms and you'll agree with Mary Devlin that she's a lovely, gentle girl.'

'That's a hard remark, Peter: one that I'm not likely to forget. To think that after all my work for you, you can call me "selfish".'

'I didn't say you were selfish: I said you were taking up a selfish attitude to this whole business. I'm not going to speak another word about it: for all I know, Miss Byrne might be engaged to someone in her home town.'

She closed her eyes and covered her face with her hands. 'To think that my own brother would accuse me of selfishness!' she cried over and over again, refusing to listen to his explanation or his apology.

In the afternoon he drove over for Nora, and in order to avoid passing his house again, they went through the town and up over the hilly road that switchbacked to the open sea. He parked the car at a tumbledown house, and carrying her basket and a rug he linked her arm and hurried her under fences and across fields till they reached the headland overlooking his favourite bay. Nora was glad to stand still, for a stitch was in her side and her breathing was sharp and quick.

'Wasn't it worth the walk?' he said, pressing her arm, and looking down at the stretch of white sand and a few children bathing at the water's edge. His eye ranged inland to the Mourne mountains, to the wide sweeping freshness of the fields, and to ladders of light stretching from a cloud's edge down to the sea. 'The freshest country in the world! When God made it He didn't insult us!' he exclaimed.

'And you running out of it to France for your holidays,' she teased.

'But I don't go to admire their scenery. I go for a change — a complete one: language, people, customs. But at the end I'm glad to come back here.'

He suddenly grasped her arm, and as they raced down through the bent grass, the cups rattled in the basket, and two pewits rose up screaming and shot down above them as Peter spread the rug on the ground.

'We'll have to shift our tent, we must be near their nest,' he said, and searching around he came upon three blotched pear-shaped eggs lying in a hoof-print among gravel and bits of snail-shells. He called to Nora, but though he stood a yard from the eggs she couldn't find them till he had stooped directly above them.

When they had moved further along the bay the birds ceased following them, and Nora sat down with her hands clasped about her knees and stared at the smooth sheen upon the sea. Her cheeks were pale, and as she breathed in deeply, a little curve of strain gathered about the corners of her mouth. She wished Peter would sit still for a while; but he was full of activity and when he had jumped over the bent grass and she could hear his feet crunching on the dry seaweed in search of driftwood to light a fire she was too weary to shout to him and tell him she hadn't brought a kettle.

In about ten minutes he was back, his auburn hair fallen over his brow, and a bundle of sticks in his arm.

'It's a flask of tomato soup Mary put in the basket,' she said, and smiled up at him. He let the sticks fall at his feet, unloosed his collar, and sat beside her: 'But we must have a fire. We couldn't say we had a picnic without a fire of some sort.'

'You'll not mind much, Peter, if I don't bathe. I think I'll postpone my first dip till the summer. I'm an awful coward in many ways.'

He coaxed her for a moment and then suddenly desisted. She'd paddle her feet in the water's edge and watch him — that's the bravest effort she could make.

He went into a hollow to undress, and after he had raced over the sand and had lunged into the water she took off her shoes and stockings and followed after him. There was nothing domineering about him, she thought: he had respect for her wishes and didn't try to wrench her to his own way — she loved him for that.

He was a powerful swimmer, and presently the smooth water was alive with little rafts of light. She swirled her feet in the water and watched the tiny flat fish with sand on their backs skim over the bottom. He swam towards her and she saw his strong shoulders gleam like polished wood. He disappeared below the surface and rose near her, flinging back his hair.

'It's lovely,' he said, standing beside her, the water wriggling like tiny eels upon his shoulders. His breathing was loud and deep, and she sensed its strength in the rise and fall of his chest. He plunged into the water again, and coming out he stripped the water from his arms and ran along the strand to dry himself.

She sat on a flat rock, her feet in a warm pool, and saw the tide come in: little waves, like long bars of shadow, running in towards the shore and darkening deeply before breaking and flattening upon the sand. She daubed her eyes and forehead with the salt water and raised her face to the warm sun. She felt at rest now, and a great peace spreading round her. He called to her a few times before she heard him, and when she turned round she saw his towel drying on the bent grass and smoke from a fire rising straight into the air.

He watched her intently as she came across the sand in her green serge frock, her shadow walking beside her. He ran to meet her and carried her over the stones above tide mark.

'I'm sorry I didn't go in, after all.'

'You missed it. But we'll come again soon.'

'You'll be hungry now after your swim,' and she walked over the rug in her bare feet and took the cups and sandwiches from the basket. Her black hair lying loose upon her shoulders shone in the sun, and as she turned and caught his glance he said: 'Nora Angela Byrne!'

'That's my full name. They used to nickname me Nab in the convent school.'

'There was something I wanted to say to you yesterday evening, but I didn't get the chance.'

'And are you sure you've got it now?'

'For one thing there's nobody near us painting a gate. Listen, Nora, do you think you could grow fond of me?'

'No, I don't think I could,' she said, making creases in the rug

208

with a spoon. 'I'm beyond that, Peter. The plain truth is that I love you.'

'Could you think of marrying me, then?' and he put his arm round her and drew her towards him.

'I could — but there are difficulties.'

'Difficulties about our age, Nora?'

'No, Peter, it's not that. It has nothing to do with yourself in any way.'

'Has it something to do with Helen?'

She shook her head.

'Luke Murphy?'

'Hardly.'

'Then it's nothing at all,' he said, kissing her till she broke away from him.

'I love you, Peter; God knows I do — much more than I've a right to.'

'Say yes — you'll marry me?'

'Give me a week or so.'

'I'll give you a year, if you like, as long as you say yes.'

'Perhaps the final yes will rest with you.'

'To hear you one would think you'd a few children hidden somewhere up the country.'

'Peter, we'll not talk any more about it now.'

He smoothed the grey parting on her brow and held her head firmly; he tried to get her to look steadily at him, but she lowered her eyes and rested her head against his breast. What she wanted to say she couldn't say; she had no strength against his strength; no strength to crush the power that held her to him against her will. She would wait, but not for long. It would come — and all would be revealed to make or break this love between them.

The sun had swung low when they were leaving, the tide coming in, the headland's shadow lengthening itself on the sand, and startled rabbits racing back to their burrows. He shook the sand from the dried towel and draped it round his neck, and as they climbed to the top of the slope the two pewits screamed around them and larks rose singing into the bright evening air.

Nora's face was red from the sun, and as she came in that evening Elizabeth said she had never seen her looking better. She had been sitting out on the lawn for the warmer part of the day, and though it was Sunday she had done her crocheting and given herself a dispensation because the work was for the Foreign Missions. She was glad to hear that Nora didn't bathe, for she didn't believe that the water was warm enough yet for that kind of nonsense.

Nora was drowsy and they persuaded her to go to bed and round off the day with a long sleep.

'Since the day she stepped across our threshold I've never seen a girl so well improved,' Elizabeth said, draping a skein of wool over the back of a chair and commencing to wind it into a ball.

'I'm after saying I've never seen Nora so well improved.'

'Yes, Elizabeth.'

'You seem to regret she isn't. What's wrong with you at all?'

'Nothing, Elizabeth dear.'

'Well, if you're going to sit there like a dumb crow you'd be much better in your bed.'

'Don't be vexed with me. For a long time I've wanted to tell you a little thing — a thing about Nora.'

'Something she told you or something you've surmised?'

'Don't interrupt or muddle me, please. I'm worried.'

Elizabeth sighed with heavy impatience, wound up the ball grimly, and glanced from the shaking skein of wool to Mary's bowed head. She pursed her lips, and shut her eyes in bored contempt as Mary shuffled about with words as if they burnt her tongue.

'You've said nothing sensible so far. I'm not a bit eager to hear the rest of the riddle-raddle, for I'm sure it's some nonsensical trash that wouldn't upset a child. If you could tell me in plain language what your trouble really is I might be of some help.'

'It's about Nora.'

'So I've gathered.'

'It's about her parents.'

'They're both dead, so they're not likely to harm you in this world.'

'She had a sister.'

'That's news — and is she in jail or what?'

'She's dead too.'

'Why couldn't you say that fifteen minutes ago and have done with it?'

'The poor girl died in a sanatorium — her sister did, and so did her poor mother.'

'Oh,' and Elizabeth finished her winding and placed the ball in her work-basket. She remembered Nora had told her of her mother but had made no allusion to the manner of her death or had even hinted that she had had a sister. She removed her spectacles, fixed them slowly in her case, and snapped it shut.

'From whom did you get this piece of information?' and her voice changed from irritable impatience to cold sharpness.

'Nora.'

'When?'

'I can't remember exactly.'

She released a volley of questions and Mary rose to escape from them.

'You're not leaving this room till I've tracked down everything. Your own sister must be your first consideration in this matter. If there's deceit and secrecy going on behind my back I'll stamp it out as I would a fire.'

Within an hour she had dragged everything from Mary except the visit to Father Lacy, and she was surprised and peeved that Mary had concealed this news since before Easter.

'The girl always looked delicate and it was likely that she, too, was a consumptive. She would have to seek other apartments after the summer. In all justice they couldn't keep her any longer than that,' Elizabeth said.

'We are at the heel of our days,' Mary pleaded, 'and it's little harm, but much happiness, she can bring to the likes of us.'

'She'll have to go.'

'The house will never be the same.'

'We'll lapse into our old ways again after she's gone. I don't want any tears. I love her as much as you, but we must be prudent in this matter. Does Peter know about this?'

'I don't know,' Mary cried.

'Well, he should know, and it's our duty to inform him. He's an old and trusted friend.'

'It's unwise to meddle in people's love affairs.'

'What do you know about love affairs? You that seldom read anything stronger than *The Irish Messenger*. Leave all this to me. I always knew there was something sly and secretive about that girl. But to think she runs to you with her paltry secrets! Being a teacher, she should have more sense in her head. She's beginning to contaminate you with her weasely ways — I can see that. But I'll not live in a house where there's one shadow of deceit — I will not.'

'Promise not to say anything hurtful to her, Elizabeth dear.'

'Don't dare to stand up and dictate to me what I should do or what I shouldn't. I'm the head of this establishment. You can go now. I'll quench the lamp and make my way upstairs in my own time.'

'What will Father Lacy say if we turn her out of our house?'

'It's we who have to live with her, and we'll decide this for ourselves.'

'I'd go away with her tomorrow if I could.'

'Go upstairs at once, and don't aggravate me any more with your nonsense.'

✿ 16 ✿

THE following evening Peter was looking out at the first swallows skimming low across his garden when he saw Mary and Elizabeth passing on the road on their way to May devotions in the chapel. He knew Nora would be alone in the house and, without hesitating, he decided to go across and spend the evening with her.

As he turned in at the gate he saw her resting on a deckchair on the sunny lawn. Her arms were under her head, a book face-downward on her lap, and her eyes closed. He stood still and stared across at her. Her arms showed through the transparency of her white blouse, and her face had a strained expression that disturbed him. The shadow of a silver birch stretched as far as her feet, and behind her, dragged against the hedge, was a chestnut bough that had been cut down, all its upright blossoms tilting sadly towards the sun. There was not a sound, and as he watched her slow breathing his own pulse beat wildly in his breast. He withdrew on tiptoe to the road, his face flushed, fearing she'd waken and catch him spying on her. But she didn't hear him or see him; and coming back again he whistled and rattled the pebbles on the path and she sat up with a jerk and sent her book on to the lawn.

'I'm sorry I've frightened you.'

'No, no,' she said, pulling on a grey cardigan. 'I was just dozing in the last of the sun. Mary and Elizabeth went to devotions and left me in charge.'

'I saw them and knew you'd be alone.'

'And you came to keep me company,' and she plumped up a cushion on a deck-chair beside her. He sat down taking her hand and locking his fingers in hers. She had a chestnut blossom in her other hand and she held it up to him to catch its faint perfume. He took it from her and tossed it on her lap, determined to make the most of their meeting.

213

'Have you thought over what I asked you yesterday?'

'I have, Peter,' and she looked at the hand that held hers, its fine hairs catching the sun. 'I have,' she sighed, 'but it will not be easy for me to tell you.'

'It'll be as easy now as it will ever be. It's no use measuring out the days like a calendar and deciding on such and such a date. Come on, Nora, we'll thrash it out now together.'

'I love you; you know that.'

'That's a lovely beginning for a story — the rest will come easy.'

'But it's not my love for you that worries me. It's myself. What I am, what I may become, what I may not mean to you.'

'How, Nora?'

'An invalid!' she withdrew her hand from his. Her lip trembled and she squeezed the chestnut stem till its sap stained her fingers. Her moment of truth had come; she bowed her head, and as her fingers picked the white petals off the stem she strove to efface from her soul every lie or half lie, every concealment of the truth, that had lain so heavily upon her. He listened to her like a priest in the confessional. She tore up everything from her soul — everything connected with her love for him: how her mother and sister had died in a sanatorium; of her broken engagement, and of her periodic visits to her doctor because of the fear that continually hung over her.

'And he discovered nothing, Nora?'

'Nothing. I was to stop thinking about it and to avoid strain.'

'And will you, Nora?'

'Will I what?'

'Cease thinking about it; and let us go forward together, happy in each other's love.'

'You're not afraid, Peter?'

'I love you and I want you. You mean everything to me. And you'll stop fretting and eating your heart out. If only I'd known months ago.'

'But I wasn't sure, then, that you loved me as you do.'

'You're sure now?'

'I am, Peter. And for your sake I'll try to push aside all my anxieties.' She tried to look at him steadily and without confusion; her brown eyes were wet with unshed tears, and the kiss she gave him expressed the sweetness of her love for him. She shuddered as if with cold, and he lifted her to her feet and arm in arm they paced the lawn, their long shadows now in front of them, and now behind them. They halted and gazed at the chestnut tree, at the hack-marks in the trunk where Johnny's ladder had rested when he was sawing off the bough.

'Elizabeth thought it was darkening the house and gathering flies, and it was she who ordered it to be cut off,' Nora explained, and was surprised at the husky tone of her own voice. 'We'll gather up the cushions and go inside before the dew falls.'

'And you'll play for me?'

'I'll play any piece you like, for I feel I'll never play better than I'll do this evening.'

He left before Mary and Elizabeth came back, and he met them trudging home while there was light still in the sky.

'You did some praying this evening?' he joked.

'It was Helen who delayed us. She's always so kind and brought us in for a little refreshment,' Elizabeth said and went on to speak of the wonderful spell of weather that had set in and how well the crops were thriving and of the sleepy scent of the hawthorn that was oozing out on all sides from the hedges. Mary stood a little behind her, downcast and weary-looking.

'You're very quiet, Mary,' Peter remarked.

'Indeed, she has been like that for many a long week past. I'm glad somebody else has noticed it besides myself.'

'Ah, she'll soon be hearing a bit of news that will rejoice her old heart,' and he strode off, leaving them puzzled.

The light was slinking away from the top fields, a corncrake calling in the coolness of the grass, and blackbirds in no hurry to finish their last songs. The stream at the roadside was speckled with petals like confetti, and here and there on the slopes the whins glowed yellow as if they had stolen patches of sunshine. From a wooden gate he looked back at the house but could scarcely see it for the thickness of the trees and the shadows hanging among the branches.

Helen was seated in the sitting-room, and a tray with cups and cake-crumbed plates was still on the table. She always tidied things up immediately, and he was wondering what it was that had upset her usual routine.

'That's a glorious evening, thanks be to God,' he said, taking his pipe from the mantelpiece.

'You should have been out at your devotions. To be a head teacher you set a nice example for the countryside, I must say.'

So that's the mood she's in, he thought, as he tapped his pockets for his matches. 'I had a nice little job to do, Helen.'

'Not more important than looking after your soul!'

'I was ministering to it in a very special way. I'm going to marry Nora Byrne.'

She stared at him, but he was gazing at the fire and blowing into the shank of his pipe. For a few minutes she said nothing, waiting for him to continue. But he remained exasperatingly silent, slowly stuffing the bowl of his pipe and rolling up his pouch.

'When you hear what I have to say it will put that foolish notion out of your head. This very evening — it was like an answer to prayer — Elizabeth informed me that Miss Byrne is a consumptive. Do you hear me, Peter? She's in consumption.'

'Yes, I hear you,' he said quietly.

'And her mother and sister died in a sanatorium!'

'I know that. Nora told me,' and he held a match over his pipe till it burnt down to his fingers. 'But as to being in consumption, that's untrue. There's only one thing wrong with her: she's too good for the likes of me.'

He rose and switched on the light. She detested the easy calm of his manner; and she braced herself to break it down and force him to listen to reason.

'Peter, you must exercise prudence in this matter — it is one of the cardinal virtues.'

'Don't meddle in what doesn't concern you, please.'

'But it does concern me. I'm your sister.'

'If you are, you should be happy to see me happy.'

'But you can't expect me to sit as dumb as a milestone and see my only brother brought to ruin by an unscrupulous girl.'

'If she were unscrupulous she'd have hidden this from me and from all of us.'

'She held it up till you were as helpless in her hand as a piece of thread she'd twine round her finger.'

'I'm going to marry her and I'm not going back on my word to her.'

'So it's a sense of honour that drives you.'

'Don't misunderstand me. I'm not in the mood for cynicism. I love the girl.'

'May God direct the unwise!' and she passed her hand across her brow. She shook her head: 'I know you too well. I'll save you from her. We were happy till this schemer came along, and we'll never be at rest till she's gone back to wherever she came from.'

He took a book from the shelf. She fixed him with a cold stare and entreated him to put the book away and to give her a few minutes of his precious time.

'Don't take it so brokenly. If you knew . . .' he stopped, choosing his words carefully. 'If you knew how much Nora loves me and I her, you would congratulate both of us.'

'Never! The whole affair is against right reason and sound judgment. It'd be madness to marry a girl of her stock. She has no charity in her to allow this to go on.'

'You've said too much. Let that be the end of it.'

'It's only the beginning. I'll save you in spite of yourself. And I'll save your precious honour with it. To think that our lovely home is on the edge of ruin — a home that we made together.'

'I hope you'll continue to make it what it is and that you'll stay with me and Nora in it.'

'Me! And to be turned into a nurse for your delicate wife.'

'Don't be so cruel — and you only an hour or two out from the chapel. Why don't you pray for what I desire and not for what you desire?'

'I pray that you'll do the right thing.'

'And it's you who are the supreme judge of what is the right thing.'

'Everybody agrees with me.'

'Everybody?'

'Elizabeth for one.'

'She's not everybody.'

'She represents wise opinion.'

'And Mary?'

'Who would give heed to what she would say? She has as much sense in her head as a hen.'

'Helen, you only get from people what you seek in them. And when you stir yourself to know Nora Byrne you'll find that she's a lovely, sweet-natured girl.'

'I'll never stir myself to do that. Good night now, and think over the advice I've given you,' and rising to her feet she carried out the tray and left him.

He relaxed in his chair; he smoked slowly, watching the smoke rings rise and spread like blue jelly-fish in the light. He had controlled himself, had crushed back his anger, the struggle leaving him weary but not unbalanced as anger would have done. He hated these scenes and he knew there would be more of them in the next few months. She was making things harder for herself and for him. We make life more difficult than it is by our own foolishness, and that which would bring us peace we turn from, and in its stead we make twisted shapes out of our own wilfulness. It was difficult for her, he'd admit, to receive another into this house, but half the difficulty came from her unchanging, hard-moulded habit. The Devlins, much older than she was, had opened their door to Nora, had received her against their will, and the change, as far as he could judge, gave new life to them. Helen would experience all this if only she would relent and give room to the word of welcome. He would lead her to it quietly, and with the help of God he would avoid these clashes with her. Everything would come right in the end, and when it would come he'd never cast up to her anything she did or said against them.

CLASHES between himself and Helen, instead of subsiding with the succeeding days as he had hoped, blazed up with distressing frequency; and time and again he implored her, in God's name, to repress her bitterness — a bitterness that would recoil upon herself and on all of them. Whether it hurt him or not she would speak of it, she maintained, and would continue to do so till he allowed common sense space enough to scatter his stupid folly. Surely it wasn't madness for a man of his years to marry; no one but an unreasonable self-willed woman would deny that! Oh, could he not understand it was the girl he was marrying that she objected to? — an unhealthy girl, not fit for any marriage; if the girl were stronger and a little older it would all be different, and she'd be able to congratulate them both and work her fingers to the bone to make them happy. Could he not be convinced of that? No, he couldn't. He loved the girl and he'd marry her whether Helen approved of it or not.

He was glad he had his school hours to escape for a while from this sickening wrangling. But even there her unceasing nagging tormented his mind; and often, as he stood in front of his class, he found his memory slipping out of his control, reliving one of these scenes, presenting him with words he should have said and filling him with remorse for what he actually did say. The boys in the front desks heard him muttering to himself, perceived his constant staring, and it was they, breaking freely into chatter, would bring him back with a shudder to the small changeable world of the classroom. Out of habit he darted at them a round of questions but was so inattentive to their slow replies or impatient with their stammerings that he would allow false answers to pass unnoticed. He tried to regain his customary energy and enthusiasm but after a few minutes his spirit would slacken, and he would sit on his chair, one arm drooped over the back of it, the other resting on the table in front of him. When he relaxed the class relaxed with him, their buzz of talk adding to his annoyance. He glared at them, feeling the taste of rage upon his lips. He controlled himself and hid away his heavy cane. They were not to blame and it would be unjust to unloose this knot of anger upon them. If he punished them it would do no good, it would only drive them to remain at home out of fear or to go mitching among the hills till school-time was over. Their heartlessness was innocent and unwilful. The sickness was in himself and not in them.

He would give them a page or two of arithmetical problems to keep them quiet, and when he would see them copying whole-sale from one another, almost brazenly transparent in their trickery, he realized how quickly his class could slip from his control. At composition time he walked between the aisles of the desks, lifting a composition here and there, only to find himself handing them back after reading a few sentences. 'I'll correct them at the week-end,' he'd say, 'I haven't the time now.' He would walk round the room, make a pretence of looking over the boys' shoulders at what they were writing, and though words of ridicule and belittlement were nearest to his lips he always managed to say: 'That's a good effort. A good improvement' — utterly unaware of what he was praising.

Nora noticed he was sad and unhappy in the schoolroom and that, on the evenings when he walked with her among the hills above the estuary, much of his gaiety of mood had shrunk from him. It puzzled her, and she suspected that he was brooding upon the sickness that had killed her mother and sister and was fearful now that the same sickness would in time catch up with her.

And one evening as they stood at the Devlins' gate before parting for the night she rested her hands on his shoulders and said: 'Peter, look at me and tell me straight what's the matter with you. You're not the same with me as you used to be. If you feel you've made a mistake in asking me to marry you, break it off now — before it's too late! You're worried and I know it and feel it: it hurts me to see you like this. If it has anything to do with our love, tell me. I'm well used to sorrow and disappointment.'

'Nora, Nora! As sure as God's above me it has nothing to do with the love between us. Surely you've no doubt that I love you?'

'But there's something on your mind, Peter. Give me a share of it so that the two of us can destroy it. There should be no great secrets that we can't share together. I can't help blaming myself for seeing you so sad.'

'It's Helen that's the cause of it, Nora. I'd rather have hidden that from you but you've forced it from me.' He explained that Helen didn't want him to get married. They had lived so long together as brother and sister she could not accept the idea of his marrying anyone. Things like that were always happening at a time like this in every family, but in the end they worked out satisfactorily.

If Nora could do anything to help him — no matter what it cost — she'd do it gladly. She'd go up to see Helen any evening he'd arrange. He shook his head at that suggestion. It was wiser, he maintained, to let this wild storm of Helen's exhaust itself against him; it was in spate at the moment and he'd let it rush on till it was as dry and weak as chaff.

But it surprised him how long Helen could keep it up. And one Friday morning towards the end of that June she asked him squarely if he had bought the engagement ring. He hadn't — and that pleased her. But he intended to do so very soon — and that exasperated her. Conscious that the long summer vacation was approaching she advised him to postpone his engagement till September at least. If he would agree to that it would please her greatly. He didn't agree or disagree with it. He would give no promises except to the girl he loved.

'You've grown very hard and disagreeable with me, Peter,' she answered him.

'You're very hard on yourself,' he declared and hurried out into the bright morning to his school.

It was early — more than half an hour before his usual time of leaving. The sun shone warmly and the angular shadows of the school lay sharp and black on the playground. He wound up the clock in his room, lit a cigarette, and took his roll-books from the press. There was great stillness and peace in the room: flies crawled on the sunny pane, the nail-heads on the floor shone likes silver, and the boys' water-colours, hanging round the walls, brightened the room with vigorous splashes of reds and yellows and greens and blues. He gazed round at them with admiration, gave a sigh of contentment and watched the cigarette smoke whorl round in a beam of sun that slanted down upon the yellow desks.

He swayed back on his chair and read a poem by Edward Thomas that was written on the blackboard since the previous afternoon.

> Tall nettles cover up, as they have done
> These many springs, the rusty harrow, the plough
> Long worn out, and the roller made of stone:
> Only the elm butt tops the nettles now.
>
> This corner of the farmyard I like most:
> As well as any bloom upon a flower
> I like the dust on the nettles, never lost
> Except to prove the sweetness of a shower.

That poem of Edward Thomas reminds me more of the Devlins' yard than it does of my own: my own house is too new yet to have character. For some of the boys on the hillside farms those lines will rouse deeper and sweeter feelings than they do for me: they have been reared with those things around them and I haven't. Now that the hot weather is here — making arithmetic obnoxious to them — I must give them more poetry and more painting. As the holidays approach the lads are growing as lazy as myself. But they can't accuse me in their own minds of coming in late these mornings!

Presently he heard the iron gate whinge outside, a slow step move across the yard, a tentative lift to the latch in the porch and then the noise of surprise to find the door was open. Malachy Maguire came in, wearing an open shirt and trousers, and his patchy hair cropped close because it was summer time.

'Good morning, Malachy.'

'Good morning, Sir.'

And Malachy stuffed his bag below his desk, lifted a duster and began to dust the room. Peter, bent over the roll-book adding up attendances, smiled to himself as he recalled Malachy's behaviour in the singing class and thought how his love for Nora had grown from such an unpleasant incident.

Malachy jumped down from a window-ledge he was dusting: 'Sir, there's a woman standing outside at the door.'

'See what she wants, Malachy.'

'Sir, it's Jimmy Doran's ma and she says she wants to see you.'

Peter went out to the porch and shut his room-door behind him.

'Good morning, Mrs. Doran.'

'You told Jimmy to bring his wee twin brothers to school, next week. Well, Master Lynch, I don't intend to send them to this school.'

'That's a matter entirely for yourself,' he said quietly, not asking or wishing to wait for an explanation.

'Just a minute, Master. I've no fault to find with you. It's just that I don't want a girl in galloping consumption to be teaching my wee ones.'

'There's no teacher in this school with that complaint.'

'Miss Byrne is — from what I hear.'

'You shouldn't listen to a rumour of that kind. There's no truth in it. I'm engaged to be married to Miss Byrne.' He tried to turn aside but she held his sleeve.

'I'm sorry, Master Lynch, for what I've said. I'll send the pair of them with Jimmy on Monday. I hope you'll be happy, Sir. I'm more than thankful to you for all you've done for our Jimmy.'

He was only half-listening to her; his mind was burrowing forward into the mound of difficulties that a rumour of this kind could pile up. But he'd soon put an end to it — he'd scatter it aside in a day or two.

The woman at his side stared puzzledly at him: 'You're not affronted by what I said, Master?' she asked, penitently. 'I don't know what made me come up to bother you like this. I'd let nobody say I'd send my twins past your school. I would not, Master Lynch. Do you hear what I'm saying to you?'

'That's all right, Mrs. Doran; send them on Monday. We'll be glad to take them in. Good morning.' He watched her go out through the gate and glance back at him with a downcast look. Presently Brennan came with slow steps across the yard, a little boy carrying his attaché case. Then Murphy arrived, riding through the gateway on his bicycle and freewheeled round to the shed at the back. A few boys were playing marbles in the sun, their schoolbags lying in a heap on the ground.

Peter walked out on to the road; he saw Nora in a dark green frock with a white collar hurrying towards him and he went to meet her.

'Is there an inspector here?' she asked, breathless.

'The whole ministry of education is here to examine the infant department! No, Nora, you needn't hurry. It's just that I've a plan in my mind that just won't wait. We'll drive up to the city tomorrow morning. I want to buy you a present — a little ring for your finger. Tell Brennan and Murphy at lunch-hour that we're engaged. A bit of gossip like that will speed on these slow weeks before the holidays!'

At lunch-hour as she was pouring out tea for Murphy and Brennan she told them.

Brennan folded his newspaper: 'And that means you'll be leaving us for good?'

'It does, but not immediately. You might have to put up with me for another year.'

'It means we will save money on this transaction,' Murphy laughed. 'We'll only have to stump up for one wedding present and not for two.'

'That part of the business never struck me,' Brennan said.

'Surely you didn't think of sending them off without a present?' Murphy winked at Nora.

'You took me up wrong, Mr. Murphy. I meant to say that the idea of having only to buy one present and not two didn't occur to me.'

'I see, or rather, I understand.'

'I hope you'll be very happy,' Brennan said.

'And that all your troubles will be little ones,' Murphy added. 'And I hope Mr. Brennan won't let your successor slip so easily from his fingers. That's one of the abuses of newspapers.'

Murphy went out with her into the sunlit yard. Waves of heat flared up from the asphalt, and cloud-shadows strode across the sloping fields. It was too hot for walking and they stood together watching the boys whipping tops, playing marbles, and four or five of them trying to read the one comic. He noticed a tiny speck of iron-rust on the tip of her white collar, and because she was always so flawlessly dressed it pleased his mischievousness to say: 'There's a tiny tea stain on your bib.'

'I'm sorry to say it's not a tea stain — a pin did it, but nothing will remove it.'

'This love's a queer business. Here's Mr. Lynch coming back again already — he doesn't take time to finish his lunch these days. And he needn't be afraid of me. I tried to win you by my charms but he knocked me out. And I suppose you've told him all the lovely things I've said about him from time to time?'

'No, Mr. Murphy, I haven't. But he'd laugh if he heard them.'

'I never suspected it would turn out like this.'

'Has it surprised you as much as that?'

'It's a terrible blow to my vanity. I used to think you were

226

struck on me. And now I'll have nothing pleasant to look at at lunch-hour for I'm sure they'll appoint some old gargoyle in your place. If they do, I'll bring my tea in a thermos and leave her in Brennan's safe and silent keeping. I'll go over now and pay my obsequies to Peter before he blows the whistle.'

☙ 18 ❧

WHEN Peter arrived back from the city the following evening Helen was out in the garden spraying the roses and in the fields around the school people were working at the hay, though a mist was now obscuring the sun that had shone brightly all the afternoon. Peter stepped into the house, and as he felt the stifling warmth of the rooms he raised the blinds for they still retained the heat of the day. Through the open windows he heard the cool noise of Helen's spray and saw the drops hanging from the roses. She knew he was watching her but she took her time, turned her back to him, and didn't move towards the house to make the tea till every drop of spray in the bucket had been used.

At the table, sitting opposite one another and hearing the sound of the reaping machines in the nearby fields, he told her he had bought Nora an engagement ring. He didn't expect her to congratulate him — and she didn't. Not a word did she say. She poured out the tea as if she hadn't heard him. But in her own mind she was reliving an incident that had occurred when he was away with Nora in the city.

She had been clipping the edges of the lawn when Father Lacy strolled past and stopped to speak to her. He asked about Peter and she told him he had no time now for gardening — that he was too busy hanging around with Miss Byrne.

'A nice pleasant girl,' Father Lacy had said.

'But a delicate girl, Father.'

'I never saw any sign of that.'

'Oh, but we're sure of it! Her mother and sister died in a sanatorium: since hearing that I've warned Peter to keep to his own side of the fence. But in spite of all I say he still goes around with her. Maybe, Father, you'd give him a word of sensible advice. You're the only one he'd listen to.'

'You wouldn't expect an old man like me to meddle in a love affair.'

'His whole life will be ruined if he marries her.'

'I'd marry them gladly if I were asked. But as to telling him not to marry — that's not my business. He's marrying a good Catholic girl.'

'I'll not live a day longer in this parish if that happens.'

'You don't expect me to interfere with your freedom?'

'I don't know what I expect, Father Lacy. I only know that a word from you would save my poor brother.'

'I've seen many a so-called delicate girl rear a strong and healthy family.'

'Miss Byrne doesn't spring from healthy stock! Peter wasn't ordained for a life with her.'

'What do we know what we are ordained for? Nothing in this life happens by chance if our motives are good. You should accept your brother's intention.'

'I can't! I can't! He's doing wrong and the thought of it is destroying my health. I'm not sleeping well. This very day the doctor ordered me to rest more and to get out in the air.'

'Heed what he says. And, Helen, leave your own will aside for once and make a gentle sacrifice of this upheaval. I know how you must feel. But if you work for what Peter wants and not for what you want, you'll be at rest.'

'But it's Peter I'm thinking of all the time and not myself.'

'Sometimes we can be deceived in that: we think we are acting for others when it is only our own selves we are acting for. Our own selfishness drives us to dominate and control.'

His words, spoken quietly, marched in front of her with firm precision. But she shrank from saying anything to Peter about Father Lacy's visit. In her own heart she felt that Father Lacy was wrong and that if it were a brother of his own who was marrying into a sickly family he wouldn't be so sweetly generous in his attitude. It was always easy to toss off advice when you weren't entangled in the result. Indeed she'd be a right fool if

229

she listened to him! Some day she'd seek advice from a younger priest and not from an old man like Father Lacy, who always sought peace at any price. But peace and imprudence make a shaky companionship! She'd go her own way, and in her own time. Elizabeth Devlin was the only one who understood her.

'That was a nice supper, Helen. And a very quiet one,' Peter said with a smile as he folded up his serviette.

'Was it? I hope you noticed I ate very little.'

'I did, and I felt uncomfortable at the way I enjoyed it.'

'I was with the doctor today. It might interest you to know I'm heading towards a complete breakdown.'

He laid aside his plate, joined his hands, and rested them on the table. He gave her a long, tender look. 'What about going away for a month? Up to Dublin, for instance. It's lovely there at this time of the year.'

'I'll do nothing of the kind! You don't think I'd leave you to fend for yourself! What state would this place be in when I'd come back?'

'The same state of perfection as it's in at present. I guarantee you'll not gather a salt-spoon of dust when you come back.'

'Stop this refined persecution, please! And do take that satisfied grin off your face. I know what's in your mind only too well.'

'Monotony would break anyone's spirit. Do, Helen,' he pleaded, 'take a holiday.'

She closed her eyes at him. 'You're very cruel. You're trying to blame me for my own pitiable condition. You did it. God Himself knows what I've suffered since that mannequin of a trouble-maker pranced into the school.'

'Keep Nora's name out of this. She has nothing to do with the suggestion I've made. You need a change, a rest — that's plain to anyone.'

'She's at the back of every suggestion you make, everything you do, all the cutting things you've said these past months. It's her you consider — first, last, and all the time. You throw me aside like an old shoe after I've used up the best years of my life to make you comfortable.' She burst forth in tears, covered her eyes with her hands, and sobbed: 'God in heaven, what am I to do?'

She stared across at him, and in the pained wildness of her gaze he glimpsed the injury she was inflicting on herself. He said nothing — to utter a single word of blame or sympathy would only unloose all the twists of her angered mind. He made ridges on the tablecloth with his thumb-nail and brushed away a fly that had settled on his plate. He stretched out his hand and touched her bowed head: 'Helen, for goodness' sake don't distress yourself like this.'

'Don't touch me!' and she flung up her head. She brushed back a strand of grey hair that had fallen over her brow. If you're not marrying her out of some stupid sense of honour you must be marrying her for her money.'

'I hope she hasn't a solitary penny to her name,' he said calmly.

'You know perfectly well she has plenty — her dress alone would convince you of that.'

'You know rightly I never went after money in my life. Don't ever say that to me again!'

'I will say it because it's true! There's nothing else could drive you.'

She saw him rise from the table, push in his chair quietly, and go out of the room. She heard the sitting-room door close gently and she knew he'd take up a book and his pipe but knew, too, he'd enjoy neither after that rap she gave him. She glanced at the clock — it was just eight. The reaping machines had fallen silent and a mist was sifting through the trees in the back garden. She'd go across to the Devlins' and have a talk with Elizabeth — she was the only one in the parish with a stitch or two of sense in her old head.

Without waiting to tidy away the dishes she put on her coat and hurried out. The evening was mild and a soft rain like broken cobweb fell among the dark spaces in the trees. She could

231

hear the mournful moo of a ship's horn rising at the back of the hills and she knew a mist was settling down upon the sea. The grey road in front of her was already damp and swallows zig-zagged across it with a cheetering sound. She held out her hand but felt no rain upon it, yet when she looked at the deserted fields the hay lying in rows was covered in rain like a frost. She halted where the roadside stream tumbled into a pool and she gazed at the brown water, seeking distraction from all thought. Clusters of bubbles formed like frog-spawn, squeezed between two stones and sailed under the briers that scratched the surface of the water. Through the hedge she could see the cattle tear and snuffle at the grass, their breath rise up like smoke. At her feet a black snail stretched at full length on the moist grass and she touched it with her toe and watched it shrink into a tight ball.

What will I do if Miss Byrne is there? What will I say to her? she asked herself, but did not wait for an answer. She reached the Devlins' gate and with a firm unhesitating step approached the door.

Mary and Elizabeth were in but Nora had gone for a walk around the quay. A few logs were burning with a hiss in the grate.

'It's not cold and I'm just burning those bits of the chestnut for I like the smell of them. Take off your coat, Helen, and stay for a while,' Elizabeth said.

'I only dropped in for a minute. I was working in the garden all day and the heat has given me a bit of a headache.'

Elizabeth noticed the dragged huskiness of her voice and noticed, too, a look of distress in her eyes, and fearing lest Mary, at any moment, would start to describe the beauty of Nora's ring she sent her off to the kitchen for a few pieces of coal.

'Oh, don't waste coal on my account,' Helen protested. 'I only ran in for a few minutes.'

'Coal's the only thing that'll make those green logs burn. Go on, Mary.'

'I'm upsetting you both,' Helen said, half-rising to her feet, for she had no patience to listen to their evasive tittle-tattle when both of them knew full well why she had called.

'Do stay for a while,' Elizabeth said. 'The evening's young yet. I've something special to show you.' She put on her spectacles, took a piece of lacework from a drawer and spread it out on Helen's lap. 'What do you think of that design?'

Helen sighed; she was tired of her and was in no mood for flattery. She raised the edge of the lace with lackadaisical fingers: 'I've seen you do much better than that. Of course, Elizabeth, your work at its poorest is superior to any done in this parish.'

'I hope I never do poor work, Helen dear. Even the tiniest portion receives my fullest attention. My own mother would never have allowed shoddy work to pass from my hands. Indeed she'd have made me do it all over again . . . I was thinking that piece would help to make a bridal veil for some young lady.'

'But Helen doesn't mean that your work is poor,' Mary said, conscious of the dry peevishness in her sister's voice. 'She only means she doesn't care much for the design of that new piece. We've all our likes and dislikes in matters of that kind. Isn't that so, Helen?'

'I suppose so,' Helen said without enthusiasm; and, at that moment, hearing the front door being pushed open and a stick rattling in the umbrella-stand she rose to her feet.

Nora came into the room, loosening a green scarf from about her neck. She greeted Helen with unabashed cheeriness. Her brown eyes were shining, and the tiny seeds of rain clinging to her hair made its blackness and greyness almost indistinguishable from one another. With her hands she wiped the misty rain from her sleeves and her ring shone in the light from the window.

'I really must go now,' Helen said.

'Stay for a little while,' Mary coaxed. 'We could give you a nice glass of wine.'

'I never take spirits at this time of the year, thank you.'

For a moment there was a harsh silence in the room, and then with startling unexpectedness Nora said in a warm tone:

'I'll leave you along the road a bit, if you don't mind.' And as Helen walked out Nora went with her.

At the foot of the drive a blackbird screeched from the hedge and Nora waved back to Mary and Elizabeth who stood together in the doorway.

They walked abreast in silence for a while and then Nora spoke: 'Helen,' she entreated, 'I always wanted to meet you alone. I love Peter, as you know, and because of that I want you to let me know you.'

'Miss Byrne, I'll never allow you to know me!'

Nora felt the blood rush to her face. She took Helen's hand, but Helen wrenched it from her.

'No, Miss Bryne,' she said in a cold, impervious voice. 'No, I'm not as soft as my unfortunate brother. You're too sly for the likes of us. You only told him all when you had possessed all.'

'Believe me, Helen, that's untrue.'

'I'll not believe you. Why did you allow all this to happen to Peter and you knowing all along the kind of weak stock you came from?'

'I wasn't sure that Peter loved me and saw no reason to speak about a matter that concerned no one only myself.'

'That's a lie, you liar! But it's not the end yet. I can tell you Peter's marrying you because he wouldn't go back on his word.'

'Did he say that?'

Helen hesitated, shrinking from the intense open look that held her.

'He had no call to tell me. I know him better than you do. He considers it his moral duty not to turn back. Of course I don't wonder that you are ignorant of that part of his character,' and she gave a shrug of scorn. 'He'll never break from you, but you, in all justice, should break with him. You haven't the health — though it's no fault of your own — for the haulings and pullings of married life. You know that, of course?'

'No, Miss Lynch, none of us is certain of that. The only thing we're certain about is the certainty of death.'

'Nothing short of a miracle would make you strong enough for married life.'

'I believe in miracles. And I believe we could all be happy together. It's what I live for. Never in my life have I felt so strong and so convinced that this will be for Peter's happiness, for yours, and for mine.'

'For my happiness! What do you know about me? — nothing!' She gripped Nora's wrist and Nora felt the pincers of her fingers squeeze numbness into her arm. She saw the ugliness of anger in the face uplifted towards her. She saw particles of food in the crevices of her teeth and caught the unwholesome smell of her breath. Whether her wrist, at that moment, was still being held she could not say for she was suddenly afraid.

'No one wants you here. And you'll not be wanted by anyone in the school when the truth about you gets around.'

'I'll go away. I'll not live amidst hate and jealousy.'

'Don't hold this against me, for God's sake,' Helen softened. 'I'm not well these days.'

'No one will hold it against you except your own conscience.'

'I'm acting for the good of us all. You'll not realize that now, but years later you'll look back and know that this advice is what your own mother would have given you if she were here. I've slaved for Peter and he couldn't live without me.'

Nora hastened away from her, and behind her she heard Helen's footsteps recede in the distance, and when there was nothing but the deep silence of the fields around her she stood under a tree that guarded a dry patch upon the road. She shuddered, clenched her hands, and prayed to God to still the throbbing in her mind.

She heard shuffling footsteps on the road and she pressed close against the dry trunk of the tree. Old O'Brien passed her, bareheaded, smiling to himself, an empty can bouncing on his shoulders as he made playful spurts along the road. At that moment she envied him and then was immediately ashamed of herself for envying his lapses of reason. No, she must be brave and pray for courage. She took the ring off her finger, glanced at it, and slipped it on again.

To no one: not even to Mary would she say anything of what had passed between herself and Helen. In the silence of her own heart she would bear it patiently. Maybe Helen was right: maybe I did withhold all till I was sure of all. God forgive me if I did that. I didn't mean to fall in love that way. I didn't! I didn't! In three weeks' time the school will close for the long vacation. I'll see it to the end. And then I'll look out for a new school.

She raised her eyes and stared at the hedges reflected darkly on the wet road. Then the rain fell heavily, pattering rapidly on the leaves above her, streaming down the tree's trunk, and dancing like midges on the wet surface of the road.

✿ 19 ✿

SHE was awake for hours that night and a sweat — cold as a child's slate — lay flat upon her forehead. Her pulse throbbed wildly like a captured bird's she had once held in her hands. She tried to pray herself to sleep, to possess it, but sleep all the more avoided her. She did not grow alarmed or rush out to waken Mary. In these long summer nights darkness was lean and sparse and the blessed dawn came early: there was comfort in that, small though it was, and comfort, too, in glancing at the mirror and measuring the passing of night by the light she saw there. But these distractions were feeble friends, and there was no use, at her age, pretending that they would shield her from the thoughts that swarmed round her in the dusk of the room. 'Postponements were my undoing,' she said to herself.

Yes, that was too true. If only on the first day in this house she had not wilfully hidden from Elizabeth the melancholy truths about her family she might not now be lying here with terror hammering like a fist upon her mind. Nor would Helen's agitation be the tortured thing that it is. And what of Peter: what must he be suffering, day in and day out, from a sister so fiercely bent on wrecking the purpose of his love? Not until a few hours ago did she really see into the heart of his sister — and yet from that short meeting, here she was with all her confidence and hopes strewn round her like torn paper.

But maybe she shouldn't blame Helen entirely for it all. Much of it arose from her own foolishness, from her own cowardly shrinking from a simple truth — a truth that no one should be ashamed of. God alone knows why she didn't tell Peter about it long ago; if she had he might have turned away from her — and he and Helen and herself would have been spared this. She only told him all when she had possessed all! — Helen had said that. Perhaps there was truth in it if she could rein in her mind to examine it calmly.

She pushed back the weight of bedclothes from round her breast and lay limp. Her lips and throat were dry and she yearned for a glass of cold water. But she lay on, afraid of wakening Mary on her journey downstairs. She moistened her lips with her tongue, tried to think back over the past year, and strove to hold in isolation the first occasion when she was aware of Peter's love for her. But scene after scene, like things glimpsed from a speeding train, fled headlong through her mind, and rushing with them were jumbled phrases of music that beat and baffled her into utter weariness. If only her mind could stay quiet for a moment she could sift out what she wanted from it. But it wouldn't lie still or do her bidding — it was as noisy and as confusing as a fairground. And so to escape from its pressure she sat upright in the bed and stared at the window and at a few pale stars above the chestnut trees. She pushed back her damp hair from her brow, and as she slowly lay down again the pillow seemed cool and her back pleasantly cold.

She lay on her side and watched the stars above the trees. There were four of them. It was peaceful to look at them and to half shut her eyes and count their spikes of light. They reminded her of the Christmas tree they had had in the school. Yes, that was one of the happiest days she had spent there — there was a mysterious joy that day and a hush in the children's eyes that she'd love to see again. 'If only I lie still, the mood of that day will come back to me,' she whispered. But her voice dispersed it and she found herself fully awake again and thinking, not of the children, but of the hatefulness she had witnessed in Helen's eyes.

She breathed deeply, blessed herself, and dragged all her strength into her clasped hands: Oh, God, strengthen me, guide me, and enlighten my foolish ways. Teach me what to do. I do not know what all this means but I do know that it has a meaning. Help me to accept it with patience and without ill-will towards anyone so that I can serve Thee always with a quiet mind.

She stretched herself full length in the bed and slowly relaxed. But still she did not sleep. Outside a bird gave its first slow warbling and the narrow brow of dawn appeared above a hill. She did not care now if sleep did not come. The sun would soon rise, the cattle would be calling across the hillsides, and she'd no longer feel herself alone. She put her arms under her head but her left wrist pained her and she rubbed it gently with her fingers, and as the light in the room brightened she saw a dark bruise on the whiteness of her skin. No one will be told that Helen caused that! Her anger must have given her the strength of a man.

Well, Helen, you'll have your wish. I tried to win you but I failed. And since I haven't the strength to stand up to tensions of this kind how could I be expected to face a marriage? Here I am laid flat at the first fearful glimmerings of what lies ahead. You're right, Helen: I haven't the health for marriage — if I had I'm sure I could brazen this with a lighter conscience.

She heard the bell ring out for first Mass, heard Mary tap at her door, but she lay on. She dozed, and the noise of footsteps on the road and Mary and Elizabeth talking outside on their way home from chapel wakened her. She would go to second Mass and she'd delay her dressing as best she could and so give herself little time to take a breakfast. The thought of breakfast filled her with nausea and she'd have to think up some excuse to Mary for refusing to take it.

Mary called her. She answered her in a sleepy voice that she was getting dressed. She sat on the edge of the bed. She felt dizzy and as she gazed at the trees, diamond specks, like bits of tissue paper, floated towards her eyes. She dressed slowly, timing everything by her watch, and not paying heed to Mary, who was calling out every five minutes that her breakfast wouldn't be worth taking if she didn't hurry.

'I'm sorry, Mary, I'm so slow this morning. I'll just take a cup of tea and run on. Maybe Johnny could take another breakfast.'

The tea made her perspire freely, and at Mass she sat near the door so that if she'd feel faint she could slip out without much attention or commotion. All the windows were open but the air around her did not seem to move; it had a sour smell like the children's school coats on a damp day. She breathed it in shallowly. She couldn't pray and when she closed her eyes she was surprised how sleep, now that she didn't want it, could so easily overpower her.

She was one of the first out of the chapel and she walked off quickly, not wishing to meet anyone. She did not halt until she reached the Devlins' gate, and then she walked quietly, almost on tiptoe, to the bench outside the sitting-room window. The front door was open to the sun and she could hear the noise of cutlery from the kitchen. She put her missal and gloves beside her on the bench, took off her hat, and sat relaxed, her eyes closed and her hands folded on her lap. She dozed for a few minutes, and on realizing that she'd fall asleep in the heat of the sun she got up and went into the cool of the house.

'I think I'll lie down for a while,' she said to Mary. 'The heat of the chapel has given me a headache.'

'You do look a bit pale, and the rest will do you a world of good. I'll call you when the dinner's ready.'

'I couldn't touch it, Mary. I'll take a glass of water up with me and two aspirins. I'll get up in the evening if my headache lifts.'

'It'll pass off before then. It's the excitement of buying the ring that has done it. Any day I ever go to Belfast I always come back with a thumping headache too. Pull down the blind when you go up, it will help to cool the room.'

She took off her shoes and skirt, lay down on top of the bed and in a few minutes she was asleep. When the dinner was ready Mary slipped upstairs to call her. She opened the door quietly and peeped in. Nora lay without moving, her arms loose by her sides and an anguished expression on her face. Mary stared at her, feeling a sudden pang of terror at the death-like pallor of her face. She lifted the corner of the blanket and placed it gently over her. She withdrew backwards from the room, keeping her eyes fixed on Nora in case she'd stir. The drawn blind moved a little in the draught of the open door and let in a line of sunlight that leaned across the bed. But Nora did not move.

'Let her sleep till she wakens,' Elizabeth said to her when she came downstairs. 'It's this infernal heat that's caused it.'

'But she took no breakfast and now she'll be going without her dinner.'

'Sleep's better for her than an appetite at the moment. When people don't eat you always think they're going to die.'

'Elizabeth, there's something on that girl's mind. I feel that Helen said something hurtful to her last night.'

'Nora would have told you if she had. It's not in the nature of young girls to keep their worries hidden. And anyway she always runs to you with her troubles. Stop annoying yourself and take your dinner.'

At five o'clock Nora wakened; she felt feverish and her head-ache was worse. She undressed quietly and got into bed. She heard Peter's car crunch over the pebbles on the path, heard him get out, and heard his voice in the hall. Mary came up again, opened the bedroom door and called her name out in a whisper. She felt her crouch over the bed and put her cool hand on her forehead.

'Peter's in, Nora.'

'Mary, I don't want him to see me like this. Tell him I'm sleeping — please do that for me. I feel all clammy and un-washed. But I'll be all right in the morning and he'll see me in school as usual.'

In the morning despite the warnings of Mary and Elizabeth she got up for school.

'I haven't missed a day the whole year,' she said, 'and I don't want to miss one so near the holidays.'

'The school will be there when you're not,' Mary said. 'Take our advice and don't go. I can send Johnny over with a message to Peter. Be sensible.'

'I'll go over to the school and if I feel I can't last out the whole day I'll leave early. Will that please you?'

'You're a headstrong little girl!'

She was late arriving at the school and when she came in, pale and thin-looking, Peter pleaded with her to take the day off.

'Don't worry about me, I'll be all right.'

He told her to take the children out to the playground and keep out in the air as much as possible. He saw the ring on her finger as she placed her hands on the roll-book to sign her time of arrival. He turned his back on his class, caught her hand and said in a low voice: 'I'll go down to see you as soon as I set these fellows some work to do.' She raised her eyes to his and went off, screwing the top on her fountain pen.

He went outside to her when he saw her seated on a chair in the playground and her class arranged round her in a semi-circle.

He sent her class off to play themselves and when they had scattered from them in all directions he advised Nora to go off at lunch-hour and he'd run her home in the car.

She smiled gently at him: 'I'm not as far gone as all that. It'll pass off in a day or two.'

'I'll close the school a week earlier than arranged. I asked Brennan and Murphy and they're in favour of it. What do you think?'

'I'd be agreeable too,' she said, and wished in her heart that it were closing tomorrow.

'You haven't decided where you'll spend your holiday?'

'Not yet. As you know I'll stay for a while with my aunt and later I might go for a while to Donegal or Kerry.'

'We'll try to spend a fortnight together somewhere. But we'll settle on that later.'

Shortly after two o'clock he came into her classroom and asked her to go out early and he'd get a big boy to look after her class.

'It wouldn't be worth while,' she said. 'The children would

spread the news around that I was sick. And really I don't feel as bad as I must look. Don't be annoyed with me, Peter, I'll be all right.'

Murphy walked home with her. He was more subdued than usual and she read in his occasional glance of concern that she must be a pitiful-looking sight. She forced herself to talk, but the effort wearied her; and she was conscious that the tonelessness of her voice uncovered the fatigue she wished to conceal.

But at the dinner-table she could no longer disguise her lack of appetite. And to lessen the anxiety of Mary and Elizabeth she suggested that it was a touch of flu that was the matter with her.

'You'll just have to stay in bed till you're better,' Elizabeth said. 'And since the doctor is coming to visit me in the morning I could get him to kill two birds with the one stone.'

'All right,' Nora agreed, realizing that in all justice she should do whatever would ease their minds. 'I'm sorry for all this trouble I'm giving you.'

'What trouble?' they both said at once.

'I was a fool to let you go out this morning,' Mary said. 'But this time you're not putting a foot under you till you're better,' she added playfully. 'You'll just lie quietly in bed and not think of us. Isn't that so, Elizabeth?'

'Yes, that's right. You'll have to be sensible. Take a page out of my book: sickness always needs a little patience.'

After Nora had gone to her room Elizabeth said in a whisper: 'She's not eating as much as a wren these days. It wouldn't be *it* that has come for her?'

'It — what do you mean?'

'The first beginnings of decline.'

'God forbid! She has no cough. It's the heat that's causing it; and then there's the foul air in the classroom to contend with.'

'Didn't I get that in nicely about the doctor?'

'You did, Elizabeth. You're great when there's trouble. I couldn't manage without you — indeed I couldn't.'

243

'I'll send Johnny to the doctor with a note. And when he calls in the morning I'll have a quiet chat with him about her mother and sister. It might help him to diagnose quickly.'

In the morning he arrived and Elizabeth drew him aside and had her quiet chat with him. He stayed with Nora longer than they expected and, on coming down, Elizabeth and Mary led him into the sitting-room and closed the door behind them.

'She needs a long rest,' he announced.

'In a sanatorium, Doctor?' Elizabeth said.

'No, not at all! It's nervous exhaustion that's wrong with the girl.'

'That's what I've always maintained, Doctor,' Elizabeth said, turning to Mary for corroboration. 'I always felt there was nothing consumptive about her in spite of what she told us about her poor mother and sister. But I'm glad to hear you confirm my beliefs, Doctor.'

Mary, with her arms folded, lowered her eyes and said nothing.

'I've told her to take things easy for a while,' the doctor said, lifting his hat from the table. 'These women teachers are far too conscientious about their work. She needn't return to the school till after the summer holidays. She's not sleeping too well and if you send Johnny down to the surgery I'll make up a nice tonic for her.'

'Indeed I heard her call out a few times last night, Doctor,' Mary said, rubbing her hands. 'But when I went in to her she seemed to be in a feverish sleep.'

'Don't let her see that you're anxious about her. I notice she's wearing an engagement ring — some girls don't wear them with a light heart,' he smiled, stepping towards the door. 'I'll have a look in again in a day or two.'

That evening Peter walked over to see her. She was propped up on the pillows and she was wearing a black satin jacket with lilac lining. Mary had arranged her hair for her, but before he had arrived Nora had taken off her ring and had put it in its box inside an envelope. He noticed she wasn't wearing it and he noticed too that her brown eyes were losing their strange hunted look. There was a limp but sad contentment about her.

He sat on the edge of the bed and not on the chair that Mary had drawn out for him.

'Well, Nora,' he said, after Mary had gone from the room, 'you look much better.'

'I feel a good bit better, thank God.'

Her hands lay loose on top of the eiderdown. He stroked the long fingers of her left hand, stroked them slowly like the un-hurried drawing-off of a glove. They always felt cool no matter how warm the day was.

'No, Peter, I'm not wearing it,' she said. 'I've thought much these past few nights about our love and I feel now that I wouldn't be strong enough to be your wife.'

'So you don't love me any more — is that what you're trying to tell me, Nora?' and his hand no longer held hers.

'It isn't that, Peter; God knows it isn't. I love you and always will. And I'll always remember the great evenings we've had. But don't you realize I haven't the health to be your wife? I can't rid myself of that fear — fear that I'd turn out a semi-invalid. Marriage requires something more than love.'

He raised his head to the window; a sunny wind rustled in the trees and green clusters of chestnuts swung stiffly on the branches; beyond them he could see a field of haycocks, each sitting squatly on its own shadow.

'Listen, Nora,' and he turned round and caught each of her hands in his. The stinging pressure of his fingers froze the strength in her arms. 'You mustn't come to a decision like this while your mind is tired and depressed.'

'But, Peter darling, you don't understand. It's only since I've made this decision that I am able to shake myself free from a worry that has almost smothered me.'

'I love you, Nora, and want no one else. You know that?'

'I do, I do! But marriage is something we just can't arrange for a year or two years and then withdraw from it should the worst happen. It would be senseless and selfish for one like me to go on with it. I wasn't made for it. I can't stand up to strain.' She looked at him twining a blanket-thread round his finger like a strand of grey hair. 'Peter, look up and don't make it harder for me. What I am doing I don't want to do; but yet I know — deep within me I know it — that it will be for your good and for my own. I will go away to another school and that will make it easier for both of us.' Her lip stiffened and she could not finish what she wished to say.

He held her firmly in his arms, and in the pressure of his hand against her back she was aware how thin she must have grown within the past few days. His voice rose in spite of himself; he wasn't going to listen to her; he didn't want the envelope she was holding out to him; he wanted no one only herself.

There was a knock at the bedroom door and Mary entered. She had heard Peter's raised voice and afraid that they might be quarrelling Elizabeth sent her up.

'Excuse me,' she said. 'I came up to see if Elizabeth left her crochet needle here,' and she made a pretence of searching for it on the dressing-table and mantelpiece. 'I'll bring both of you up a nice cup of coffee.'

'No, thanks, Mary. I'll be going now.'

'Don't let me chase you. Sit down till I tell Elizabeth her needle's not here.' On her way out of the room she smiled anxiously at Nora.

'I'll come back tomorrow evening, Nora. You'll consider all this again.'

She shut her eyes and shook her head wearily: 'I have considered it and I know I'll not change.'

'You will change — I know it and feel it.' He smoothed back her hair and kissed her brow. 'Before I go: did Helen say anything to you on Saturday evening?'

'She only stayed for a few minutes. She didn't congratulate me if that's what you mean.'

He stared at the envelope lying on the bed and at the raised imprint of the box inside it. Nora lifted it loosely in her hand and motioned it towards him.

'I'll not take it. We needn't go over all that again and make you ill. And if Helen has said anything to you against our marriage we'll both go away and I'm the one that will look out for the new school.'

With those words, spoken with all his urgency and determination, he went away from her. She lay and listened to his footsteps going down the drive, heard them echoing on the dry road outside, and in her own mind followed them up the hill to the wooden field-gate where he would halt and look back at this house and see the ribbed fanlight above the door. Her lip trembled, and she clenched her fists in an effort to keep back her tears.

Father Lacy called to see her the following morning.

'This is a nice how-do-you-do,' he said cheerily as he came into her bedroom. 'Getting sick out of season.'

'I'm afraid, Father, that my kind of sickness is always in season.'

'Your kind! There's nothing special about it as far as I can hear. You needn't pride yourself in being unique. Peter Lynch was worried about you so I rang up the doctor to find out all the ins and outs about you. You're suffering from nervous exhaustion — and a good holiday will cure that.'

'He didn't recommend any particular place, did he?'

'What kind of a place?'

'A sanatorium.'

'No, he did not!'

'Did you ask him, Father?'

He smiled, and in that smile she guessed that he had asked.

'You seem to be disappointed that he hasn't recommended a sanatorium.'

'But why am I so tired, so fagged out? It even tires me to lift up my arms like this,' and she raised them and let them drop down like dead things on the eiderdown. 'I should be back with my aunt and not be lying here giving trouble to Mary and Elizabeth.' She praised them for all they had done for her and she told him of how happy she had been in the school.

'And you'll continue to be happy in it, please God.'

She made dents on the eiderdown with her finger: 'Happy as I have been in the school I don't want to come back to it after the holidays. Please, Father, don't ask me what the reason is.'

'Nora, I know what the reason is without having to ask. But there's nothing time can't mend on that score. A girl of your age must take delight in living and you must start right now and oppose this tragic outlook of yours. You can't choke your girlish happiness like this without doing yourself an injury. Your own father wasn't like this and he'd be grieved to see his daughter like it. Life indeed is a strange puzzle — an insoluble one to those who seek for continual happiness in it: it is not as easy as we wish to make it, but we make it more difficult when we wish to escape from it. Everything that lives has to struggle and that which struggles lives longest and strongest. And here you are giving in at the first sign of trouble.'

'I can't help it, Father.'

'You mustn't say "I can't"; you must begin saying "I can". You must rid yourself of this sinful sorrow. Your sorrow isn't the kind that finds favour either with God or man. You must be more thankful for what you have.'

'I am, Father.'

'Then stop brooding on yourself and on your health. And thank God for what you have instead of living in fear of what you haven't.'

'I'll try,' she smiled sadly.

'And when Peter Lynch comes to see you, for the love of God make him smile.'

'That's a different story, Father Lacy. I love him but he has a sister who also loves him.'

'But you're not marrying her!'

'The actions we do affect other people.'

248

'But if you think of actions in that way you'll never act at all. Helen's at an age when it will be easier for her to make a sacrifice than for you.'

He crossed to the window. Two young thrushes were hopping about the lawn with ungrown tails and they dropped their wings and opened their frog-like mouths as the mother bird alighted beside them.

'Mary and Elizabeth have a nice place here,' he said, still looking out. 'But it's a pity they sawed the bough off that old tree. It's like a cow with one horn.'

'Elizabeth thought it darkened the place and encouraged flies.'

'You've enough swallows around to eat up all the flies from here to the coal-quay and back. She shouldn't have meddled with it.'

'I wouldn't be the one to tell her that,' Nora laughed.

'Neither would I for that matter. Don't be telling her what I said. She doesn't like criticism.'

'Indeed I'll tell her, Father,' she joked.

'If you do she'll never let me hear the end of it. I must go now. Goodbye,' and he shook her hand. 'No going back on your promises?'

'No going back,' she repeated with a smile; and as soon as he had gone she tore open the envelope that was under her pillow and took the ring out of its box.

On his way home Father Lacy called in the school to have a quiet word with Peter; and at lunch-time Peter released his class ten minutes earlier than usual and rushed over in his car to the Devlins'. Elizabeth was crocheting in Nora's room as he entered, and Nora was sitting up in bed taking a glass of milk and biscuits from a tray.

'What do you think of her this morning?' Elizabeth said brightly. 'Amn't I making a good job of her?'

Nora looked up at him with an easy smile and patted the side of her hair, displaying the ring on her finger.

'We're not going to get rid of her as easily as we thought,' Peter said, leaning over the brass bedrail.

'She's talking about going off on Saturday to her aunt. You don't think she'd be fit for a journey like that?' Her reel of cotton rolled on the floor and Peter picked it up for her.

'I'm a nuisance to everyone and I really must set out then.'

'You're a very impatient patient,' Elizabeth said, taking the tray from her. 'Peter hasn't long to stay so I'll leave you in his hands for a few minutes while I help Mary in the kitchen.'

Nora stretched out her arms to him and he leaned over and kissed her: 'I was impatient to see you, Peter, though I didn't expect you till this evening. I had Father Lacy in to see me this morning.'

'He told me about it.'

'Already?'

'Yes, already.'

'He has been very good to me. Will I tell you all, Peter?'

'No, Nora, you needn't go back on anything.'

'And Helen?'

'She'll have to allow us to live our lives in our own way. But you needn't dwell on that.'

'I won't,' and she gave a slight smile and gripped his fingers.

'And when you're leaving here for the holidays I'll drive you home. I'd like to meet your aunt and uncle.'

He heard one o'clock strike and he scrambled to his feet. 'I'm dead late. But I'll be back this evening.'

'I'll probably get up for an hour or so then.'

He rushed home quickly and into the house. Helen was seated at the table taking her own lunch.

'I suppose you've had yours over in the Miss Devlins'?'

'No, I hadn't time. Just pour me out a cup of tea. I'll not sit down.'

'Well, is the patient going to die?' she said with dry disdain.

'She's very much alive.'

'So she has fooled you again, Peter.'

'No, it's herself she has been fooling all along. You'll not see her again for six long weeks.'

'I wish it were six long years — it wouldn't be long enough!'

He said nothing.

'I'll go away from here,' she went on. 'That'll be my choice in this matter.'

'You're free to do that,' he answered, rattling the empty cup down upon the saucer. 'And you're also free to stay.'

She rose abruptly and caught his sleeve as he made towards the door.

'Please, don't keep me late, Helen,' he said, detaching her hand from his sleeve.

'Peter, you've broken my heart and she'll break yours. And when I go away you needn't send for me when your troubles come.'

He took his whistle from his pocket and hurried out into the bright sunlight that was alive and noisy with the shouts of children playing in the school-yard.

The Choice

by
Michael McLaverty

A fine subtle novel of human goodness and frailty

POOLBEG

The

Brightening
Day

by
Michael McLaverty

A finely crafted and passionate novel that tells of one
man's striving for personal justice and happiness

POOLBEG

The Silken Twine

A Study of the Work of Michael McLaverty

by

Sophia Hillan King

A comprehensive critical survey of the novelist in his
time and place

POOLBEG

In Quiet Places

The Uncollected Stories, Letters and
Critical Prose of Michael McLaverty

Edited with an Introduction
by
Sophia Hillan King

POOLBEG